"I don't want you falling in love with her, Daddy," Lindsey explained

"Why not?" he asked.

"She's not right for you," Lindsey said. "She's a star. You don't understand about stars, Daddy. They're different."

"You're the only star I care about," he murmured. "Susannah isn't a star anymore. And I'm not in love with her. Okay?"

She was reassured. "Okay."

"Do you want me to miss Daddy School tonight? I'll stay home if you need me to," he said, loosening his hold on her.

"No, that's all right. I've got homework ~~to do~~ anyway." She didn't want to do her homework, but she figured saying it would ~~cheer~~ ...

It did. He ste... ...ledged smile. "Okay, ...nd I'll go to class. A... ...an."

"I'm not worrie... ...er. She's cool. She's terrific. She's just..." *More than you can handle*, Lindsey wanted to say. "She's different."

"Yeah," he agreed, "she's different."

Except Lindsey knew for sure he *didn't* mean it the way she did.

Dear Reader,

Two years ago, I wrote a trilogy of books about the "Daddy School," a program that taught men how to be better fathers. The three "Daddy School" books were so popular I was asked to write another "Daddy School" book.

The result is *Dr. Dad,* a story about a widowed doctor and his lovely but exasperating ten-year-old daughter. Toby Cole has always been close to his daughter, but now Lindsey is changing, both physically and emotionally. These changes intensify when the woman who moves into the house next door is Lindsey's idol, a TV star who isn't at all what Lindsey had always dreamed she would be.

We all know that romantic love can be the best medicine for healing the human soul. A father's love for his daughter can be equally powerful. This is a lesson I learned from my own father, who would probably make an excellent Daddy School teacher himself!

I hope you enjoy *Dr. Dad.* And please visit my web site: www.superauthors.com.

Happy reading!

Judith Arnold

DR. DAD
Judith Arnold

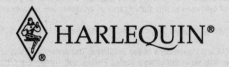

HARLEQUIN®

TORONTO · NEW YORK · LONDON
AMSTERDAM · PARIS · SYDNEY · HAMBURG
STOCKHOLM · ATHENS · TOKYO · MILAN · MADRID
PRAGUE · WARSAW · BUDAPEST · AUCKLAND

ISBN 0-373-70894-7

DR. DAD

Copyright © 2000 by Barbara Keiler.

This edition published by arrangement with Harlequin Books S.A.

® and TM are trademarks of the publisher. Trademarks indicated with ® are registered in the United States Patent and Trademark Office, the Canadian Trade Marks Office and in other countries.

Visit us at www.romance.net

Printed in U.S.A.

This book is dedicated to the wonderful pediatricians
who have kept my sons healthy and happy.

CHAPTER ONE

THE MOVING TRUCK had been sitting in the Robinsons' driveway when Lindsey got home from school, and it was still there three hours later. It took up the entire length of the driveway, with the cab hanging out into the street. Brawny men in brown uniform shirts and blue jeans walked back and forth, lugging cartons and sofas and weird-shaped objects wrapped in quilted gray cloth across the lawn to the front door or straight into the garage.

Lindsey sat on the cushioned window seat in the study, spying on the movers. She was hoping for a clue, something to tell her about the family moving into the Robinson house.

Some baby items—a stroller or a tricycle or one of those pudgy plastic basketball hoops designed for toddlers—would indicate that the new neighbors had little kids, which meant maybe they would hire her to babysit for them. She was going to turn eleven in July, and eleven was old enough. According to her friends, babysitting meant getting paid three bucks an hour to watch TV and eat potato chips while the kids slept. Lindsey could definitely handle that.

But she would sacrifice baby-sitting jobs for the chance to have someone her age moving in next door. A girl, so she and Lindsey could be friends. Cathy Robinson used to be her very best friend—and she still was, even though her family moved to Atlanta in December and she and Lindsey had to use e-mail to stay in touch with each other. But Lindsey would sure like it if another girl moved in next door, someone she could hang out with and go to the mall with and stuff. Or a boy, as long as he was cute and a year older than her, because boys her own age were such jerks. If he was a year older, he'd be going into seventh grade while she went into sixth, but they'd both be taking the same bus to the middle school. So maybe they could be friends.

Especially if he was cute.

For as long as Lindsey had been watching, though, nothing the movers hauled out of the truck offered a single hint about the new neighbors. A car was parked by the curb in front of the house, one of those updated Volkswagen beetles the color of pea soup, with a California license plate attached to the bumper. Lindsey couldn't understand why people thought those new beetles were so cool. She thought the car in front of the Robinson house looked disgusting.

She dug her finger inside her sneaker to scratch an itch below her ankle bone. She wasn't supposed to be wearing shoes when she had her feet propped up on the window seat, but she didn't care. Dad was going to be pissed at her today, whether or not she put her feet up with her shoes on.

She wished her feet didn't sweat so much. In another month it would be warm enough to go barefoot, but not yet. It didn't make sense that her feet should be too hot in shoes and too cold in sandals. Sometimes it seemed like nothing about her body was working right.

One of the moving men came out the front door, with a woman following him. The new neighbor, Lindsey thought, sitting straighter. She squinted, trying to size her up, to see if she looked friendly and, more important, if she looked old enough to have a kid Lindsey's age or young enough to have toddlers in need of a baby-sitter. Her long blond hair was pulled back in a sloppy braid, and she wore a big sweatshirt and tight jeans. She had really slim legs. In the late-afternoon shadows, it was hard to see her—until she turned and the sun hit her in the face.

"Oh, my God!" Lindsey shrieked. Her heart shimmied inside her chest, beating so hard it felt like it was going to break out of her rib cage. She surged to her knees and shielded her eyes to get a clearer look at the woman.

It was her! It had to be. Even though her hair was just a little lighter, and she looked a little thinner, and her coloring was just a little paler without makeup, but... "Oh, my God," Lindsey whispered. The words came out sounding like an actual prayer.

It made no sense that someone as famous as she was would actually be moving to this boring little corner of Arlington, Connecticut. Nothing exciting ever happened around here, especially not to Lindsey. Never in her wildest dreams would she have imagined meeting someone so extraordinary, let alone having someone so extraordinary move into the house next door.

It must be fate. A giant swoosh of destiny. Lindsey's life was going to change forever because of this. It was going to become important and meaningful, maybe even spectacular. Everything would get better.

"Daddy? Daddy!" She leaped off the window seat and tore out of the study, down the hall to the kitchen. "Oh, my God, Daddy, guess what?"

Her father was standing beside the kitchen table, his

tie loose and his blazer draped over his arm. She didn't know why he even bothered to have a blazer with him, since he always took it off as soon as he got to work, and then maybe he put it on to drive home but he stripped it right off again the minute he entered the house. Lindsey was glad she wasn't a guy, because she thought blazers were really stupid, especially with those little notches in the collars that looked like a penguin had taken a bite out of the fabric on each side.

Ties were stupid, too. Her father's tie was loosened, his shirt collar unbuttoned and his shirt comfortably wrinkled. He hated ironing.

He was holding a piece of paper, studying it, and when Lindsey realized what it was, she almost forgot about the new next-door neighbor. He was going to be so pissed when he finished reading it. She was going to be in major trouble, and no swoosh of destiny was going to rescue her from it. If she'd gotten into a fight or talked back to the principal or something, her father would be angry for a while and then get over it. But grades were a whole other thing. He took grades *very* seriously.

She wondered if she could get him so excited about the new neighbor he'd forget all about her midterm report. "Daddy, you'll never guess who's moving into the Robinson house! Come on, guess!"

He lowered the paper and peered at her. He was furious. She could have been standing two towns away, and she'd still have felt the waves of anger rolling off him. He waved the paper at her. "This is not good, Lindsey."

She already knew that. She'd read the report. And being the honest daughter she was, she'd bravely left it on the table for him to see first thing when he got home, even though she knew that was like suicide. If she hadn't been honest and brave, she would have hidden it until later, when he was half-asleep in his easy chair, and then said, "Oh, by the way, Dr. Dad, you have to sign this for tomorrow," and he might have been so sleepy he'd have signed it without looking too hard at it.

Fat chance. He would never sign anything without reading it thoroughly.

All right, so he was angry and she was in trouble. Big deal. The most incredible thing was happening practically right outside their door! Did they really have to discuss her midterm report right now?

Apparently, they did. Her father lifted the paper and stared it as if it were a love letter he wanted to memorize. Or a hate letter, given how grim his face was. "'Math,'" he read. "'Lindsey is a gifted student, but she isn't putting forth the necessary effort. Science. Lindsey is missing two homework assignments.'"

"I can make those up," she mumbled.

Ignoring her, he continued reading. "'English. Lindsey seems distracted and uninterested—'"

"Well, the story we've been reading is boring. It's about Hitler and this stupid stuffed rabbit—"

"'History,'" her father read. "'Homework has been sloppy. Spanish. *Muy bien.*'"

"See?" she said hopefully. "I'm doing real good in Spanish."

"Really well," he corrected her, then lowered the midterm report to the table. "What's going on, Lindsey?"

"Okay, so it isn't as good as usual." Her feet felt fidgety, and she nudged the floor with her toe to keep herself from running away, back to the study to spy

on the new neighbor, or maybe straight out the door
to see her in person.

"As good as usual?" He jabbed the report with his
finger. "This stinks, Hot Stuff. It isn't like you at all."

Maybe it *was* like her. Maybe she wasn't Hot Stuff.
Maybe she wasn't Little Miss Straight-A, like she used
to be. Maybe other things mattered more to her than
being perfect all the time.

For instance, the new next-door neighbor—*she* mattered more. "Look," she said, racing through this discussion so she could steer her father to the more important issue. "I can make up the missing homework.
If Ms. Hathaway wants me to redo the history homework, I'll redo it neat."

"Neatly," her father said.

She tried not to roll her eyes. This wasn't a good
time to let her father know she thought he was being
a major pain. "Neatly," she echoed. "This is just the
midterm report. It doesn't actually count."

"No, but it tells me something's not right. Your
schoolwork is deteriorating. The midterm report exists
to warn us when there's a problem—and there's clearly
a problem here, Lindsey."

"I'll fix it." *Please, Daddy, don't turn this into a
big thing. Please.* "It's not a problem, I promise. I can
talk to Ms. Hathaway and fix everything."

"I think that perhaps *I* should talk to Ms. Hathaway."

"You don't have to do that. It's not like I'm failing
or anything. I'll do the missing homework, and that'll
be that."

He gave her the Look: a deep, stern, narrow-eyed
frown that announced: *You have disappointed me.* She
hated the Look. She had no defense against it.

Except today, maybe she did. She had the new neighbor, which was so much more significant than anything going on in her useless, idiotic fifth-grade class. "Susannah Dawson is moving into the Robinson house," she said.

Her father scowled. "Who?"

Sheesh! He thought history homework was more important than having a celebrity as your next-door neighbor. "Susannah Dawson! From *Mercy Hospital*!"

"Mercy Hospital?" He was still frowning. "Where's that? I've never heard of it."

"It's a TV show, Daddy. *Mercy Hospital.* Susannah Dawson plays Lee Davis on it. *Dr.* Lee Davis," she added, because she thought that might impress her father.

"She's not a doctor. She just plays one on TV," he muttered, then smiled wryly.

Lindsey wanted to shake him hard. He could be so dense. Didn't he realize what a big thing it was to have someone as famous as Susannah Dawson moving into their neighborhood? More than their neighborhood—right next door!

Obviously, he didn't think it was a big thing at all. He was her father. Totally clueless.

"So, she's a TV star?" he asked. He looked like he was pretending to be interested.

"Yes, she's a TV star. If you ever paid any attention to anything—" Lindsey cut herself off. She couldn't mouth off to her father. He was already steaming mad because she'd blown her midterm report. She couldn't risk making him even madder.

Once you were famous, fifth-grade midterm reports no longer mattered. Lindsey would bet Susannah Dawson never gave hers a moment's thought. And as soon as Lindsey walked out of Elm Street Elementary for the last time in June, she was never going to think about fifth grade again, either. She was going to start middle school next fall, and after that high school, and after that she was going to be a star, like Susannah Dawson. She'd appear on some wonderful TV series every week, and she'd be beautiful, and girls all over America would wish they were her. And she'd get to kiss men who looked like Lucien Roche, who had been having an affair with Dr. Davis until they started fighting on the show.

Lindsey couldn't wait to be old enough to have guys like Lucien Roche falling passionately in love with her. Once you had someone like Lucien Roche in your life, fifth grade was pretty meaningless.

"So, what are we going to do about this?" her father asked, gesturing at the midterm report. Evidently, he didn't think having Susannah Davis of *Mercy Hospital* moving onto their street was anywhere near as significant as Lindsey's missing a couple of homework assignments. "I think I should make an appointment to meet with Ms. Hathaway so we can review your work together."

Lindsey shrugged. "Really, Dr. Dad, you don't have to. Ms. Hathaway is a jerk."

"She's your teacher. Whether or not you like her is irrelevant. You've got responsibilities as a student. You've to get the job done."

Lindsey shrugged again, this time letting out a long sigh. Her father was always saying things like that— *You've got to get the job done*—as if he were a coach addressing a football team. As if school were a job like his job as a pediatrician. As if the fate of the universe rested on whether or not Lindsey got her job done.

He just didn't get it. A famous, gorgeous actress was moving in next door, and he thought Lindsey's school-work was the only thing worth caring about. He really was hopeless.

TOBY HAD BLOWN IT. He knew he had even before Lindsey had slouched out of the kitchen with her shoulders hunched and her gaze on the floor. She'd bounced in so full of energy, bright-eyed and exuber-ant—and he'd come down on her like the Lord High Executioner wielding an ax. And now she was gone, off to contemplate how very much she despised him.

Would it have made a difference if he'd given her a hug first? She seemed so prickly these days he was hesitant about touching her. Maybe he should have said he loved her—but she tended to recoil from all shows of affection, verbal or physical.

He didn't know how to reach her.

Obviously, Ms. Hathaway didn't, either.

Lindsey had always been a good student. Even Ms. Hathaway had admitted on the midterm report that she was gifted. But the report showed that she was slacking off in nearly every subject. It wasn't like Lindsey to do that.

He sank onto one of the kitchen chairs and reread the report, although he already knew its troubling con-tents. His day had entailed the usual ups and downs—treating sick children could be both rewarding and de-pressing. But nothing was as rewarding as raising his precious daughter. And lately, nothing was as depress-ing, either.

For not the first time, he suffered the gnawing worry

that he was losing Lindsey. She wasn't the girl she used to be, and he was scared out of his wits.

As a doctor, he understood the changes theoretically. He knew about hormonal upheavals, about the moodiness and restlessness that assailed children with the onset of puberty. Physically, she was already beginning to show the signs. Her body was developing a mature femininity that frightened the hell out of him. Even worse, her face was different. The last layer of baby fat had melted from her cheeks and chin, leaving behind a face of sculpted beauty—a face that resembled her mother's in an unnerving way. Every time he looked at Lindsey these days, he saw Jane, and it made him realize how desperately he needed Jane right now, and how alone he was.

Sighing, he shoved away from the table and crossed to the sink. He rolled up his sleeves, washed his hands and unwrapped the salmon steaks he planned to broil for dinner. The mechanics of preparing the evening meal couldn't distract him from his worry about Lindsey. That she had budding breasts and a new roundness to her hips, that she looked like the reincarnation of her mother, that she'd recently discovered the sublime thrill of sarcasm—it was all unsettling, but there was nothing he could do about it. He had to focus on what he *could* do something about: getting her back on track in school.

If only the Robinsons hadn't moved away, he could have turned to Diane Robinson for help. Her daughter Cathy had been Lindsey's best friend, going through every developmental stage Lindsey was going through. And Diane was a mom. Lindsey used to be able to go to her with questions and problems she refused to discuss with Toby because he was a man. He wished there were someone like Diane in her life now, when she needed a woman's guidance more than ever.

He sprinkled parsley flakes and lemon juice on the salmon, added a few modest pats of butter and slid the tray into the oven. It didn't seem fair that Lindsey was shutting him out just because he was her father. Denying him access to her because he wasn't a woman struck him as outrageously sexist. If he could be standing over the stainless-steel sink, rinsing and tearing lettuce leaves for a salad while the salmon broiled, his daughter ought to be willing to confide in him.

If he were a woman, perhaps he'd understand why the possibility that some boob-tube personality had moved in next door meant more than getting a satisfactory midterm report. What was her name? Susan something? He'd never even heard of *Mercy Hospital*. But then, he rarely had a chance to sit down in front of the television before the eleven o'clock news came on. The only way he was able to get home before six in the evening was by bringing paperwork with him. After dinner, he would review files, take notes, assess his patients' progress. On those occasions when he didn't have to work in the evening, he usually pried Lindsey away from the TV and they did something together—drive to Paganini's for ice cream, or bicycle around the neighborhood, or work together on a special project for school. He didn't want to waste those valuable minutes watching an inane TV show.

Maybe he shouldn't have given up the baby-sitter this year. Maybe that was why Lindsey was screwing up in school. She'd said she was old enough not to need an adult waiting for her at the house when she got off the bus, and Toby had agreed. But maybe Mrs.

Clarkson's presence had been essential to Lindsey's academic achievement.

Mrs. Clarkson had been a gentle, grandmotherly type, kind and patient. But kindness and patience didn't count for much with Lindsey these days. She was at an age when she considered anyone older than thirty an idiot. Older than sixty, Mrs. Clarkson probably qualified as doubly idiotic. So when she'd been offered another nanny job, Toby had wished her well and sent her on her way.

He was going to have to break through to Lindsey himself. Whatever was going on with her, between them, at school and in her fertile, mysterious mind, he was going to have to figure it out. He was going to have to grab hold of her and drag her back from the edge of disaster. Even if the falloff was only a few feet and the disaster was only a lousy report card, Toby was her father. He was going to have to save her.

FINALLY, thank God, the truck was gone. Susannah gazed around the living room. Although her furniture was in place, the room looked stark. The couches had been purchased for a very different house in a very different place. Maybe she should have ditched all the old pieces and purchased new things when she moved here.

But she didn't want to burn through her money. There would be more coming in, and she'd probably saved enough so that she would never have to work again if she lived frugally and budgeted carefully. Of course she would go crazy if she didn't work again; fortunately, she had those writing contracts waiting for her. They wouldn't pay what she'd been earning before she'd quit the show, but that was fine with her.

Trying to decorate a Victorian farmhouse in bucolic northwestern Connecticut with the sleek modern furniture she'd purchased for a sprawling ranch in a canyon north of Los Angeles was a challenge, but Susannah wanted challenges—new challenges, not the same old garbage she'd been battling for as long as she could remember. That was why she was here.

"What do you think, MacKenzie?" she asked her plump, sulking cat. He glowered up at her, then meticulously licked a paw. He was not pleased with the move—not yet. In time he'd get used to the new house. He'd discover that it was more fun to romp across a soft green lawn than the strawlike, drought-stricken grass of Southern California. He'd learn that curling up in front of a fire on a winter's day was more fun than never even knowing what a winter's day was. He'd come around.

For now, however, he clearly had no intention of offering her any input on the decor.

The air wasn't particularly warm, but she felt sticky and grimy. Strands of hair had unraveled from her braid; she could feel them tickling her cheeks and chin. Her lower back ached, even though she hadn't done much heavy lifting. Just standing all day, monitoring the movers as they unloaded her life from the back of their truck, had been enough to fatigue her.

"You think I made a mistake, don't you," she muttered to MacKenzie.

He gave her a supercilious stare that seemed to say, "Do you even have to ask?" Then he went back to grooming himself.

All right, so she'd made a mistake in deciding not to renew her contract, selling her house and moving all the way across the country to a town that, one

month ago, she'd never even heard of. A colleague
from Manhattan had told her Arlington was a charming
place—not too big, but not so small she'd feel isolated.
Less than two hours by train or bus to New York City,
less than two and a half to Boston. A bustling downtown just minutes away from rolling countryside, hills
and woodlands and crystalline ponds. "The half of the
city that doesn't have weekend homes in the Hamptons
has them in the Arlington area," her friend had told
her.

She didn't want to live surrounded by weekend ex-
iles from Manhattan. So she'd asked a real-estate agent
to find her a nice, manageable house in an established
neighborhood. And now here she was, wondering if
moving to Arlington was the most brainless thing she'd
ever done.

Nah. She'd done so many other brainless things in
her life this one might not even make the top ten.

"We've got a nice porch here, Mac," she told her
cat. "I picture you sitting out there on the porch,
watching the world go by. Maybe I'll get a hammock.
What do you think? Is that what folks in New England
do?"

MacKenzie gave her another contemptuous look.

Irritated by his lack of supportiveness, she bent over,
scooped him up and left the echoing living room,
weaving around a few unopened cartons and heading
down the hall to the door. Once Mac saw the porch,
maybe he'd fall in love with it the way she had when
the real-estate broker had faxed photos of the house to
her. He cradled himself in the crook of her arm—he
might think she'd made a mistake in moving here, but
he didn't mind letting her carry him around as if she
were his slave. She pulled open the front door, then

pushed open the screen door. The screen door would take some getting used to. She hadn't had one in California. There were no bugs out there, and when it was warm enough for screens it was warm enough for air-conditioning, so most people kept their doors shut.

It was not warm in northwestern Connecticut. It wasn't exactly cold, but it was bracing, the evening sky a delicate sunset pink and the air infused with the scent of greenery. She crossed to the porch railing and propped MacKenzie on it. "What do you think, Mac? Tolerable?"

Mac sniffed, less disdainful than curious. He could smell it, too—that exotic perfume of growing grass and budding azaleas and daffodils spearing through the humid soil.

"We're not in California anymore, Mac," she murmured. "Get used to it."

He meowed thoughtfully.

A movement to her right caught her attention. The garage door of the tidy brick colonial next door slid open with a mechanical rumble, and a man emerged dragging a wheeled garbage can. Her new neighbor.

Even in the dusk light she could see him clearly enough to observe that he was handsome. Not plastic handsome like most of the men she knew in L.A., with their perfect tans, their impeccable coiffures and their surgically improved features. There was something endearingly genuine about what she could see of his face—the prominent nose, the broad chin, the shock of dark, thick hair tumbling down over his forehead. He wore pale slacks and a blue shirt, the sleeves of which were rolled to his elbows.

This must be what real America is like, she thought—a quiet residential neighborhood of attractive

houses, the sunset lending the springtime air a chill, a
husband wheeling the trash down his driveway to the
curb. And here she was, a witness to this American
panorama, practically a part of it—a lady on the porch
with her cat in a quiet residential New England neighborhood.

"Hi," he shouted over the hedge that formed a bar-
rier between his driveway and her property.

It wasn't just a scene she was witnessing. She *was*
a part of it, as much his neighbor as he was hers.
Sooner or later, she knew she'd have to meet her
neighbors. Perhaps later would have been better.

Fortunately, she wasn't well-groomed. Her sweatshirt was wrinkled, her jeans old and fraying at the
hems. She was tired and washed out, and she looked
it. In the fading daylight, the man might not realize
who she was.

She was going to have to be friendly with him. Reserved, cautious, but pleasant. After hoisting Mac-
Kenzie off the railing, she descended the three steps to
the lawn and crossed it, the soft grass springy beneath
her sneakers. When she reached the row of dense,
waist-high shrubs separating her from the man, she
paused and gave him a closer look.

Damn. He was *really* handsome. If his personality
matched his looks, his wife was one lucky woman.

He extended his right hand to her above the shrubs.
"Toby Cole. Welcome to Arlington."

What a sweet smile he had. Slightly shy, slightly
crooked, his teeth straight and white and one cheek
creasing into a dimple. "Sue Dawson," she introduced
herself, slipping her hand into his. His long fingers
wrapped around her in a warm, oddly possessive grip.

He shook her hand and released it. "Welcome to the neighborhood. How did your move go?"

"Nothing broken so far," she said. Either he hadn't recognized her or he didn't care who she was. Maybe this would work out after all. "I haven't unpacked everything yet, so we'll see."

"It's a nice house. My daughter was best friends with the girl who used to live there, so we know the house. It gets lots of sun."

"Good." In Southern California, getting lots of sun in the house meant having to crank up the air conditioner to high power.

"If your cat likes to doze in the sun, he'll be happy. Is it a he?"

She nodded, digging her fingers into the beast's dense, soft fur to scratch his ribs. "His name is MacKenzie," she said. The cat eyed the man suspiciously, then emitted a rumbling sound, half purr, half growl. "It may take him a little while to get used to the boundaries of my yard. I hope you won't mind if he accidentally strays onto your property. If he does, just send him back. He thinks he's tough, but he's harmless."

"Cats don't bother me," Toby Cole assured her. His smile was so genuine, so utterly natural, she couldn't stop staring at it. It seemed almost foreign to her, a mysterious local idiosyncrasy. She was used to people who smiled in such a way that the skin around their eyes didn't crinkle. Laugh lines turned into wrinkles, and wrinkles meant plastic surgery. Actors smiled very carefully in Los Angeles.

"So," he said, then angled his head toward the garbage can. "Trash pickup is Friday morning. They'll take recyclables, but you've got to bag them separately.''

"Okay.''

"You have to call the company and set it up. They provide the trash can.''

"Okay.''

"Or you can buy a pass to the town dump and take care of your garbage yourself.''

She grinned, partly because he was trying so hard to be helpful and partly because his smile was contagious. "I think I'll go with the service you use.''

"I've had no trouble with them.'' He gazed at her for a long moment. "If you want their number—or if you have any other questions—just give me a call.''

Me, she noted. He hadn't said, give *us* a call. Was there no lucky wife in the picture? He'd mentioned a daughter—there had to be a wife somewhere. Maybe he was an obnoxious philanderer, flirting with the new neighbor while his wife was washing the dishes inside.

Susannah hoped that wasn't the case. She really liked his smile.

He dug his wallet from his hip pocket, then plucked a pen from his shirt pocket. He pulled a business card from the wallet, flipped it over and scribbled a phone number on the back. "Seriously, anything you need to know,'' he offered. "The best dry cleaner, the best take-out Chinese, the best auto shop. The best doctor in town,'' he added with a smile. "Just give me a buzz.''

"Thank you.'' She took the card from him and flipped it over. Dr. Tobias Cole, it said. Arlington Pediatric Associates. "You're not the best doctor in town?'' she asked.

"I'm the best pediatrician. If you have any kids—''

"No kids," she said laconically.

He nodded and gave the trash can a tug. "Well. I guess I should get this taken care of."

She tucked the business card into her pocket and stepped back, as if to give him permission to leave her. MacKenzie issued another guttural purr.

Toby Cole glanced at him. Then, flashing Susannah a farewell smile, he took the trash can by the handle and started dragging it down his driveway to the street.

She started back across the lawn, hearing the squeaking wheels of the can and a chorus of honks as a V-shaped formation of geese flew across the sky. Back on the porch, she pulled his business card from her pocket and turned in time to see him walking back up his driveway to his garage. He didn't look at her.

Fool, she thought. He was a friendly suburban father, a doctor, a family man. Sinfully good-looking, but so what? He wasn't available, and he hadn't been coming on to her. And even if he had been, she wouldn't have been interested.

She wanted peace and quiet. No excitement, no passion, no demands, no pressure. No photographers, no directors and producers, no managers and handlers. No greedy, needy people telling her what they expected her to do for them.

She'd come to Arlington to get away from everything that had been wrong with her life. That included men, work, family and pretty much everything else.

Dr. Tobias Cole could direct her to the best dry cleaners and the best take-out Chinese. More than that she didn't need.

CHAPTER TWO

"YOU DID WHAT?" Toby gaped at Lindsey, who stood in the kitchen doorway, clad in jeans and a long-sleeved T-shirt that he was certain had been big on her a few weeks ago but now fit her alarmingly well. Her eyes were the color of milk chocolate, just as sweet and just as hazardous to one's health.

"I asked her over for dinner."

"Tonight?"

Lindsey almost smiled, almost smirked. He couldn't tell whether she was glad or sorry she'd invited the new neighbor to share their evening meal, whether she was upset by his reaction or secretly pleased by it. Sometimes she seemed to do things for no other reason than to rile him.

He was exhausted. He hadn't slept well last night, and that morning he'd had the painful task of informing the parents of a seven-year-old boy that their son had leukemia. He'd spent all morning at the hospital with patients, and he'd devoted the few free minutes he'd had before his afternoon clinic appointments to a telephone conversation with Lindsey's teacher. He'd told Ms. Hathaway he wanted to schedule a meeting with her to discuss Lindsey's schoolwork, and Ms. Hathaway had argued that she didn't see why she should put any effort into teaching Lindsey if Lindsey wasn't willing to put any effort into learning.

"Frankly, I don't know what to do about her," Ms. Hathaway had lamented. "She used to be one of my top students, but she seems to have lost her motivation. I don't see what good a meeting would do."

Toby hadn't persuaded her that a meeting would do any good, but he'd gotten her to agree to a conference the following Wednesday at 7:30 a.m. That gave him five days to figure out what he could possibly tell her about Lindsey's inexplicably vanished motivation.

He wished the only reason he'd been racked with insomnia last night had been his worry about Lindsey's midterm report. Or his concern about Andy Lowenthal, the little boy whose blood work had come back positive for leukemia. But more than just a seriously ill patient and a frustrating daughter had kept him awake into the gray hours of early morning.

Sue Dawson had been on his mind.

Her alleged fame hadn't been what held his thoughts hostage all night. Lindsey believed she was a well-known actress, but he wasn't convinced. How well-known could she be if he'd never heard of her? Besides, Lindsey had used a different name for the actress—he couldn't remember what, but it hadn't been Sue Dawson.

He hadn't noticed anything particularly celebrity-like about the new neighbor. She didn't exude wealth or glamour or elegance. She'd looked like nothing more or less than a suburban homeowner.

She was just a woman, he told himself. A remarkably attractive woman. But Toby came in contact with attractive women fairly often, and on occasion dated them, so having one move into the house next door shouldn't have kept him tossing and turning. He could admire a beautiful woman in an aesthetic way and in a shamelessly lustful way, but his reaction to Sue Dawson after chatting with her for a few minutes yesterday evening hadn't fallen into either of those convenient categories.

Yet she'd haunted him all night. Closing his eyes, he would see her; opening them, he would feel her presence, even though she wasn't anywhere close by. During their brief conversation over the hedge, he'd managed to chat easily with her, but something inside his soul had been buzzing, hissing, a quiet, constant static he couldn't tune out. He'd been unsettled by the contradictions of her: delicate yet strong, slight of build yet vividly present, as distant as the sun but just as radiant. Her large blue eyes had seemed both crystalline and opaque, friendly and wary. Even her hair varied from dark blond to cornsilk pale, as if it couldn't quite commit to a single color.

He had neither the time nor the energy for a distraction like her. He was too drained to entertain anyone—let alone someone who was practically a stranger—over dinner. And he hardly had any food in the house, certainly nothing suitable to serve a guest. During his drive home, he'd fantasized about throwing on some old jeans, pouring himself a cold beer and sending out for pizza. After he and Lindsey had eaten, he'd intended to talk to her about how he could help her turn things around in school.

But there she stood, wearing a small, defiant smile as she gauged his reaction to her announcement that she'd invited the new neighbor to dinner.

"Why did you invite her? What happened?" he asked, tossing his jacket onto the nearest chair and rolling up his sleeves.

"I was walking home from the bus stop, and she

was in her yard chasing a cat. And the cat ran straight to me, so I picked it up. It's a beautiful cat, Daddy. Its name is MacKenzie." Lindsey let out a dreamy little sigh. "Isn't that a cool name? I wish I had a cat. I wish I had any kind of pet. Even fish would be okay, but they aren't as cool as a cat. Especially a cat like MacKenzie, all gray and soft like a dust bunny..."

Toby steered her back to the subject at hand. "So, you caught the cat."

"And Susannah Dawson walked over and said hi."

Susannah. That was the name Lindsey had said yesterday. Sue Dawson, Susannah Dawson. Maybe she used her full name professionally, but when she was hanging out in the 'hood she wanted to be just plain Sue.

"She was so friendly, Dad. It was like she could have been any old person, not this famous TV star."

"Are you sure she's famous?" he asked.

Lindsey clicked her tongue. "If you ever watched TV, you'd know. *Mercy Hospital* is like the coolest show. But you wouldn't know, because you never watch it."

He sensed Lindsey was baiting him, but he refused to bite. "She didn't say anything about being a TV star when I talked to her yesterday."

"You talked to her? When? Why didn't you tell me? What did she say?" Lindsey babbled like a fan possessed.

"We talked about the garbage pickup." At Lindsey's groan of disgust, he added, "And I welcomed her to the neighborhood, more or less."

"So you didn't talk about her show?"

"Of course not. Why should I? I was taking out the garbage, and I saw her and said hi."

"Well, if you already met her, you can't mind me inviting her over for dinner."

"Lindsey, I've been working hard all day. And the fridge is close to empty. You know we're always low on food by the end of the week." Toby did the grocery shopping on the weekend.

"I'm sure we can scrounge up something," she said, circling the table to the refrigerator and swinging it open. It was indeed almost empty. Sighing, she yanked on the freezer door and peered inside. "Here," she said, digging out a package of frozen shrimp. "You can make something with this."

"Are you sure she actually said yes?" he asked, taking the shrimp from Lindsey and staring at it dubiously. "Maybe you misunderstood her." If she was the celebrity Lindsey seemed to think she was, why would she want to spend her Friday night at a yawnfest at the Cole house?

"I think she liked me," Lindsey confessed with a modest shrug. Her shoulders used to be bony, but not anymore. She'd added a layer of muscular flesh to them in the past few months. Her body was more solid, more substantial. The skinny little kid she used to be no longer existed.

"Of course she liked you. You're very likable," he said, although at the moment he wasn't sure he liked her. He swung open a cabinet door and searched the shelves, hoping for inspiration. "When did you tell her to come?"

"Six o'clock."

He swore under his breath. It was five forty-five now. No time to race out to the supermarket. What could he do with frozen shrimp? "Spaghetti," he said.

"She won't eat that. It's too fattening. You know what they say about TV—it adds ten pounds."

"Ten pounds of what?"

Lindsey gazed at the ceiling and groaned "Dad," as if she thought he was just pretending ignorance. But he had no idea what she meant about ten pounds, and he had no time to chisel through her sarcasm. Whether or not the new neighbor wanted to eat spaghetti, that was what he would be serving. It was either spaghetti or pizza delivered from Luigi's.

He pulled out the big pot, filled it with water, set it on the stove and turned on the heat under it. Then he tossed the package of shrimp into the microwave to defrost and grabbed a jar of marinara sauce from a shelf.

Five years ago, no one could have convinced him he could fix a dinner so efficiently. Neither he nor Jane had been particularly talented in the kitchen; they'd cooked edible meals, but they'd never been the kind to experiment with exotic ingredients or collect bizarre appliances—like state-of-the-art garlic presses and vegetable steamers and candy thermometers. Because he'd worked long hours, Jane had done most of the cooking. He'd known the basics of food preparation; during his bachelor days, he'd somehow managed to keep himself from starving to death. But she'd been the boss in the kitchen. He'd been the assistant.

Now he was the boss, receiving minimal culinary assistance from Lindsey. He used to ask her for help, but lately he'd been hesitant. Asking her for anything meant running the risk of tripping some invisible switch inside her, sending her into one of her sulks or igniting an argument.

He didn't have time to argue with her tonight. Sue

Dawson would be over in—he glanced at his watch—ten minutes. But it was Lindsey's fault that he had to throw this last-minute dinner together. She ought to do something to help out. "Why don't you set the dining-room table," he suggested in as mild a voice as he could manage. "If we're having company, we might as well eat in there." The kitchen table currently held his briefcase, his jacket, Lindsey's backpack from school, a stack of as yet unopened mail and a dirty plate left over from breakfast. He didn't have time to neaten up the place.

Without a quibble, Lindsey exited into the dining room. She had a new way of walking, he noticed—a kind of slinky, slouchy motion, using her hips more than her feet to propel her. He wondered if her back-pack was too heavy, damaging her posture, or if this was simply the way preteen girls walked, thinking they looked sexy.

God, he was tired of worrying about her all the time.

Right now, he couldn't spare a minute for worry. He rummaged in the refrigerator for lettuce, tomatoes and a stalk of celery. He didn't have any Italian bread—he hoped spaghetti with shrimp and a salad would be sufficient.

Would Sue like wine? he wondered. The thought of lingering over a glass of wine with her appealed to him. He felt guilty about that. And he felt stupid for feeling guilty.

The wine rack built into the cabinet near the micro-wave wasn't well stocked. He'd never considered wine a beverage to drink in solitude, and the last time he'd had guests for dinner was the office holiday party, which he'd cohosted with his partners. The food had been catered, but he'd bought a case of assorted wines, and he had a few bottles left over.

He found a bottle of Italian table red and pulled it out, then grabbed a couple of goblets from the adjacent cabinet and carried them to the dining room. To his amazement, Lindsey had done a meticulous job of setting the table. She'd spread a dark-green linen cloth over the mahogany oval and rolled matching linen napkins into the silver napkin rings. She stood at the open breakfront, carefully gathering the good china dishes they would need for their meal, and the silver chest was open on the sideboard, the flatware inside glinting in the light. Fresh white tapers were wedged into the silver candlesticks Toby and Jane had gotten as a wedding present from Jane's aunt Laura.

Seeing him in the doorway, Lindsey smiled sheepishly. "Does it look okay?"

"It looks magnificent," he said, hoping she would accept the heartfelt compliment without rolling her eyes. It *did* look magnificent. He was surprised that she'd done such a fancy job of it. Maybe she wanted to impress the famous TV star.

"I think the water's boiling," Lindsey said. "I can hear it from here."

"Right." He set one wineglass near his chair at the head of the table and the other at Sue's place. Resisting the urge to give Lindsey a hug, he returned to the kitchen to add the spaghetti to the boiling water.

He was lifting the lid from the pot when the doorbell rang. Whatever pleasure he'd felt from Lindsey's efforts vanished in a wave of panic. Spaghetti and salad seemed too mundane to be eaten on fine china. Sue Dawson might think they were trying too hard, or not hard enough.

"Lindsey, can you get the door?" he shouted over his shoulder as he emptied the box of pasta into the water. Their guest would think whatever she thought. He was doing the best he could under the circumstances.

He heard Lindsey's footsteps as she hurried through the living room to the front door. He stirred the pasta, then pulled the defrosted shrimp out of the microwave. Voices floated down the hall to him, Sue's and then Lindsey's. He tossed the shrimp into the tomato sauce, gave it a stir and set it on the stove. He wasn't nervous, he told himself. He wasn't under any obligation to bedazzle the new neighbor.

She preceded Lindsey into the kitchen, and for a moment he was the one bedazzled. Again he was reminded of the sun—its light, its heat, its ability to burn. There was no one thing about Sue Dawson that was so bright—her eyes were lively, her hair shimmering as it fell loose past her shoulders, her smile relaxed and her body graceful in a white tunic-style top and slim-fitting gray slacks—but put it all together and she practically shimmered with warmth. Small diamonds winked in her earlobes, discreet and utterly tasteful, and a silver bangle circled her wrist. She carried a plate heaped with something, wrapped in aluminum foil.

"I brought brownies," she said. "I hope that's all right."

"Brownies," Lindsey murmured reverently, hovering near the table and gazing worshipfully at Sue. "I *love* brownies."

"Well," Toby said, "since I didn't plan dessert—" hell, he hadn't even planned dinner "—it's a good thing you brought some with you."

"I'll put them in the dining room," Lindsey offered,

taking the plate from Sue and disappearing from the kitchen.

Toby smiled. Sue smiled. The water resumed its rolling boil, filling the room with a gurgling sound. "I hope you like spaghetti," he said cheerfully.

"Spaghetti's great." Her smile was luminous, altering her cheeks and brow, her eyes, her entire body. Did they teach people how to smile that way in acting school? "It was so nice of you to invite me over. It looks as if you've barely gotten home from work." She gestured toward the tie still knotted tight at his throat.

He grinned and tugged the knot loose. "It was my daughter's idea to invite you," he confessed, giving the sauce a stir. "It happens to be a fine idea, though." It was, he realized. Now that he knew she thought spaghetti was great, he intended to relax and enjoy himself.

She gazed around the kitchen, and he wondered whether he should apologize for its clutter. Besides the detritus scattered across the table, the refrigerator was decorated with shopping lists and school calendars. A broom was propped in a corner, left out from when Lindsey had spilled a box of Cheerios yesterday. The pleated shades at the windows had been raised to different heights that morning, and he'd never bothered to adjust them.

But no, he wasn't going to apologize for the disheveled state of the room. He wasted too much energy worrying about whether he ought to apologize to Lindsey for transgressions real or imagined. He wasn't going to worry about his neighbor, too. One difficult relationship with a female was all he could handle.

"Um..." Sue peered through the doorway into the

dining room, then glanced behind her toward the hall.
"Will I be meeting your wife?" she asked delicately.

The question jolted him, although he realized it was
a perfectly natural one. She'd met him; she'd met his
daughter—why shouldn't there be a wife in the picture?

He set down the spoon he'd been using to stir the
sauce. "My wife died five years ago," he said with a
wry smile. "So no, I don't think you'll be meeting
her."

"Oh!" Sue looked chagrined. "I'm so sorry—"

"That's all right." There was a great deal he hated
about Jane's death, but one of the worst things—which
had never occurred to him until he'd experienced it—
was the constant need to break the news to others. For
years after Jane had died, he would run into old ac-
quaintances who hadn't heard, and they'd ask how she
was, and he would have to tell them and revisit his
grief. And when he met new people, like Sue Dawson,
he would have to go through it all over again.

The pain wasn't acute anymore; after five years he'd
gotten used to the idea that Jane was no longer with
him. But whenever he told new people, they would
become upset and he'd feel an obligation to comfort
and reassure them. Instead of receiving their sympathy,
he'd be knocking himself out trying to make them feel
better.

"Am I going to meet your husband?" he asked, in
part to direct the conversation away from himself and
his loss and in part because he assumed a beautiful
supposed celebrity like her had to be married or attached, or at the very least in a hot relationship with
the Hollywood heartthrob of the moment.

"No husband," Sue said laconically, her voice dipping into the subzero range.

Okay. No more questions in that direction.

He found a salad serving utensil in a drawer and placed it in the salad bowl. As he shut the drawer his gaze drifted back to her, standing near the windows, the evening light sloping through the panes and glazing her hair with an amber shimmer. She was single; so was he. Interesting.

But impossible. She was his neighbor, and becoming involved with a neighbor would be a serious mistake. Besides, Lindsey deserved the bulk of his attention right now. He couldn't fritter away his time or emotions on anyone else.

She reentered the kitchen and he thrust the salad bowl into her hands. "Would you take this to the table, please?"

She eyed Sue. "He treats me like a slave," she muttered, then headed back to the dining room with the salad.

Sue grinned. "How old is she?"

"Almost eleven—physically. Mentally, she's anywhere from three to forty, depending on her mood." The sauce had begun to bubble. He eased a strand of spaghetti out of the water with a fork and tested it for doneness. "I've got a bottle of wine for dinner, if that's all right with you."

"Great."

Lindsey reappeared in the doorway. She glanced at Toby, then turned to Sue, who exchanged a smile with her. He had a sense they were communicating privately in some secret female code. Lindsey was probably saying, *My dad is really a jerk,* and Sue was saying...what? *All dads are jerks,* or *I'll teach you how*

to get around him, or *Your dad just offered me wine,
so he can't be that much of a jerk.*

Trying to ignore them, he drained the spaghetti and
dumped it into a serving bowl. "Yes, Dr. Dad," Lindsey singsang before he had a chance to ask, taking the
bowl from him to bring into the dining room. He
poured the shrimp-laden sauce into another serving
bowl—entertaining a guest meant using dishes he
hadn't used in ages, but given how nicely Lindsey had
set the table, he wasn't going to serve dinner in pots
and pans. At last, he opened the bottle of wine, then
gestured Sue ahead of him into the dining room.

There, he thought, gazing at the food arrayed on the
table, the gleam of silver and china, the teardrop-
shaped flames crowning the two candles, which Lindsey must have lit. Either the meal would go smoothly
or it would be a disaster. He'd done his best under
pressure, which seemed to be the way he did everything these days. No one could ask more of him.

A REAL HOME, Susannah thought. A father, a child,
warmth and love. It was almost enough to make her
weep.

She was an actress, and she knew how to weep—or
remain dry-eyed—on cue. But a sentimental sweetness
filled her as she soaked it all in—Lindsey's sardonic
jokes and long-suffering sighs, Toby's forbearance, the
simple, filling food, the tart wine. She couldn't recall
the last time she'd eaten spaghetti. Out in California,
it was always *pasta,* and it was never served in anything as basic as tomato sauce with shrimp mixed in.

She wouldn't have come if she'd known this dinner
party had been his daughter's idea. The poor man! He
was a doctor; he shouldn't be entertaining a guest after

a full day of racing around, pushing gurneys up and down hospital corridors, barking orders, holding patients' hands, demanding tests and equipment and facing a crisis every thirteen minutes, just before the commercial break. That was how it worked on *Mercy Hospital,* anyway.

After such hard work, he deserved better than to have Susannah appear on his doorstep with nothing more to offer than a plate of brownies that she hadn't even baked from scratch. She wanted to beg his forgiveness—except that she was through with accommodating everyone else, making others happy, doing what they wanted her to do. It was her turn to do what *she* wanted—and what she wanted right now was to be eating spaghetti mixed with slightly rubbery shrimp and bland sauce, in this pretty dining room with its old-fashioned furniture and expensive china.

And the candles. Were they on the table for a reason? Surely he hadn't been thinking of a romantic dinner, not with his sassy daughter present. And why was Susannah even thinking about a romantic *anything* with Toby Cole? He was just her new neighbor. An unconscionably good-looking man, but so what? She didn't want a romance with him or anyone else.

He was describing a new therapy he hoped to try on a patient of his, a six-year-old with asthma. Every now and then, he'd glance at Susannah and say, "You don't really want to hear this, do you?" and she would insist she did. She wanted to hear every word of it—not because she was a polite guest or because she longed to increase her knowledge about what doctors did beyond what little she'd learned from the TV show, but because when Toby talked about the promise of a new asthma drug, his eyes glowed brighter than the candles, fiery with passion.

Would he be as passionate in bed as he was when he talked about helping a six-year-old to breathe more easily?

Stupid question. Stupid thought. He was a neighbor, for crying out loud, a little girl's daddy.

"So," he asked, "what brings you to Arlington?"

"I was looking for a change of pace," she said vaguely.

"You're leaving *Mercy Hospital,* aren't you," Lindsey said.

Susannah turned to the girl. She'd liked Lindsey when they'd met in the front yard that afternoon. She liked anyone MacKenzie approved of, since Mac-Kenzie tended to be quite selective in bestowing his approval. The moment Lindsey had caught Mac and scooped him off the ground, the cat had sighed and snuggled into her arms, melting into a purring ball of fuzz—his signal to Susannah that the kid was okay.

The kid was a little less okay right now. She'd brought up the one subject Susannah really didn't want to talk about: her acting career.

She was going to have to talk about it. Sooner or later, people were going to recognize her. She could introduce herself as Sue Dawson—or Mary Smith or Sally Jones or Hazel Berrybush, for that matter—but anyone who watched TV or read showbiz magazines was going to realize she was Susannah Dawson, the onetime star of the top-rated TV show *Mercy Hospital.*

Lindsey was staring at her, her eyes wide and glistening with curiosity, or maybe awe. Susannah had to say something. "I've already left the show," she murmured, infusing her voice with a note of finality.

"See?" Lindsey swung toward her father. "I told you she was a famous actress! I told you! I can't believe she's living right next door to us! This is so exciting!" She turned back to Susannah, who felt her appetite slipping away. "I *love* that show! It's the best show on TV. I thought you were great in it. I read you were leaving the show, and Dr. Lee Davis was going to be written out during the May sweeps. I don't know why you left, except that now you're here and that's so incredibly cool."

"Well..." She wished Toby would bail her out, steer his daughter in another direction, talk some more about the appalling increase in pediatric asthma cases over the past decade. But why would he? He was probably just as fascinated by her career as Lindsey was. People always thought working on a television series was more exciting than it actually was, more glamorous, more stimulating. He was probably just as curious as Lindsey to learn why Susannah Dawson had abandoned the show and transported herself all the way across the country in an effort to get as far from that whole scene as she could. She couldn't expect him to stifle his daughter.

"I was looking for a change," she said again.

"But it's the most popular show on TV," Lindsey said. "And I bet you made gazillions of dollars, and people all over the world watched you every week. Plus, you got to kiss Lucien Roche—"

And an unfortunate experience that was, Susannah thought bitterly, although she didn't say so. She hadn't fled from *Mercy Hospital* with the intention of bad-mouthing everyone else connected to the show. The producers still wanted her writing scripts for them, which was generous of them and a wonderful oppor-

tunity for her. As for the actors…they were doing their
jobs, and she'd made the choice to do that job for
many, many years. She took responsibility for her life,
the way she'd lived it then and the way she hoped to
live it now. She wasn't going to put down anyone else.

"I'd die if I could be a TV star," Lindsey gushed.
"I bet it's so much fun, having all those people fussing
all over you all the time, and making all that money
just by pretending to be someone else."

"Obviously, Ms. Dawson decided she'd rather do
something else," Toby interrupted, gently but firmly.
He *had* rescued Susannah from his daughter's inquis-
itiveness after all.

She sent him a grateful look. His smile was enigmatic but reassuring. She wondered if he used that
smile in his medical practice, if by smiling at his patients he was able to ease their symptoms and make
their medications work more effectively.

"But—everybody wants to be a star, and Susannah
Dawson *is* a star." Lindsey returned her adoring gaze
to Susannah. "There are so many people in the world
who would give anything to live that kind of life."

"Those people don't know any better," Susannah
retorted. "If they did, they'd run screaming in the opposite direction. Stardom is a lot nicer to dream about
than to live through."

Lindsey seemed to deflate, and Susannah regretted
her harsh words. She wondered if there was a way to
apologize without making the girl feel worse.

"Sometimes what seems like one thing when we
view it turns out to be quite different when we live
it," Toby gently explained to his daughter. "Lots of
people want to be doctors, but they don't realize how
much hard work and stress come with the job. You

know because you live with me. But other people might not see that. They might think being a doctor is more like—like what you see on TV medical dramas." He sent a smile Susannah's way.

Lindsey said nothing. Her eyes downcast, she pushed back from the table. "Can I be excused?" she asked.

"Would you like some dessert? Ms. Dawson brought those brownies," he reminded her, gesturing toward the foil-wrapped plate.

"Maybe later." Lindsey stood, gathered her empty plates and stomped out of the room.

Susannah turned to Toby for an explanation of what terrible thing she'd done. Perhaps she'd spoken sharply, but had she really been curt enough to send Lindsey fleeing from the room?

"Forget about it," he said, as if sensing her dismay. "You never know what's going to set her off."

"I guess she was a little starstruck, and I didn't live up to her expectations." Susannah sighed. She'd spent far too much of her life trying to live up to people's expectations—and she couldn't even live up to a ten-year-old girl's.

"Storming away from the dinner table is one of her favorite activities. She likes to be dramatic. Maybe she's got a bit of showbiz in her." He lifted the wine bottle. "Would you like some more?"

She appreciated his effort to make her feel better. "Thanks, yes," she said, lifting her empty glass toward him.

He filled it, then added more wine to his goblet. "She's disappointed in me because I didn't even know who you were," he said with a self-deprecating grin. "Yesterday you told me your name was Sue, so I thought maybe she was confusing you with someone else."

"She wasn't," Susannah admitted. "I..." She didn't know Toby enough to confide in him—and one thing she'd come to Connecticut for was privacy. But she still felt bad about his daughter, and about her foolish attempt to deny who she was. "My name is Susannah. I just had this crazy idea that if I left Los Angeles, people might not recognize me."

"People like me won't," he said, his smile growing. "I watch the eleven-o'clock news, basketball and a little football on TV, and that's it. *Mercy Hospital* wasn't on my radar screen until Lindsey started jabbering about it yesterday." He sipped some wine, his eyes clear and piercing as he studied her. "Susannah's a lovely name, but I kind of like Sue, too."

"I like Tobias," she admitted, recalling the name printed on the business card he'd given her. "But I gather you prefer to be called Toby?"

"You can call me anything you want, as long as it's clean." He grinned and sipped a little more wine. "Anything but Dr. Dad. That's Lindsey's special nickname for me."

"She's a wonderful girl," Susannah said, wishing she could bring Lindsey back into the dining room and make things right with her.

"When she's not being a pain in the butt." He lowered his glass. "Would you like a brownie?"

"They're not that good," she confessed, then laughed. "I made them from a mix. I'm a terrible cook."

"Lindsey will love them. She'll probably pig out on them later tonight."

He trailed his index finger around the rim of his

glass. His wrists were bony, his hands large yet surprisingly elegant. She imagined him patting the shoulder of his young patient with asthma and soothing that
child. She imagined him wiping a tear from his daughter's cheek or writing her a note, signing it "Dr. Dad"
in a smooth, sleek script. She'd seen him loosen his
tie, and she imagined his nimble fingers tugging the tie
completely free of his collar, moving down the front
of his shirt to undo the buttons, gliding over a woman's
skin, lifting her hair from the nape of her neck so he
could plant a kiss there....

She blinked to rid herself of the vision. "I should
probably be going," she said, externally calm, giving
no hint of what she'd been thinking, or how those
thoughts had made her feel. She was warm inside,
tense, restless in a disturbing way. Tobias Cole was an
easy man to like, but she didn't want to *like* him.

He glanced at her refilled wineglass, then lifted his
gaze to meet hers. His smile faded and he nodded.
Apparently, he recognized that she needed to leave.
She only hoped he didn't understand why.

"I really enjoyed dinner," she added.

"Maybe we'll do it again sometime." He stood as
she did, and his smile seemed slightly rueful. She
wanted to assure him that yes, they definitely would
do it again sometime. Lots of times, if he wished. She
would love to have dinner with him—and his daughter,
too. She'd love just to observe a normal family, the
affection between a father and his daughter, the simple
rhythms of ordinary life.

She wanted him to know she was sorry she had to
go—but she couldn't stay if merely glancing at his
hands filled her with erotic ideas.

But she had to stop feeling sorry about everything

she did. Smiling, she let him usher her through the
kitchen to the hall that led to his front door. "Thanks
for coming," he said, opening the heavy oak door and
letting the cool evening spill in.

So formal, so stilted. Straight from the book of eti-
quette. But his gaze wasn't formal. It wasn't even polite. It was dark and bold, reaching inside her, searching, touching places she'd thought she'd sealed up
tight, places that had been wounded and not yet healed.
He was a doctor. Did he know how to heal her? Could
those profoundly dark eyes of his perform a miracle
cure?

She didn't want to know. But when she returned his
steady, probing gaze, she couldn't help wondering.

CHAPTER THREE

FROM HER BEDROOM window, Lindsey had a view of the whole side of Susannah Dawson's house. Susannah hadn't hung any curtains yet, and glaring light filled most of the windows. Perched on her bed, Lindsey could see inside the living room—a couch, a few chairs, a colorful area rug on the hardwood floor—and the dining room—a circular table and matching chairs, the light a little less bright in there. On the second floor she could see into the bedroom that used to be Cathy's.

She and Cathy used to communicate between their windows at night, after their parents had sent them to bed. They'd worked out their own secret system using flashlights. They'd tried Morse Code, but that was too complicated, so they'd invented a code of their own: moving the beam up and down meant yes, moving it from side to side meant no, swinging it in a circle meant "call me tomorrow" and zigzagging meant "I don't know." Sometimes they'd prop up their dolls in the windows and pretend the dolls were playing with each other. Sometimes they'd draw pictures and display them for each other, although it was really hard to see drawings when the light was coming from behind them.

Mostly, though, it hadn't mattered whether they were communicating clearly. Just being connected to each other had been enough.

Lindsey wondered whether Cathy knew that a famous TV star was living in her old house. Had Cathy's parents told her they'd sold the house to Susannah Dawson? Did they even know who Susannah Dawson was, or were they as out of it as Dad?

Every now and then Lindsey spotted movement in the house next door. Susannah walked through the living room, her shadow following her. She paused at the dining-room table, then moved away. MacKenzie the cat sat on a windowsill in the living room, staring out at the night, flicking his tail back and forth. He was such a beautiful cat, almost as beautiful as Susannah.

The living-room light in Susannah's house went off. Lindsey sighed and flopped across her bed. It was ten o'clock, which was past her bedtime, but there was no school tomorrow so staying up late didn't matter.

Restless, she padded barefoot out of her room and down the stairs. Through the open doorway of the study she heard her father's voice. She knew from the droning sound of it that he was leaving a voice-mail message for one of his partners. They all took turns working on the weekends, and her father liked to leave information about his patients for whoever was on call. He'd sit and yak into the phone as if he was talking to an actual person. It was kind of weird, but Lindsey was used to it.

She slipped past the study and entered the kitchen. The pots from dinner were turned upside down on the drying rack, shining in the light above the sink. The forks and knives lay glistening on a towel next to the rack. The china was stacked on a counter, waiting to be returned to the breakfront in the dining room. Her father's jacket and the stack of mail were gone from the table, although Lindsey's backpack was still there.

She felt guilty for having not helped her father clean up after dinner. She really ought to help more. She always meant to help, but then other things got in the way—like a TV show was on, or one of her friends phoned, or she was angry with Dr. Dad.

She'd been angry tonight, not with her father so much as Susannah. Didn't the woman appreciate that she'd had the chance to live everybody's fantasy? To be a star... It made you more real somehow, more alive. If everyone knew who you were, even when you died they'd remember you, and that was almost like not dying.

Lindsey didn't want to die. If she became a star, maybe it would be like never dying.

She spotted the foil-wrapped dish of brownies on a counter near the refrigerator. She hadn't had any dessert earlier. Just seeing the plate convinced her she was starving.

She crossed to the counter to get the brownies, thinking she'd bring them up to her room and maybe eat a few while she flipped through a magazine or something. Tiptoeing so as not to alert her father that she was prowling around the house this late, she headed out of the kitchen.

Her father must have finished lecturing into the phone. A rectangle of golden light spilled into the hall through the study doorway, but she didn't hear his voice. She didn't hear anything at all.

She crept down the hall and peeked into the study. Her father was standing in front of the window seat, staring out at the house next door. He had his hands in his pockets. His slacks were just baggy enough not to look dorky, and his shirt was wrinkled. He needed a haircut. But she kind of liked when he looked sloppy.

Right now he looked more than sloppy. Something
in the hunch of his shoulders and the angle of his head,
something in his utter silence and stillness, made him
seem terribly alone to her. "Daddy?" she whispered.

He spun around, startled. Then he relaxed and
smiled. "What are you doing up, Hot Stuff?"

"I was hungry." She padded into the room. The
oversized T-shirt she slept in fluttered around her
thighs, and her hair felt heavy on her neck. She was
so ready for summer. She wanted to wear T-shirts all
the time, and shorts, and go barefoot.

She peeled back the aluminum foil on the plate.
"Want a brownie?"

"Thanks." He helped himself. She took one, as
well, and put the plate on the window seat.

"Were you leaving messages on the phone?" she
asked, taking a bite of her brownie. It was dry.

His mouth full, he only nodded. Once he swallowed,
he said, "I was thinking, before I go to the supermarket
tomorrow I'd like to stop by Arlington Memorial to
visit a patient of mine."

"Who? How come?"

"He's a very sick little boy. He was diagnosed this
morning with leukemia. Do you know what that is?"

"It's a kind of cancer, isn't it?"

"That's right." He popped the rest of the brownie
into his mouth. "He's under a specialist's care now,
but I'd still like to see him, just to cheer him on. He's
got a rough stretch ahead of him."

"Chemo?" Lindsey asked. She knew more about
medicine than any of her friends, mostly because of
her dad, but a little bit because of her mother, too. And
maybe a little bit from watching *Mercy Hospital*.

"Chemo and radiation both. Not much fun, huh?"

"Poor kid." She took another bite of her brownie and sat on the window seat, bending her knees to her chest and pulling her T-shirt over them so it covered her to her ankles. "Is he going to be all right?"

"I promised him he would be, so I guess he'd better."

Lindsey chewed thoughtfully. "Maybe you should bring him some brownies."

Her father smiled, but he still seemed sad to her. "I don't think he'll have much appetite. But you're a sweetheart to suggest it."

"Actually, these brownies aren't very good," she said as she reached for another.

She got a laugh out of him. "Sue warned me they weren't. Susannah," he corrected himself, then took a second brownie, too.

"Did she tell you to call her Sue?"

"Originally. I think she was trying to hide her identity from me. Little did she know I'd never heard of Susannah Dawson." He joined Lindsey on the window seat, the plate of brownies between them. He'd taken off his shoes, she noticed. He had on dark socks, but with the desk lamp providing the only light in the room, she couldn't make out the color.

"Why would she want to hide who she was? It's so cool being famous."

"Maybe she doesn't enjoy it as much as you would."

"I wish I could trade places with her," Lindsey admitted with a sigh. "On top of being famous, she's so beautiful."

"You're beautiful, too."

Yeah, right. Fathers always said icky things like that. It was like some obligation, a clause in the Daddy contract: Even if your kid has three eyes, green hair and zits, tell her she's beautiful.

"You look more and more like your mother every day," he added quietly, and Lindsey felt her skepticism slip away. She knew her father wasn't just doing the standard dad routine. He was telling her something important.

Her own memories of her mother were sometimes vivid, sometimes blurry. But in her dreams her mother came to her perfectly clear. Maybe Lindsey did look like her. She didn't remember her mother as being beautiful, though. Sure, she was beautiful because Lindsey loved her, she was beautiful the way mothers always were. But she wasn't beautiful like a TV star.

"Her eyes were the same shape as yours, and just as dark," he told Lindsey. "And your nose is exactly like hers."

"She had a big nose, huh," Lindsey muttered. If she was going to take after her mother, at least her mother could have had a little nose.

"She had a perfect nose. So do you," her father said. He looked as though he wanted to put his arm around her, and she hoped he would. It would be nice. He hadn't hugged her in a while, which was probably her fault. She would have liked a hug now.

When he got this way, his voice kind of hushed and his eyes distant, Lindsey understood how much he missed her mother. She missed her mother, too, but not the same way. She missed her when all the other kids had their mothers in class, like during the Native American festival, when the class had been broken into groups of four and each group had to research an American tribe and make a presentation. Lindsey had been in the Lakota group. They'd drawn a couple of posters about the Lakotas, and they constructed a tee-pee out of sticks and this fabric that looked like cow-hide, and Abbie Croce dressed one of her dolls as a Lakota maiden. The mothers of Lindsey's classmates would stop by their table at the fair, and she and Abbie and Robbie Crofton and Christopher Chou, who were both jerks but their names started with a C like hers and Abbie's so they'd gotten stuck working together, would explain how the Lakotas hunted and what their weapons were, and how they roamed the northern plains and what good horsemen they were. Every mother in the whole class, and quite a few fathers, too, came to the fair.

Her father hadn't been able to come. He couldn't sneak out of work for even an hour during the day. But if her mother had come, Lindsey would have been so happy. It was hard being the only kid in class without a mom.

Her father had to miss her mother even more than Lindsey did. If it was hard for her to be the only kid in class without a mom, it must be just as hard for him to be the only dad she knew without a wife. Except for the divorced ones, of course, but they still had their wives around, to talk to and argue with and stuff.

He must be so lonely. All those years when she'd been talking to Cathy at night through their windows, who had he been talking to? His partners' answering machines?

Maybe he and Susannah Dawson could be friends, so he wouldn't have to be as lonely. Not romantic friends—that would be so weird, a nobody Connecticut doctor going with a famous TV star—but just friends, so he could talk to someone real instead of voice mail.

"Do you like Susannah?" she asked.

He peered at her, curious. "She seems very nice," he said.

"Do you think Mommy would have liked her?"

"Absolutely."

"Mommy wasn't glamorous, was she?"

He shook his head. "Neither is Susannah. Look." He gestured at the plate. "She baked brownies. That's not glamorous."

"Especially when they're bad, like these. You'd think someone as famous as her could have done better. Unless maybe she's used to having maids cook for her."

Her father shrugged. "It's possible."

"Could we maybe invite her over again sometime?" Lindsey asked, noticing a crumb on her finger and licking it off. "I'd love to talk to her about *Mercy Hospital*. I wouldn't press or anything, but, I mean, Lucien Roche was so cute...."

"Who's Lucien—what?"

Lindsey checked the urge to give him a hard time for being so clueless. "Lucien Roche. The guy she fell in love with last season. That's the name of the character, anyway—and her character had an affair with him."

"They *are* just characters, you know," her father reminded her. "You shouldn't confuse Susannah with the character she played on TV. She isn't really a doctor. She's an actress."

Lindsey pursed her lips. "Duh. I *know* that," she said, then regretted her sarcastic tone. "Anyway, she probably never wants to talk to me ever again because of the way I bolted after dinner. She probably thinks I'm like a creep."

"No, she doesn't."

"She probably thinks I'm obnoxious."

"Lindsey." Again he looked on the verge of putting his arm around her, but he didn't. "She probably thinks you were done eating and wanted to be excused."

Lindsey snorted. She hadn't made a good impression on Susannah Dawson, and she knew it. "If she comes over again, I promise I'll be better," she said, hoping that Susannah would come back at least once more, if only so Lindsey would have a chance to stick around after the meal was done, and act like a proper hostess.

And she would. She swore to herself she'd be as good a hostess as she could, just for the chance of getting Susannah Dawson to like her.

"Maybe it's time for you to start practicing being better by climbing the stairs and getting into bed," her father said with a teasing smile. "It's late, Lindsey. Time for you to get some sleep."

"I'm old enough to stay up till ten-thirty. Everyone else in my class..." She bit her lip to silence herself. She knew what her father thought about everyone else doing something: he didn't care. And if he felt like it, he could give her a very long speech about why he didn't care.

She hoped he would spare the speech tonight.

He did. "I'll be heading up to bed myself soon. I'll give you a five-minute head start, okay?"

"Maybe you should stay up and watch *Mercy Hospital*."

"Is it on tonight?"

"No, but I've got it on tape. It's always on too late, so I have to tape it." She eased her legs out from under the T-shirt and stood. She could have found a better way to argue about her bedtime, but not tonight. Not when her father was looking so wistful. Not when he was missing her mom.

"Don't forget to brush your teeth," he reminded her.

"Yeah." Her teeth had chocolate grit in them from the brownies. "Good night, Dr. Dad."

"Good night, Hot Stuff. I'll be up in a few minutes."

She went upstairs, brushed her teeth, used the toilet and went back to her bedroom. Checking through the window, she noticed that the lights were off downstairs in Susannah's living room and the dining room, but Cathy's old window was still bright. Lindsey couldn't see Susannah, though. She couldn't even see MacKenzie.

She tugged the string to lower her shade, then sprawled out in bed. The house was as quiet as midnight. She closed her eyes and listened for her father's footsteps on the stairs, but she never heard them.

He was probably still in the study, staring through the window at the house next door.

OVER BREAKFAST Saturday morning, Lindsey announced that she wanted to go to the supermarket with him. According to her, the music store two doors down from the supermarket was selling a CD by the latest sixteen-year-old singing sensation at a three-dollar discount. "She is so cool," Lindsey rhapsodized. "Everybody at school has her CD. I've got to get it."

"If everyone already has it, why don't you borrow someone's CD and tape it," Toby suggested.

She rolled her eyes. "It's not the same."

"It's at least ten dollars cheaper."

"But it's not the same. Don't you know anything?"

The girl who had been so open to him last night, so generous and friendly, had disappeared. The surly Lindsey Beast was back.

He sighed. He'd felt so close to Lindsey last night. Like old times, when they could talk about anything—even Lindsey's mother—and share a snack, without borders or barriers. She used to be so affectionate, so transparent. If she was angry she yelled. If she was sad she cried. If she was hungry for love she climbed into his lap and wrapped her arms around him.

She was too old to climb into his lap now. But why did she have to keep retreating behind walls? Why couldn't she let him reach her?

"If you want to come to the supermarket with me, be my guest," he said. "But I'm not going there directly. First I'm stopping at Arlington Memorial to see how my patient with leukemia is doing."

"Yeah, sure, whatever. As long as you don't spend like forever with him." She shoved a handful of dry Cheerios into her mouth and stood. "I'm gonna go get my wallet."

Watching her flounce out of the kitchen, he suffered a stabbing pain in the vicinity of his soul. Why couldn't she always be the sweet, loving girl she'd been last night, when she'd wanted to bring Andy Lowenthal brownies? It wasn't as if he believed she shouldn't change and grow and shed her child's skin like a chrysalis, emerging a butterfly-lovely woman. All he wanted was for her not to be so nasty on her journey from here to there.

There was a limit to how much he could blame on hormones. Some of it was just plain Lindsey, a kid who was bored with school, fed up with her teacher and vexed by her father, a girl whose best friend had moved a thousand miles away and who resented the universe because of it.

A fine drizzle hung in the air as they left the house. He tried not to glance at Susannah's house as he drove past, but he couldn't resist the temptation. Maybe he'd catch a glimpse of her moving about inside.

He saw no sign of life at all, though. All the windows were dark.

Next to him, Lindsey slumped in her seat. She was wearing jeans, a snug-fitting sweater and a windbreaker with Arlington Soccer stitched across the back. She'd played soccer for the past four years, and he'd signed her up for spring soccer again, but he sensed no excitement in her about the impending season. He couldn't imagine her getting revved for it, charging out onto the field and dominating the game the way she had in seasons past. The possibility that she was outgrowing the sport broke his heart.

"So, what's the name of this wonderful new singer again?" he asked, hoping to start a conversation.

She gave him a withering look, then turned on the radio and pressed one of the buttons she'd preset for her favorite stations. "Listen awhile, they'll probably play her song."

All right, he could take a hint. She didn't want to talk to him. From the radio came the nasal voice of a man wailing about how sometimes life goes sour and a person just needs to explode. Toby wished the windshield wipers could drown out the song.

Traffic was light, and he reached the hospital in ten minutes. He parked in the staff lot. "I'll wait in the car," Lindsey announced.

"No, you won't. You're coming in with me. I might be a while."

She frowned, her exasperation obvious. He himself was close to snapping. He wanted to remind her it had been *her* idea to accompany him on this outing when she knew damned well what it was going to entail, and she'd better not complain if he spent a few minutes with Andy Lowenthal. But lately he'd found that arguments with Lindsey were pointless, all heat and no light, and he never felt any better when they were over, even when he won. To lash out at her now would likely spoil the rest of the morning.

So he held his tongue and returned her frown, certain that she'd see just as much exasperation in his face as he saw in hers. Then he shoved open his door and climbed out.

"I'll wait in the gift shop," she said as soon as they entered the hospital's main lobby.

"You'll come upstairs to pediatrics with me," he told her. She was not going to set the agenda, especially not after she'd been so snotty in the car.

Pouting, she followed him down the hall, shuffling her feet and affecting that slouching posture he'd noticed yesterday. They reached the elevator and he jabbed the button. When the doors slid open, he saw a familiar face inside: Allison Winslow, a nurse in the neonatal unit of the pediatrics wing.

"Allison!" he greeted her with a rush of relief. Here was a friend, an ally, someone who wouldn't get into a snit over nonsense. He'd known Allison for as long as they'd both been practicing at Arlington Memorial. She'd watched over many of his youngest patients, the newborns and day-olds who remained at the hospital while their mothers recuperated from childbirth. As far as he was concerned, Allison was the heart and soul of her department.

She grinned. "Hey, Toby, what brings you here? Did you pull a Saturday shift?"

"No, I'm just stopping by to see how a patient of mine is bearing up. Do you remember my daughter? Lindsey, this is Nurse Winslow," he introduced them. "Or is it McCoy?" Allison had gotten married a year ago.

"Still Winslow," she told him. "It's a tradition in my family. No matter what—or *who*—happens to us, we always remain Nurse Winslow."

"Allison is the third generation of nurses in her family," Toby told his daughter, who looked painfully bored by the conversation.

Allison smiled at her. "Of course I remember you, Lindsey. You were at the July Fourth barbecue last year, weren't you?"

"Yeah, right," Lindsey mumbled, studying her thumbnail. As soon as the elevator doors slid open, she bolted, shouting over her shoulder, "I'll be in the kiddy gift shop," as she jogged down the hall.

Toby let out a long, weary breath. It was one thing for her to be rude to him, but quite another for her to be rude to Allison. "I'm sorry," he murmured. "She's in a foul mood this morning."

Allison gazed down the hall after her. "She's changed so much since last summer."

"Tell me about it." Dejection echoed in every word.

"She's practically a teenager."

"She hasn't even turned eleven yet. She's too young to be a teenager. She's just acting like one." He scruffed a hand through his hair, wondering whether Lindsey was deliberately trying to embarrass him by behaving like a brat in front of his colleagues, or whether she was completely indifferent about how she came across to others. "I wish I knew how to get through to her. Sometimes…" Like last night, he thought. "Sometimes she's the most wonderful kid in the world. Other times, it's as though her body has been inhabited by some alien creature."

"I bet she feels that way, too," Allison remarked thoughtfully.

He turned to her, puzzled. Attired in a powder-blue T-shirt under a white coat and white slacks, with her stethoscope draped around her neck and her long, curly hair held back from her face with a barrette, she looked both professional and blessedly confident, not the least bit offended by Lindsey's behavior.

"What do you mean—she feels that way?"

"As though she doesn't know who's in her body. Or what happened to her old body. Or who she is."

"I survived adolescence," he argued. "I don't recall it being all that confusing."

"You're you," Allison pointed out. "Lindsey's Lindsey. Besides, you're a guy, which makes a big difference."

He swallowed a groan. This was part of it, he knew, part of what troubled him about his daughter. "I haven't got a wife to help her through this," he said, trying not to sound bitter about that miserable fact. He didn't want sympathy; he was just stating the truth.

"I know, Toby." Allison gave his arm a gentle pat. "Maybe that makes it harder for you. It's possible she'd be behaving just as badly with a mother as she is with you, but if you had a wife for moral support, it would help."

"Well." He shrugged and forced a smile. "I guess I'll have to do without moral support, then. Unless you've got some to spare," he added hopefully.

She smiled. "As a matter of fact, I might. Why don't you try the Daddy School?"

"The what?"

"The Daddy School. It's a program my friend Molly Saunders-Russo and I started two years ago. We give classes on parenting designed just for fathers. I work with expectant fathers and fathers of newborns. Molly offers classes to fathers of older kids. You'd probably find it useful."

He probably would. It certainly couldn't hurt. "When do these classes meet?" he asked, acknowledging that taking them *could* hurt his already overburdened schedule.

"I think Molly has a couple of evening sessions for fathers of older children. I'm not sure when she holds them, but I can give you her number and you can call her yourself." Allison gestured for him to follow her to the nurses' station in the neonatal department. Once there, she grabbed a notepad with a pharmaceutical company's logo printed on it and jotted down her friend's name, along with a phone number. "This is the number of the preschool she operates, so don't panic when you call and hear lots of screaming toddlers in the background. It's really a top-notch preschool. Molly knows her stuff."

"About preschoolers," he said dubiously.

"And older children, too."

"Does she have any kids of her own?" he asked, still skeptical. Who could possibly understand what he was going through, other than someone who'd gone through the same thing?

"A three-and-a-half-year-old stepson and a baby on the way," Allison said with a smile. "I know—you think that means she's no expert. But I'll tell you, her stepson was quite a handful when he came into her life. His parents were divorced and he had some serious issues to work through. He was smack in the middle of the Terrible Twos, which is the same thing as adolescence except that the kid is shorter. Molly fell in love with Michael before she even fell in love with his father. She knows how to handle the tough cases. Trust me—you're in good hands with her. And really, what have you got to lose?''

Nothing, he thought. His daughter was already half lost to him. He was clinging hard to the other half, but he felt her slipping like sand through his fingers.

He'd already lost his wife. He couldn't bear to lose his daughter, too.

''I'll call this friend of yours,'' he said, taking the slip of paper and tucking it into his shirt pocket. ''Thanks.''

Allison scrutinized him for a moment, then impulsively reached out and hugged him. ''You know, when I meet women about to give birth, they're usually frightened. They think their baby is going to come out wrong, or labor is going to hurt too much, or they're not going to be able to deliver for some reason. And I tell them, many, many millions of women have gone through this before they did, and it almost always turned out all right. Now I'm telling you the same thing, Toby. Millions of parents have gone through what you're going through, and most of the time it's turned out all right. Especially when the parent loves his child as much as you love yours.''

In spite of himself, he smiled. ''When did you become a psychologist?''

''I'm not a psychologist. I'm a cheerleader.'' She

gave his shoulder a final comforting squeeze. "You're going to be okay, Toby."

Her encouraging words echoed inside him as he strode down the hall to the pediatric ICU, where Andy Lowenthal was awaiting his first grueling round of chemotherapy. What Toby was going through with Lindsey was nothing compared with what Andy would be going through over the next several weeks. Besides, Allison was right. Plenty of people before him had raised adolescents successfully. He wasn't such an ignoramus that he couldn't master the necessary skills, as well.

Still, it would be easier if he had Jane by his side, fighting the good fight with him. Or any woman. Someone who understood the way a girl's mind worked. Someone who could help him make sense of it. Someone Lindsey could confide in, and trust, and admire.

Someone who could whisper to Toby, when desperation threatened to drag him under, that he was a good father and a good man, and his daughter was going to turn out fine.

CHAPTER FOUR

SUSANNAH HOOKED the pot of impatiens on the beam in the porch of the overhang and stepped back to look. The delicate pink blossoms spilled over the edges of the pot, soft and drizzly. It still amazed her to think she had managed to escape from one life and transport herself all the way across the continent to another, entirely different life, one with mint-fresh spring afternoons and porches with overhangs from which a person could suspend a pot of flowers. Along with disorientation, she felt a kind of pride that she'd accomplished this.

Her life was really hers. She could do what she wanted—sleep late, read every page of the newspaper over a leisurely breakfast, discuss worldly matters with MacKenzie and shop for groceries at midnight at the all-night supermarket. She'd done that last evening and discovered the store nearly empty at that hour. In her eyeglasses and with her hair pinned up, she'd gone unrecognized by the drowsy cashier.

Sooner or later, she would emerge from behind the eyeglasses and let her hair down. Sooner or later she'd allow the small, safe world of Arlington, Connecticut, to learn who she was. Eventually, she hoped, she would become yesterday's news and no one would give a damn that she'd once been a familiar face on TV.

She heard the high-pitched babble of young voices drifting down the street on a breeze. Turning, she saw a throng of children spilling out of the yellow school bus that had stopped at a corner several blocks away. They separated into twos and threes, chattering, giggling, the boys shoving and chasing one another, the girls conferring in private huddles. A trio of girls walked slowly along the sidewalk. As they drew nearer, Susannah recognized one of them as Lindsey.

The other two girls peeled off, veering onto a side street, and Lindsey continued on toward her house alone. She wore a snug-fitting T-shirt and even snugger jeans that displayed a body just beginning to emerge from gawky little-girl skinniness. Her hair was held off her face with a headband, and her eyes were large and dark above delicate cheekbones.

She was awfully pretty, Susannah thought. In a few years, Toby was going to have his hands full keeping boys away from her. Susannah sensed that Toby was the sort of father who would stand guard at the front door, protecting his daughter's virtue with his fists if necessary.

She shouldn't consider the idea of a protective daddy such a turn-on. But it didn't matter how many times she told herself not to think about Toby Cole as anything more than a congenial neighbor. Merely glimpsing his daughter walking home from the bus stop caused Susannah to remember his intense gaze, his gentle voice, the sensual motions of his hands.

She ought to keep her distance from the Cole family. She ought to apply herself to her new life—writing, decompressing, seeking her own counsel and all that. She ought to steer clear of the sexy doctor next door and his moody daughter.

Every ought-to flew out of her mind as Lindsey drew near. Susannah recalled how Lindsey had bolted from the table last Friday night because of her. Maybe she could repair the damage she'd unintentionally inflicted.

"Hey," she called out.

The girl stopped at the edge of the lawn and stared.

Susannah recalled that the damage had been related to the fact that Lindsey believed she was someone worthy of being stared at. Lindsey had been disappointed that Susannah didn't think highly of her own celebrity. Perhaps, if she could convince Lindsey she was just an ordinary human being, Lindsey would relax around her and they could be friends.

When Lindsey said nothing, Susannah asked, "Do the flowers look okay over there?"

"Um…yeah. They look great."

"You think so?"

Lindsey seemed to thaw a little. "I love hanging plants. I wish we had a porch like yours so we could have hanging plants, too."

"The porch was one of the things that sold me on this house." Susannah scrutinized Lindsey across the expanse of grass. Lindsey's posture was that of a girl who'd just sprouted breasts and was a little embarrassed about them. Her smile was shy, hesitant. Her schoolbag hung from a strap over one shoulder, its waterproof purple surface bulging with lumps from books and clutter.

"I've still got some pictures to hang inside. Any chance you could lend me a hand? I can't decide where I want them. I'd love it if you could give me some ideas."

Lindsey looked behind her, as if not quite sure Susannah was talking to her. She turned back, apparently stunned. "You want *me* to help?"

"We both think this porch is nice, so we probably have similar tastes. You can tell me if I'm hanging the pictures straight."

Lindsey's face lit up. She started across the grass, then paused and glanced toward her own house. "I'm supposed to go straight home from school," she said. "Dad'll have a cow if I don't go home."

"How about if we give him a call and see if it's okay with him," Susannah suggested.

The light returned to Lindsey's smile. She bounded across the grass, running with the fleet grace of an athlete. "This is so cool," she said. "I know your house so well because my best friend used to live here. Cathy Robinson. Her dad got transferred to Atlanta and they had to move. But we used to hang out in each other's houses all the time." Bubbling with energy, she preceded Susannah into the house, her familiarity with it obvious. "We weren't allowed in the living room too much," she informed Susannah, letting her backpack slide from her shoulder and hit the hardwood floor of the entry hall with a thump. "Cathy's mother wouldn't let us. She had expensive stuff in there. White couches and stuff. It was pretty, but it seemed kind of stupid to me. I mean, what's the point of having a living room if you can't even use it? I like your living room much better," she declared, marching through the arched doorway into the still starkly decorated room and heading straight for the cat, which lay curled in a patch of sunlight on the rug. "Hey, MacKenzie! Remember me?"

Observing from the doorway, Susannah grinned. This was the Lindsey she'd met Friday afternoon, the talkative, exuberant girl full of spunk. MacKenzie seemed happy to see her, too. Usually, he didn't take kindly to being awakened from a nap, but when Lindsey stroked his back he stirred, yawning and arching against her hand.

Susannah had intended to have Lindsey telephone her father, but she was too busy stroking Mac. Abandoning them in the living room, Susannah headed for the kitchen alone. She carried her cordless phone to the desk, where she'd left Toby's business card, and punched in the number printed at the bottom.

"Arlington Pediatric Associates," a receptionist recited. "How may I direct your call?"

Susannah felt nerves pinch her nape. She didn't want to disturb Toby at work, where he might be in the midst of examining a patient. More important, she didn't want the sound of his voice to remind her of the erotic thoughts she'd had while seated in his dining room on Friday night.

But she was an actor. She could conceal her anxiety. "May I speak to Dr. Cole, please?" she asked smoothly.

"One moment." She was put on hold, and then heard another woman's voice: "This is Dr. Cole's assistant. Can I help you?"

Obviously, he was too busy. Just as well—Susannah could tell his assistant where Lindsey was and avoid talking to Toby altogether. "This is Dr. Cole's next-door neighbor," she said. "Could you please tell him I've got Lindsey over here, and—"

"Lindsey? Hang on, I'll get him."

Before Susannah could finish, she was put on hold again.

A smile touched her lips. He must have given his

assistant permission to drag him from whatever he was doing if Lindsey needed him. He was so attentive to his daughter, so available to her—the way good fathers in loving families were supposed to be.

A few seconds passed, and she heard his voice: "Susannah? Is everything all right?"

Her smile grew. If anyone had seen her, they might have thought she was a kid with a crush, grinning like a goofball at the sound of a particular man's voice. She couldn't recall ever having had a crush on anyone in her life. And here she was at the advanced age of thirty-two, having spent most of her life in the high-pressure grow-up-quickly world of television…and she felt almost as young as Lindsey, practically tongue-tied in the presence of the cutest guy in town.

"Everything's fine," she said. "How did you know it was me?"

"Mary said it was my next-door neighbor," he said, "and I knew it wouldn't be my neighbors on the other side. No one's ever home there during the day." As he spoke the tautness left his tone. "So everything's okay?"

"Yes. Lindsey just got home from school, and I invited her in to help me hang pictures. I thought we ought to check and make sure that was all right with you."

"She wants to help you hang pictures?" He sounded bewildered.

"Well, actually, I thought we could sort of make up from Friday night. If we don't get around to hanging pictures, it's no big deal."

He said nothing for a minute, then, "Are you sure you want to do that?"

"Do what? Make friends with Lindsey?" It didn't

seem like such a risky undertaking to her. "Is there something wrong with my wanting to do it?"

"No. Not at all." Again he fell silent. Closing her eyes, she visualized his thick, dark hair, his earnest smile, his lean, lanky build. "Actually, I'd be very grateful."

"Don't be. This is between Lindsey and me," she said. She didn't want to believe Toby had anything to do with her attempt to befriend Lindsey. It was just that she'd been a moody teenager once, too—a girl with two parents whose ideas of how she should live her life rarely took her feelings into account. Lindsey had a father who seemed truly attached to her, but she lacked a mother. She was facing challenges no less difficult than what Susannah had faced as a teenager.

Susannah would have been thrilled to have a neighbor who cared for her, cared enough to make sure she was all right. If she could be that kind of neighbor for Lindsey, it would be good for them both.

Toby had nothing to do with it.

"Can I talk to her for a minute?" he asked.

"Sure. Hang on." She strode out of the kitchen to find Lindsey lying on her back on the floor stroking MacKenzie, who sat happily on her belly. As soon as Susannah entered the room, Lindsey bolted upright, depositing MacKenzie onto the rug. Lindsey looked embarrassed, although there was no reason for her to be. She wasn't the first human being MacKenzie had wrapped around his paw, and she wouldn't be the last.

"Your dad wants to speak to you," Susannah said, handing the phone to Lindsey.

"Oh—okay." Lindsey pressed the phone to her ear, her wide eyes fixed on Susannah. "Yeah?" she said into the phone. "Dad?"

Susannah lifted one of the framed prints she'd been planning to hang on the living-room wall, not so much because she cared about the print but because she wanted to assure Lindsey she wasn't eavesdropping. "Just some math," Lindsey said. "I can do it tonight.... No, I promise I won't forget to do it. I know you're meeting with Ms. Hathaway. Your plan, Dr. Dad, not mine." She ran her free hand through her hair, which had gotten matted from lying on the rug. "No, I won't stay too long. I won't be a pest.... I *know,* Dad." She rolled her eyes. "Okay. Here's Susannah." She handed the phone back to Susannah, making a great show of looking exasperated.

Susannah gave her what she hoped was a placating smile and returned to the kitchen alone. "I told her not to stay at your house all afternoon," he said.

"I don't mind."

"I do." He half sighed, half laughed. "If she starts getting on your nerves, send her home."

"She won't get on my nerves," Susannah assured him.

"You don't know her the way I do. And I'd hate to destroy a good neighborly relationship over the fact that my daughter can be a pain in the butt when she wants."

Was that what he envisioned for them? A good neighborly relationship? She supposed that would be appropriate.

But did a good neighborly relationship include her having outlined a plotline for an episode of *Mercy Hospital* that revolved around a charismatic pediatrician with soulful eyes and a heart-melting smile? Did it include her sprawling out in bed, imagining what that doctor's hands would feel like twining through her hair or caressing the underside of her chin, what that doctor's mouth would feel like on hers?

Surely that wasn't what Toby had had in mind when he'd mentioned good neighborly relationships. And if Susannah was wise, she'd be satisfied with what he *did* have in mind. If she didn't want to get hurt again, if she didn't want to get caught up in other people's agendas, if she wanted simply to live a normal life as an anonymous human being in a quiet, peaceful community, she would be wise to keep things neighborly with Toby and everyone else she met in Arlington.

"I know more about pain-in-the-butts than most people learn in a lifetime," she told him. "Don't worry about Lindsey and me."

"I always worry about Lindsey. She's my daughter," he said simply. "And I'll worry about you because—" he paused as if giving his statement great thought "—you've got a generous heart."

That sounded more than neighborly. Even after she hung up the phone and went off to find Lindsey, his words resonated inside her. No one had ever told her she had a generous heart before.

She liked the sound of it. She liked even more that Toby Cole had been the one to say it.

CRUISING SLOWLY down the street to his house, he spotted Lindsey and Susannah sitting on Susannah's porch steps. Susannah's cat sat in Lindsey's lap, and she was stroking the creature and talking to Susannah. She must have heard his car, because she looked toward him, smiled and waved.

Susannah smiled, too. The late-afternoon sun made her hair shimmer with streaks of platinum and gold.

Her smile wasn't as broad as Lindsey's, but it was knowing and genuine.

Evidently, they'd made friends.

He was pleased, but other emotions mingled with that pleasure: worry that Lindsey needed more than he could give her; apprehension that it would be too easy for Lindsey to become attached to Susannah; and a strange, selfish anger because *he* wanted to be Susannah's friend.

Being her friend wasn't a good idea. And Lindsey's being her friend *was* a good idea. He shoved the anger out of his way and pulled into the driveway, pressing the automatic garage door opener as he drove.

By the time he'd parked and emerged from the garage, Lindsey had jogged across Susannah's front lawn, her backpack slung over her shoulder. Susannah followed a couple of steps behind her, holding the cat.

"Daddy!" Lindsey's voice bubbled with excitement. "We hung pictures in Susannah's house! I helped. I did my homework, too, and I ate a banana. And we played with MacKenzie—he's so smart, Dad. He's smarter than some of the kids in my class. You tell him to go and bring you his little mouse toy, and he does it."

"Only if he feels like it," Susannah interjected, her eyes bright with amusement as they met Toby's.

"And we had a problem," Lindsey went on. "Susannah wants to hang a full-length mirror on the back of a door, but we couldn't do it. It's too heavy and complicated. I told Susannah you'd do it for her. You will, won't you, Dad?"

He would have said "Yes, of course," if only Susannah wasn't looking at him that way, her eyes so blue they nearly blinded him with their beauty. If she wasn't so damned attractive, he'd have no problem hanging a dozen full-length mirrors on her doors.

But she was Susannah Dawson, and he'd been thinking about her the way he hadn't thought about a woman since Jane died. And that troubled him.

"I told her you could do it," Lindsey continued, apparently unaware of his hesitation. "You do all kinds of stuff around our house, and you're strong. This mirror weighs like a ton, Daddy. So maybe you could do it tonight."

"Your father just got home from work," Susannah pointed out. She must have noticed his reluctance.

"Well, I meant, like later. I did my math homework sheets already, so we can have dinner right away, and then we can go back to Susannah's and hang the mirror."

"The mirror can wait," Susannah insisted, directing her words more to him than to Lindsey.

"Of course I'll do it," he said, thinking her mouth might be even more beautiful than her eyes. Her lips were soft and pink, the lower lip slightly fuller than the upper. "But we do have to have dinner first. I could call you after we're done—"

"Or maybe she could eat with us," Lindsey suggested.

To his great relief, Susannah bailed him out. "I don't think so, Lindsey. Why don't you have dinner and visit with your dad. We can take care of the mirror another time."

He thanked her with a nod. "I'll call you," he promised.

"Tonight." Lindsey nudged him.

He gave Lindsey a quelling look. "Susannah and I will work it out."

Lindsey wriggled through the hedge bordering the driveway. "'Bye, Susannah. And don't forget what I told you—the movie theater on Hauser Street is much better. They use real butter on the popcorn and the seats in the front rock. Forget the other movie theater. The popcorn sucks."

"Okay." Susannah backed up a couple of steps. "Talk to you later," she said to Toby, then waved, turned and headed back to her house.

He forced his gaze away from her retreating form, her long legs and sleek curves and her glorious, silky-looking hair. He smiled down at Lindsey. "So, you had fun?" he asked.

Indeed she had. He heard about it nonstop as they entered the house, as he tossed his blazer over a chair and flipped through the mail, as he seasoned the chicken breasts and Lindsey gathered the ingredients for a salad. He heard about how cool Susannah was, how big the waves were off the coast of California, where she used to live, and how tall the palm trees grew there. He heard about how everyone drove everywhere there, and lots of people had convertibles that they drove in January because it was always so warm, and about how all the coffee bars had outdoor tables year-round. He heard about how Susannah had turned Cathy's bedroom into an office, and she was writing scripts or something, and Lindsey had wanted to do her homework at Susannah's desk, but Susannah said no because she had all these papers laid out in a certain order and didn't want them to get messed up, so Lindsey did her math at the kitchen table, instead. Susannah had a seriously cool kitchen table, according to Lindsey. It was varnished wood with ceramic tiles in the center of it, and she had a lamp with a stained-glass shade hanging from the ceiling directly above the table.

Toby listened, perhaps more closely than he should have. What scripts was Susannah writing? Had she and Lindsey discussed her acting career at all? Had she explained to Lindsey why she didn't want to talk about her work on the TV show—and if so, would Lindsey tell him? Not because he wanted to pry but because he wanted to know Susannah better.

He couldn't count on Lindsey to help him get to know Susannah. She'd done enough by inviting Susannah to dinner last Friday—and by offering his services as a mirror hanger. If he wanted to get to know Susannah better, he ought to thank Lindsey for creating an opening for him—and then walk through that opening himself.

"I'm meeting with Ms. Hathaway tomorrow morning," he reminded Lindsey. "Is there anything in particular you want me to talk about with her?"

Lindsey let out a long, weary breath. "Tell her to give me higher grades," she said. Then hastily added, "Joke, Dad."

"I figured."

"I don't care what you talk to her about," Lindsey said. "I told you I'd do better and I will. Susannah said I was a real math whiz. She was doing stuff in the kitchen while I did my homework. Rearranging cabinets, she said. She decided she didn't like the way she set them up when she unpacked, so she was moving stuff around while I did my math, and she looked over my shoulder and thought I was doing a real good job with it...."

And on Lindsey went, through dinner, through dessert, during the time it took to clear the table and wrap

the leftovers. Toby tried to recall the last time he'd
seen her so pumped up about anything. It might have
been at a soccer game last summer. Once she'd started
fifth grade, she'd gone flat, all the fizz seeping out of
her. Even at her birthday party—an outing with a
group of her friends to see a movie, followed by take-
out pizza from Luigi's and a decorated cake from the
bakery—Lindsey had been reserved and blasé.

She wasn't blasé now. Susannah Dawson had gotten
her adrenaline flowing. Toby was delighted, but also
wary. He knew that adrenaline highs didn't last forever, and once they ended a person could crash hard.

"So, are we going back to Susannah's house to hang
the mirror?" Lindsey asked as she draped the dish
towel over the handle on the oven door.

"You're not," he said. "You've been at her house
all afternoon. Maybe she could use a break."

"She said she wanted the mirror hung."

"That doesn't mean she wants it hung this minute."

"I bet she does. She's so pretty—I bet she wants
the mirror up so she can check herself out."

Toby laughed. "I'll call her and we'll set up a
time."

"You could go tonight without me," Lindsey
pointed out. "She might be sick of me, but she hasn't
had a chance to get sick of you yet."

Lindsey's perceptiveness surprised him. He was
amazed that she would acknowledge the possibility
that Susannah might be sick of her, but he was un-
nerved by her suggestion that he go to Susannah's
without her. Did Lindsey know he also considered Susannah pretty?

"I'll call her," he repeated, then asked, "What
would you do if I went over there tonight?"

"Watch TV," she said. "I've got *Mercy Hospital* on tape."

"All right." He took a deep breath, surprised by the twinge of nervousness he felt. "I'll call her."

Lindsey strode out of the kitchen. Her posture was straight, her shoulders square. Could one afternoon with Susannah Dawson have transformed her back into the Lindsey she used to be? Probably not permanently, but he appreciated the change. That was reason enough to call Susannah—to thank her for having boosted Lindsey's spirits today.

He dialed Susannah's number and listened to the phone ring on the other end. She answered on the second ring. "Hello?"

"Hi, it's Toby," he said, his nervousness ebbing. Hearing her voice calmed him. "What did you do to my daughter this afternoon?" he asked.

"Do to her?" Susannah sounded anxious now. "Nothing. We just hung some pictures and she did her homework—"

"She's in such a great mood. She wouldn't shut up all through dinner, and she was hardly sarcastic at all. What did you do, give her a drug?"

Susannah laughed. "Do you think I'd give drugs to a girl whose father's a doctor?"

"Well, whatever you did, it worked. Thank you. I'm in your debt."

"I didn't do anything, really," she insisted. Closing his eyes, he could picture her smile, her luminous eyes. "But I don't mind having you in my debt."

"I was figuring I'd pay it off by hanging that mirror for you."

"Now?"

Why not? "Sure, if you'd like."

"Okay. Come on over."

"Give me ten minutes," he said.

He hung up the phone and glanced at the wall clock. Ten minutes. He ought to change out of his work apparel. And brush his teeth and comb his hair. Not because this was a date, not because he wanted to make a good impression on Susannah, but…hell, he *did* want to make a good impression. He might as well be honest about it.

He raced up the stairs to his bedroom, exchanged his twill trousers for a clean pair of jeans and detoured into the bathroom to freshen up. Then back to his bedroom to grab his wallet and keys from the bureau, where he'd left them. He checked his watch: eight-fifteen. He'd be home in less than an hour and a half, in time to start nagging Lindsey about her bedtime.

This wasn't anything but a favor for a neighbor. He wasn't going to make a big deal out of it.

"Lindsey," he called into the den, where she was sprawled out on the couch with the remote control clutched in one hand, "I'm going over to Susannah's. I'll be home before nine-thirty."

"Whatever," Lindsey said, her attention on the screen.

He went downstairs to the basement to grab a couple of screwdrivers, in case Susannah didn't have any, and then left the house, locking the front door behind him. The sky was a rich blue, just barely dark enough to make the first few stars of the night visible. The grass had a fresh, dewy scent. Down the street he saw Don Goldman walking his chocolate Lab. Had Don met Susannah yet? Did he know she was a former TV star? Had he noticed that she was gorgeous?

Well, he wasn't blind, so if he'd seen her he'd noticed. But Don was married. Toby wasn't.

And he shouldn't be thinking about Susannah in the context of his marital status. He wasn't going to get involved with her, especially now, when her friendship had made such a difference in Lindsey's mood. Let them develop a relationship. Lindsey needed a woman in her life more than Toby did. He wouldn't do anything to complicate matters.

He spotted the hanging pot of flowers on her porch as he climbed the steps, a pretty, feminine touch. Should he have flowers around the house for Lindsey? He really didn't know much about plants.

At least he knew how to hang a mirror.

He rang the bell. Susannah swung the door wide and amber light spilled from the entry hall, making him aware of the slight nip in the night air. Her house looked warm. Her smile looked warm, too. ''Hi,'' she said, gesturing him inside. ''Are you sure you don't mind doing this?''

''If I minded, I wouldn't be here.''

''Well, you didn't have to rush over and do it tonight,'' she said, ushering him down the hall to the stairs. ''I bet Lindsey badgered you into doing it.''

''Not really. Although I think she wanted me out of the house. When I'm not home, she pigs out on ice cream in front of the TV.''

''When you're home you don't let her do that?''

''I tell her to take less ice cream,'' he explained.

''Ice cream is nature's perfect food,'' Susannah declared. ''Telling someone to take less is a crime against nature. In fact, if you decided to hang the mirror tomorrow, I could have gone out to the store and stocked

up on ice cream, so I could reward you with a bowl
of it afterward. A huge bowl of it. A pig-out bowl.''

"I'd put half of it back," he admitted. Ice cream
didn't mean as much to him as it did to Lindsey or,
apparently, Susannah.

He'd been in the Robinson house a few times, but
never upstairs. Following Susannah up, he tried not to
focus on the sway of her hips, the fall of her hair, the
tangy fragrance she wore. She glanced over her shoulder at him, and he wondered if she knew he'd been
admiring her from behind. "In any case," he said, "I
couldn't hang the mirror tomorrow night. I've got a
class to go to."

"Really? What kind of class?"

He almost regretted having opened his mouth. Admitting that he needed to take a class in how to be a
father would make her think he was inept. Which
would be a good way for him to keep anything remotely romantic from stirring to life between them, but
still... He didn't like announcing to the world that he
felt inadequate when it came to raising his daughter.

Susannah glanced over her shoulder again, obviously awaiting his reply. "Daddy School," he told her,
suppressing the urge to cringe.

She halted and turned to him. "Daddy School?"

He really wished he hadn't mentioned it. He gave a
slight nod, then asked, "Where's the mirror?"

She accepted his change of subject. "Right here,"
she said, pushing open a door and leading him into a
room. A bedroom. *Her* bedroom.

The bed was broad and inviting, with a simple brass
headboard. The mattress was covered in teal-colored
sheets and a puffy beige comforter, and teal and beige
pillows of various shapes lay scattered against the arch

of brass. It was a bed big enough for two, a bed big enough for sex.

Annoyed that the idea had even occurred to him, he turned away. A low teak dresser occupied one wall, and a small brass-trimmed vanity table stood near the window, its mirrored surface covered with crystal bottles filled with colored fluids. Perfumes? Body oils?

He felt a curse take shape on his tongue. Why the hell did the mirror have to be in her bedroom? Why did he have to be in this room with her?

Not that anything would happen. She already knew he was incompetent enough to need a class in fathering skills. If anything could turn off a woman, that was it.

"I was thinking it should go on the back of the closet door," she said, sauntering to the closet as if his presence in her bedroom signified nothing.

He trailed her across the room. She opened a door and flicked on an interior light, exposing a spacious walk-in closet less than half-filled with clothes. Didn't showbiz stars maintain huge wardrobes? Susannah had clearly left showbiz behind.

The mirror was propped up against a wall inside the closet. "It's really heavy," she warned, stepping deeper into the closet so Toby could reach the mirror.

The closet had a pleasant scent, fresh laundry blended with Susannah's spicy fragrance. The walls felt close, the rack of her clothes hanging along one side, the empty shelves and as yet unpacked cartons shoved against the other and the single overhead light illuminating her as she stood in the tiny room. It would take so little effort to shut the door, enclosing them both in the snug space.

Swallowing, he turned from her and hoisted the mirror away from the wall. When he swung it toward the door, her reflection flashed across the glass. Her poise and stance were elegant. As an actor, she'd had to use her body as a creative instrument of her craft, and it showed.

He heaved the mirror up against the door to get an idea of how it would fit. "Like this?"

"That would be perfect."

He lowered it back to the floor. "Have you got a tape measure? And a pencil. I need to get it centered and mark where the screws are going in."

"Sure." She brushed past him while exiting the closet. He felt her warmth against his back, a tickle where a strand of her hair floated against the side of his neck as she moved back into the bedroom.

He took a deep, calming breath. He felt like a teenager, as hormonal and erratic as Lindsey sometimes behaved. Susannah seemed utterly unaffected by his nearness, however. To her, apparently, hanging a mirror was the only thing going on.

She returned to his side carrying a pencil, a tape measure and a straight ruler. "Now, tell me about this Daddy School," she said as he measured the length of the door. "What is it? A school for daddies?"

All right. He had doomed himself, and it was just as well. As long as she thought of him as a blundering father in need of tutoring, hanging a mirror would define the limits of the evening. He should be glad. He'd already decided that getting involved with her would be a mistake.

"Yes," he said as he marked the door with small pencil dots where the brackets would be screwed into place. "It's a school for daddies."

"What do they teach you?"

"How to be better daddies, I hope."

He felt her smile before he saw its reflection in the mirror. "I don't think you need this school, Toby. You're a wonderful daddy."

"I wish," he muttered, hunkering down to mark the bottom of the door. At least he didn't have to look at her while he confessed his failings.

"Of course you are. Look at what a sweetheart Lindsey is. A bad father couldn't raise such a fine daughter."

"Lindsey idolizes you," he told her, measuring the width a second time. "If you told her to stand on her head and blow bubbles out her ears, she'd do it. With me, it's a whole different situation."

"I doubt that. Mac, go away—we're busy here." She turned to shoo her cat out of the bedroom, then returned to Toby's side, settling onto the carpeted floor next to him, crossing her legs and resting her elbows on her knees. "I don't think Lindsey idolizes me. I hope she doesn't, anyway. I don't want to be idolized."

"It's not just because you're a famous actress," he said. He wasn't sure that was true, but he thought it would make Susannah feel better. "It's because you're a woman. And you're not her father. Those are two big pluses."

"I bet she idolizes you, too. You're a doctor. You save people's lives."

"Not always." He fussed with the tape measure, unable to look at her. This conversation had grown too intimate too quickly. And intimate in the wrong way. He'd barely confessed his shortcomings as a father and she had deftly located his even worse failing.

"Well, of course you can't save *every* life," she said gently.

"My wife died of cancer." He didn't want to talk about this, but he couldn't see a way out of it. He was kneeling on Susannah's bedroom floor, pretending to be absorbed in the screws and brackets stored in an envelope taped to the mirror, and somehow he and she had ventured into treacherous waters. He couldn't see a way back to safety other than sticking his oars in the water and rowing hard.

He peeled the envelope from the mirror and set it carefully on the floor, then turned to Susannah. "My wife had ovarian cancer. From the day they diagnosed her to the day she died was less than six months. I'm a doctor. I work with other doctors. I'm affiliated with a hospital. And all this brainpower, all this medical expertise, all the years of research and study—none of it saved her life. Lindsey knows this. She was there. She lost her mother. She knows doctors aren't worth idolizing."

Susannah didn't look shocked or cowed. She gave him a crooked smile. "Maybe someday she'll appreciate how hard the doctors tried. Maybe she'll understand that they did their best. She'll realize that what doctors do is a hell of a lot more important than what actors playing doctors do."

"You're an optimist."

Her smile expanded. "It beats the alternative. So, what do you think they'll teach you at this Daddy School? How to win your daughter's respect?"

She seemed so forthright, so unruffled by what he'd revealed. That she could smile, not recoil from him for sharing his scars and insecurities, not dismiss him as the floundering fool he often felt he was, moved him even more than her grace and beauty.

"I'm not sure what they'll teach me," he said. "I guess I'll find out when I get there."

"They'll probably teach you that you're doing everything right," she said. "But it'll be worth it for you to hear that from the experts." She eyed the door. "Do you want me to get on the other side so I can hold it steady for you?"

"Yeah." Having the door between them would help. He felt uneasy. He wasn't used to talking about his inadequacies to anyone, let alone a near stranger. He wasn't sure why he'd opened up to her.

She stood and circled the door. "I'm ready," she called out. He positioned the first bracket and screwed it to the wall. She held the door firm against the pressure.

Other than the faint creak of the wood as the screw bit into it, the room was silent. The cat hadn't returned. Susannah didn't speak. The door stood solidly between them.

Should he say something? Find an upbeat subject to discuss? He couldn't think of anything. His mind was overwhelmed by the realization that spending a few minutes with Susannah in her bedroom was nothing like he would have imagined.

He bent over and picked up another bracket. Once he'd positioned it, he twisted the screw into place. He tried to picture Susannah on the other side, strong despite her slender build, holding the door still. "Am I pushing too hard?" he asked, hoping she wasn't straining herself.

"No," her voice came to him. "Am I?"

Not now, he wanted to say. *Before, when you asked me questions I didn't want to answer...*

Yet she hadn't really asked. And he could have

avoided answering. Perhaps, on some subliminal level, he'd wanted to tell her these things. Perhaps he needed a woman to talk to even more than Lindsey did.

No. Susannah was Lindsey's friend first. Lindsey was the one who mattered, the one he loved, the one he worried about.

"I appreciate your spending the afternoon with Lindsey," he said.

She didn't respond immediately. "We had fun," she said.

He screwed in another bracket. "Lindsey more than you, I'm sure." He fastened another bracket, then warned, "The last two are going into the bottom of the door, so there's going to be more pressure down there."

"Okay."

He knelt on the thick blue carpet and worked the last two brackets into the wall. She said nothing. Yet the tension seemed to leave him. The silence had grown comfortable, almost companionable. "Done," he called to her. "I'm going to put the mirror on now."

Susannah emerged from behind the door. "What do you want me to do?"

"Just hold the door steady from the side," he requested, lifting the heavy silver glass and fitting it into the brackets. He adjusted them, wedging their lips against the mirror to pin it to the door, and then stepped back. His image filled the mirror, and then Susannah's as she came to stand beside him.

"I had fun, too," she said quietly, addressing his reflection. "I like Lindsey."

He watched her reflection as she watched his. Her eyes were so clear he felt as if he could see straight through them to something inside her, something soft and sweet and questioning. Something that told him she was trying to communicate much more than what her words expressed.

He was afraid to find out what. So he didn't ask. He simply returned her reflected smile, pocketed his screwdrivers and said, "All done."

CHAPTER FIVE

SUSANNAH HADN'T EXPECTED to fall asleep easily that night, so it didn't shock her to find herself at two-thirty in the morning, seated at her computer in the room she'd set up as an office. A cup of herbal tea stood near her elbow, its minty fragrance soothing.

She'd been writing. Rewriting. Revising. The story line she'd come up with for the scripts she'd been commissioned to do for *Mercy Hospital* was fine, but the character she'd created, the handsome young pediatrician, needed work.

Actually, he would have served as a fine character the way she'd first written him: reserved but friendly, exuding a quiet confidence that drew women to him. But tonight, as Arlington slept, Susannah remained awake, altering him, giving him added texture, added dimension. His quiet confidence would mask deep vulnerabilities. His sexy smile would disguise a wounded heart. He would not be just some handsome dude introduced into the plot to excite the female staff of Mercy Hospital—and the female audience tuning in to the show. He would be much more complex.

Leaning back in her chair, she rubbed her eyes, which were beginning to burn from the strain of staring at the monitor. She took a sip of tea, then glanced toward the window.

Toby's house was dark.

She wasn't sure what she'd expected when he'd come to her house, but she'd sensed that more would happen than merely the mirror hanging. Maybe she'd hoped he would suggest that they get together, just the two of them, some evening. Dinner, a movie, nothing elaborate, but…just some time together, assuming he found her even remotely as attractive as she found him.

Several times that evening, she'd felt a spark. When the mirror had been hung and she'd moved beside him to judge whether it was straight and properly centered on the door, she'd seen something in his eyes, a flash of longing.

Or maybe it was just her own longing she'd seen. Mirrors could be tricky that way.

He'd left almost immediately after that moment when they'd stood side by side, gazing at each other through the medium of the mirror. She'd felt bad about his abrupt departure, wondering whether she'd made him uncomfortable. When he'd talked about his wife, she'd sensed that it was a difficult subject for him. If she were more reckless, she would have taken him in her arms and given him a hug.

The computer hummed. The tea grew tepid in her ceramic mug. She scrolled up the screen and reread what she'd written, altering a word here, adjusting a phrase there.

The regular writers on the show would have finished this scene by now. But one of them had decided not to renew his contract, and Bill Rowan, the head writer, had been worried that the scripts were getting a little stale after five years. Susannah had written two episodes in the past two years, and when she'd approached Bill with a story line that would give her character a graceful exit out of the show, he'd surprised her by saying, "You've got a knack for this, Susannah. Why don't you write me a few scripts for next season? You know these characters better than anyone. You could do it—and you could even do it long-distance, if you're really sure you want to clear out of town."

She could do it. She'd been working from scripts for so much of her life that she often found herself thinking in television rhythms, visualizing the world in scenes and camera angles and strings of dialogue. Some actors liked to stretch their creative muscles by directing television shows. She hadn't given much thought to stretching any creative muscles, but she wasn't going to slam a door on potential income. If she hadn't been supporting her parents all these years, she would be rich. But she had been, and she wasn't.

She couldn't say she loved writing, but she didn't mind it. And she could do it far from the people who'd made her miserable.

One final glance at the Cole house, and she turned back to her computer. She knew the casting department wouldn't pay much attention to her description, but she made sure she'd mentioned that the new pediatrician at Mercy Hospital was tall, with a wistful smile and thick brown hair and eyes so dark and haunted that a woman couldn't help but sigh and shiver a little inside when she gazed into them.

"REALLY? You were inside her house?" Amanda squealed. She always squealed when she got excited.

Lindsey motioned for her to lower her voice. The cafeteria was pretty noisy, anyway—the fourth-graders they had to share lunch with were so obnoxious—but she didn't want a teacher's aide showing up at their table to find out what was so exciting that Amanda had to squeal about it.

"Yes, I was inside her house," Lindsey reported. "I was in there a million times when Cathy lived there, don't forget."

"It's not the same thing," Meredith pointed out. "Cathy wasn't a TV star."

"So what was it like?" Amanda asked, bouncing in her chair. "I mean, did she have jewels lying around? Or all that gourmet stuff in the kitchen like they use in California? I've heard they cook way different in California, like with herbs and raw octopus and stuff like that."

"She's not a very good cook," Lindsey said, feeling a bit smug because she'd had such extensive personal contact with Susannah Dawson. "I've eaten her home-made brownies, and they were kind of dry."

"Yeah, but *she* baked them. I mean, that must have been so cool, eating something *she* baked, even if it tasted bad."

"She probably had a personal chef back in Holly-wood," Meredith said.

"Exactly." In truth, Lindsey didn't know if Susannah had had a personal chef, but she'd made the same assumption as Meredith. Meredith was a bit smarter than Amanda, but Amanda was okay, too. Now that Cathy was living in Atlanta, Lindsey understood how important it was to stay close to her other friends. It was hard, since they didn't live next door to her, and neither of them was in her class, but at least they could spend time together during lunch.

"Is she really thin?" Amanda asked. She was really thin herself. She was always picking at her lunch, peeling the crusts from her bread and then crumbling her sandwich and throwing it out. Lindsey knew about eating disorders, and she sometimes worried about Amanda. If Amanda hadn't been her friend, Lindsey might have discussed her concerns with her father and gotten his input, being that he was a doctor and all. But they were friends, and Lindsey would never betray a friend.

"Susannah is beautiful," Lindsey said, then added. "Really thin isn't beautiful," because she thought Amanda needed to hear that. "And she eats like a regular person. She ate spaghetti at our house."

"She was at your house?" Amanda squealed.

"Last Friday. She came for dinner."

Meredith gave her a gentle poke in the arm. "Why didn't you tell us?"

Lindsey hadn't told them because she'd acted like a jerk that night, and she didn't want to have to admit to her friends she'd stomped out of the room when Susannah implied that being a TV star was a drag. "Well, she's our next-door neighbor," Lindsey explained, giving a blasé shrug. "It's not like such a major thing if she comes over for dinner."

Meredith sank back in her chair and sighed. "I can't believe this. Nothing ever happens in Arlington. I can't believe we've got someone this famous living here—right next door to you."

"She's really just like a normal person when you meet her," Lindsey said, hearing the smugness in her voice.

"I know your dad doesn't like you making plans after school, but do you think maybe we could just come over and look at the house?" Meredith asked.

"It's Cathy Robinson's house," Lindsey said. "You

know what Cathy's house looks like. You were there when Cathy lived there.''

"Cathy doesn't live there now. It's not her house anymore,'' Meredith argued.

"And besides, maybe Susannah Dawson would stand in front of the window and we'd catch a glimpse of her,'' Amanda chimed in.

"Or,'' Meredith added hopefully, "she might even come outside, and we'd see her in person.''

"She might even talk to us.''

"I think we should form a fan club,'' Lindsey declared. She wanted to stay on top of the situation, and if she was the one who organized the club, she could be in charge. "Not a big national fan club, but our own secret club. The Susannah Dawson Admirers Club.''

"That's a great idea,'' Meredith said.

"But it's got to be kind of a secret,'' Lindsey emphasized, "because I don't think Susannah likes being idolized. You know what I mean?''

"Secret clubs are more fun,'' Amanda said.

"So it'll be just us three, unless we decide to invite someone else in—but we all have to agree to any other members,'' Lindsey said. The club was her idea, so it was up to her to establish the rules.

"And we'll have to have meetings,'' Meredith added, then bit down on a carrot stick from her lunch. "We should have the meetings at your house, Lindsey. You're the one who lives next door to her.''

Lindsey considered the risks. Not only was she supposed to go straight home after school, but her father didn't like her having friends over when he wasn't home and didn't know in advance. He claimed he trusted her, but he said he didn't always trust her friends.

He could trust Meredith and Amanda, though—if Lindsey even bothered to tell him they were over. If they came over right after school and the Susannah Dawson Admirers Club met for an hour or even two, they'd still be gone before he got home. If the club was a secret, it would have to be a secret from him, too.

Of course it would have to be a secret from him. If he knew about it, he'd probably tell Susannah, and she'd be pissed. They'd both be pissed—Susannah because she didn't seem to want people to make a big deal over her being a TV star and her father for sneaking her friends into the house after school. Lindsey would be in serious trouble all around.

"Okay," she said, gesturing for her friends to huddle across the table. "Let's meet at my house today after school. But you can't tell anyone about the club, and we can't let Susannah see us. Okay?"

"Okay," Amanda and Meredith chorused.

Grinning, Lindsey leaned back and took a crunchy bite out of her apple. She might have lost her best friend, but ironically, it was because Cathy had moved away that Lindsey was going to wind up more popular than ever. And why shouldn't she be? She was like this close to the world-famous Susannah Dawson.

She had too much energy to sit still for the rest of the school day. Ms. Hathaway gave a really boring lesson on decimals, which were so obvious to Lindsey, she didn't see why she had to pay attention. While Ms. Hathaway droned on and on about how the more digits you had to the right of the decimal point, the smaller the fraction actually was in multitudes of ten, Lindsey

doodled a trademark for the club. S.D.A.C. seemed like
pretty good initials. But maybe it should be the Susannah Dawson Admiration Society. That sounded so
much classier—societies were superior to clubs. She'd
have to discuss it with Amanda and Meredith at the
first meeting.

It was drizzling outside. Probably for the best. If
Susannah was outside when Meredith and Amanda arrived, she'd see them go into the house and tell Dr.
Dad. Lindsey was glad he'd gone to Susannah's house
last night and hung her mirror for her. She wanted her
father and Susannah to be friends. But not too close
friends—not close enough that they might be talking
about Lindsey behind her back.

After what felt like three years, Ms. Hathaway finished with decimals and moved on to the International
Fair. That was another big class event where Lindsey
would be the only kid without a mother attending.
Everyone in the class had drawn the name of a foreign
country out of a shoe box and had to make a presentation on that country. Lindsey had picked Finland, and
there really wasn't much to say, except that it was very
cold and the Finns ate lots of cheese.

Ms. Hathaway discussed the posters the students
were going to have to make for their countries. She
discussed researching the countries' flags and their major crops and industries. Lindsey drew a wedge of
cheese on the margin of her math worksheet, then drew
holes in it like Swiss cheese. She was pretty sure she'd
once had cheese from Finland with holes in it.

"Your oral presentation should last between five and
ten minutes," Ms. Hathaway was saying. "I'll expect
to see your note cards with all your research on Monday."

Great. That was just what Lindsey wanted to do for the rest of the week: research Finland and write down everything she learned on note cards.

At last the bell rang and Ms. Hathaway had to shut up and send everyone out to the buses. Kids jammed papers and books into their backpacks, two boys played catch with a pencil and four kids bolted out the door before Ms. Hathaway could stop them.

She could stop Lindsey, though—and she did. "Lindsey Cole?" she hollered across the room as Lindsey tried to sneak out the door. "Can I talk to you for a minute?"

Lindsey sighed. If she was going to get chewed out for doodling on her worksheet, she'd really be mad. She had a meeting of the Susannah Dawson Admiration Society to get to.

Hoisting her backpack onto her shoulder, she crossed the room to Ms. Hathaway's desk, praying that whatever Ms. Hathaway was going to do to her would go fast so Lindsey could get out.

"I met with your father this morning," Ms. Hathaway said.

Lindsey nodded. She knew he had been planning to see Ms. Hathaway sometime this week.

"He's very concerned about your schoolwork. More concerned than you are, I'd say."

"He has to be concerned. He's my father," Lindsey explained. Ms. Hathaway was such an idiot she had to be told these things.

"You really need to work harder, Lindsey." Ms. Hathaway had too many freckles. They spread over her nose and cheeks like splatters of brown paint. "You aren't working up to your ability, and it has him worried."

"I know." Lindsey toed the floor with her sneaker and snuck a glance at her watch. If she missed the bus she'd have to walk home, two miles—in the rain—and there would be no time for the club meeting.

"He's been through a lot," Ms. Hathaway reminded her. "I think you ought to go out of your way not to upset him, after all he's been through in the past few years."

Lindsey didn't know what to say to that. Her mother died five years ago, so all her father had been through in the past few years was dealing with Lindsey. Had he told Ms. Hathaway that being Lindsey's only parent was such a hard job? Had he made a play for sympathy?

"Isn't it amazing," she muttered, pretty steamed herself. "My father has been through so much, and I haven't been through anything at all." And then, because she felt tears forming under her eyelids, she turned and stormed out of the classroom, not caring if Ms. Hathaway thought she was rude.

By the time she reached the bus circle, she decided she hated everyone: Ms. Hathaway, her father, her mother for having died. Then she saw Amanda and Meredith standing near her bus, waiting for her in the drizzle, and she felt a little better. She still had the Susannah Dawson Admiration Society. She had the coolest next-door neighbor in Arlington, a woman who was beautiful and famous and fun, and who had the most wonderful cat in the world. Susannah had to like Lindsey; if she didn't, she wouldn't have forgiven her for being such a jerk last Friday night.

Susannah was like a queen. A goddess. She was one person Lindsey didn't hate.

"Let's go," she said briskly, leading her friends onto the bus.

TOBY DECIDED to leave the office early. His last appointment was a well-child physical at four, and by four-thirty he was done. He could have caught up on paperwork at his desk, but he had his first Daddy School class at seven-thirty that night, so he decided to go home an hour ahead of schedule and unwind a bit, maybe talk to Lindsey about his meeting with Ms. Hathaway that morning and figure out if there were any specific issues he wanted to explore at the Daddy School—assuming that the Daddy School was set up to explore specific issues.

The roads weren't as crowded at four-thirty as they were at his usual rush-hour departure time. A light rain was falling, washing the lawns and budding trees, rinsing the staleness from the air. He tuned the car radio to a soft-rock station and sang along with The Police, something he would never dare to do if Lindsey was in the car with him. She'd think he was so corny, harmonizing with Sting about how every little thing the woman in the song did was magic.

Susannah's image appeared unbidden in his mind. No, she wasn't magic—but somehow, she'd cast a spell on him last night, getting him to reveal too much of himself. He didn't talk about his insecurities with people, let alone someone he barely knew. One thing he'd learned as a single father was that he always had to project strength. Lindsey needed to know she could rely on him. If she saw his fears and worries, she would doubt his dependability.

But Susannah had seen those fears and worries. She'd heard him admit his disappointment in his own field, medicine, the discipline he'd devoted so much of his life to. Medicine was supposed to work miracles and save lives, yet it had failed when he'd been desperate for a miracle. And Susannah had also heard him acknowledge his misgivings about the job he was doing as Lindsey's father.

She might as well have stripped him naked and posed him in front of the mirror so she could see him from both sides at once.

If she'd done that, though, she might have exposed yet another secret of his: she turned him on. Stripped naked before her, he wouldn't have wanted to stand in front of the mirror. He'd have wanted to strip her just as naked and carry her to her inviting brass bed.

The Police song ended, replaced by Dave Matthews crooning that he was crazy. Once again, Toby sang along. Susannah might not be capable of magic, but lately, it seemed as if Toby skirted close to the edge of crazy more often than he'd like to admit.

He pulled into the driveway, hit the remote button and waited for the garage door to slide open. After parking inside, he grabbed his briefcase and blazer from the back seat and entered the house. He immediately heard a chorus of giggles, then a hushed whisper.

Lindsey wasn't alone.

"Hello?" he hollered.

Several pairs of footsteps clattered down the stairs, and then Lindsey and two other girls spilled into the kitchen. "Daddy, Amanda and Meredith were just leaving. Amanda's mother should be here any second to pick them up. They came over to do some homework. We were all doing homework together. A homework project."

"Hi, Dr. Cole," the blond one said. Toby was pretty sure she was Meredith.

"We're just leaving, Dr. Cole," the skinny one— Amanda—said. "Sorry." She giggled, sounding about as sorry as a lottery winner.

"It was for a homework assignment," Lindsey repeated. She was talking too fast. She knew she wasn't supposed to have friends over at the house without planning it and getting his permission. Even if the girls had come over for a homework assignment...

Which Toby doubted, because neither Amanda nor Meredith was in Lindsey's class this term. He'd been listening to Lindsey complain all year because none of her good friends were in her class, and he knew Amanda and Meredith qualified as good friends.

So she'd invited friends over without getting his permission, and now she was lying about it. He could have excused her inviting the girls over if she hadn't lied about it. The dishonesty bothered him so much he had to steel himself against erupting.

"There's my mother now," Amanda said, glancing out the window as a green minivan coasted slowly up the driveway. She and Meredith hoisted their backpacks higher on their shoulders and raced for the door. "'Bye, Lindsey!"

"'Bye, Lindsey. 'Bye, Dr. Cole," Meredith said, hurrying after Amanda. Lindsey followed them through the mud room to the garage so they wouldn't have to run across the front yard in the rain.

Waiting for Lindsey to return, Toby took a few deep, bracing breaths. He didn't want to jump down her throat the way he had when he'd seen her midterm report. He had to discuss his concerns calmly. He'd tell her why he didn't want kids in and out of the house when he wasn't home, and then he would explain how much her lying hurt him. He would remind her that he didn't expect her to be perfect—hell, he was far from perfect himself—but he did expect honesty.

She tiptoed back into the kitchen, looking sheepish and a bit scared. "Sorry, Daddy," she said, then turned to head down the hall to the stairs.

"Lindsey, come back!" Did he sound angry or frightened? Both, probably. Both emotions were sizzling inside him.

She returned slowly, her shoulders slumped and her mouth twitching. Before he could say anything, she started babbling again. "I know I'm not supposed to have friends over, but there was this homework assignment—"

"Don't," he cut her off. He couldn't bear to hear her repeating her lie. "I know there's no homework assignment, Lindsey. Those girls aren't in your class."

She drew in a shaky breath, let it out and stared past him at his jacket, which was draped over a chair at the table.

"Why don't you try the truth this time," he said, hoping he didn't sound as furious as he felt.

"Well—well, you got home early. I thought they'd be gone before you got home."

Not a good defense strategy. "If I'd come home the usual time, you would never have told me they'd been here?"

"Well…well…" A sob bubbled into her throat and she struggled mightily against it. As angry as he was, he wanted to hug her. He wanted her to trust him so much she not only told him the truth but leaned on him when she needed to be comforted. "I just had a terrible day," she confessed. "It was awful, and then when

Amanda and Meredith and I were talking, and they thought about coming over for a little while, just to make me feel better..." Tears streaked down her cheeks.

The hell with it. He opened his arms. If she was willing to take a hug, he was more than willing to give one.

She nearly fell into his arms. Loud, hiccuping sobs emerged from her. He stroked her hair and patted her back, the way he used to when she was six years old. She'd cried such wrenching tears then, missing her mother. These tears were different—tears of frustration and fury. But at least she was letting him console her.

After a minute she eased away from him and crossed to the counter to grab a square of paper towel. She wiped her face and sniffled. "Anyway, it was just a bad day," she said, which seemed like a gross understatement after the way she'd been weeping.

"Want to tell me about it?"

She shook her head.

"Did something happen in school?"

"It's just...everything."

A horrifying thought seized him: what if this was PMS? What if she was about to start menstruating? At her age, it was quite possible. He'd discussed menstruation with her a year ago, and she'd found the discussion terribly embarrassing, but it had all been theoretical then. What if he had to take her to the store to buy her sanitary pads?

He was pretty sure he could handle it. He wasn't at all sure she could.

"Listen, Hot Stuff," he said, nudging her into a chair and handing her a fresh paper towel. "I don't mind if you invite a friend or two over after school. But there have to be some rules."

"What rules?" she asked in a watery voice.

"You have to get my permission first. I have to know the friend."

"And?" She knew there was more.

"You can't lie to me about it."

"Okay."

"I mean it, Lindsey. I'm angry that you lied to me. Very angry." He kept his tone subdued, though, so she would listen to the words rather than the emotion.

"I'm sorry."

He sighed, exhausted from the conversation, from the constant strain of being a pillar-strong parent. She swabbed the moisture from her cheeks while he rolled up the sleeves of his shirt and loosened his tie. "I was planning to go out this evening, but if you want I'll stay home," he offered.

"Go out? Where?"

"To a class."

"A class? Yuck." She shrugged, her hair riding up and down on her shoulders. "If you want to go, I don't care."

"You're upset."

"I'm okay. I'll just do my homework and watch TV."

Her homework. So much for the mythical homework assignment she and her friends had been doing. "Why were Amanda and Meredith here?"

"No reason," Lindsey said with another shrug. "Just hanging out."

He studied her across the table. He suspected she was lying again, and it caused a searing ache in his soul. But he couldn't bring himself to accuse her. He needed not to be angry.

Pressing his lips together, he crossed to the sink to wash his hands. He had to get dinner on the table and be out the door by seven for the Daddy School class. Would they teach trust in the Daddy School? Would they teach lie detection? Would they teach fathers how to select the correct-size tampons for their daughters?

If the teacher was wise, she would probably teach the fathers to find women to take their daughters shopping for tampons. He wondered how one went about asking a woman for such a favor. He could have asked Diane Anderson when she'd lived next door; she could have taken Lindsey and Cathy shopping for supplies together. Or his mother could have helped him out— if she didn't live in Minneapolis.

Could he ask Susannah?

He had to suppress a wry laugh. Wouldn't that be something—telephoning the famous actress and saying, "Hey, I hung your mirror, so would you mind picking up some Kotex for Lindsey? One good turn deserves another." Sure.

His hands clean, he pulled the tray of chopped beef from the refrigerator and began molding the meat into patties. Lindsey remained at the kitchen table, watching him, swinging her legs under her seat. Since she hadn't fled, he figured she might want to talk some more. "I saw your teacher this morning," he said.

"I know." Lindsey slouched in the chair. "She's such an idiot. I hate her."

He suppressed another laugh. "She didn't astonish me with her brilliance, either," he confessed. "But you're going to have to tough it out. Only two more months and you'll be done with fifth grade."

"I hate her," Lindsey said so vehemently he wondered whether Ms. Hathaway had contributed to her teary mood.

"Any particular reason?" he asked.

"No."

Hearing the single syllable was like having a door slammed in his face. Lindsey hated Ms. Hathaway for a definite reason, and she wasn't going to tell him what it was.

"How about slicing the pickles while I cook the burgers," he suggested. Maybe if they worked side by side, he could keep a casual conversation going until he pried loose what Ms. Hathaway had done to annoy her.

She crossed to the refrigerator and pulled the pickle jar from the shelf on the door. He watched her movements, ungainly and graceful at the same time, and his heart ached for her, for her undefined misery, for the changes she was going through. "Ms. Hathaway thinks you're very smart," he commented lightly, "so I guess she can't be that much of an idiot."

"Believe me, Dr. Dad—she is."

He sent Lindsey a sidelong look. She was grinning. The girl who'd been sobbing hysterically just minutes ago was smiling now. "Anyway," he said, flattening the patties in the pan, "she thinks you're capable of amazing things, if you'll only work harder."

"Yeah, well." Lindsey shrugged.

"So work harder," he said.

"Uh-huh."

"It won't kill you."

"Uh-huh."

He glanced at her as she sliced a pickle into six even spears. God, he loved her. Loved her so much he'd gladly storm into every drugstore in Connecticut to buy tampons for her. Loved her so much he'd let her wail and rage and be inscrutable.

Even knowing that she lied to him couldn't change that. It broke his heart, but it didn't make him love her any less.

CHAPTER SIX

THE LAST LIGHT had faded from the sky by the time Susannah reached her block. She didn't mind. The neighborhood had sidewalks, and the falling darkness camouflaged her more effectively than her eyeglasses and her braided hair.

Her caution was silly, really. More neighbors than just the Coles must have figured out who she was by now. Perhaps some, like Toby, didn't watch a lot of TV, so they wouldn't recognize her. Others might just be discreet, allowing her her privacy. She shouldn't keep making midnight runs to the all-night grocery store as if she were a vampire, lethally allergic to sunlight. And she shouldn't put off taking her power walks.

That evening, when the lack of exercise had finally gotten to her, she'd waited until the drizzle had dried up and then ventured out. One car on Guilford Lane had slowed to a crawl as it passed her, but that could have been for a dozen reasons having nothing to do with her famous face. The teenage boys shooting hoops in a driveway hadn't interrupted their scrimmage to look at her, and if people glimpsed her through their windows, they refrained from chasing her down the street waving pads and pens under her nose and demanding autographs.

Maybe in Arlington she'd found the perfect place to

settle—a city where few people knew who she was and even fewer cared.

She'd left her porch light on, and that, along with the illuminated windows, gave her house a warm, welcoming glow. She loved the peaked roof, the neat white clapboard, the dark-green shutters framing the windows. She loved the sweet fragrance of buds and blossoms in the air. She loved the daffodils lining people's driveways, the moist air fragrant with the scent of blossoming magnolias and forsythia, the peaceful murmur of a car in the distance, a dog barking, the rustle of leaves as a squirrel scampered along a tree branch, the honks of migrating geese slicing through the sky. Even when she was walking at a swift pace, with weight bands strapped around her wrists and her lungs pumping with aerobic efficiency, she could appreciate the bucolic beauty of her new neighborhood.

As she neared her house, she heard a car approaching her from behind. Pivoting, she saw it slow down, signaling to turn into the Coles' driveway. Even though the driver was merely a shadow in the darkened interior, she knew who he was.

Toby steered his car up the driveway and into the garage. She knew she, too, ought to go inside, but she lingered on the front lawn, wishing he would emerge to say hi to her. God, she was like an infatuated schoolgirl, longing for a glimpse of him, a greeting, an acknowledgment that she hadn't imagined the strange intimacy she'd felt with him last night.

She waited. She heard the click of his car door closing, and then…he came outside.

She tried not to smile too broadly as she approached the hedge bordering his driveway. He approached from the other side. "What are you doing out so late?" he asked.

"Late?" She laughed. It wasn't even nine o'clock yet. Back in California, she'd be just leaving the studio at around nine o'clock, after a long day of rehearsals or taping.

"Exercising," he said, answering his own question, then running his gaze the length of her body, taking in the pale-blue sweatshirt, the black Spandex leggings, the white socks and leather walking shoes and the weights strapped around her wrists.

"How about you?" she asked, providing her own answer, as well. "Did you have that father class?"

"Daddy School," he corrected, then nodded.

"How did it go?"

He almost replied, then paused and gave her one of his crooked smiles. "Why don't you come over and I'll tell you about it? I've got cold drinks in the fridge, if you'd like one."

A cold drink sounded great. Going to Toby's house to talk sounded even better. She strolled to the end of the hedge and around it to his driveway.

They entered his dark garage together. It was cool, the cement floor echoing, the air smelling of gasoline and fertilizer. Toby touched his hand lightly to her shoulder as he threaded a path around his car, two bicycles, a gas grill and a hose coiled onto a spool. She felt the warmth of his palm, his certainty and protectiveness as he escorted her past the obstacles to the inner door. When he let his hand drop, a chill took its place.

He reached around her to unlock the door, then hit the button to close the garage. As they walked through the mudroom into the kitchen, Susannah unstrapped her weights from her wrists. She flexed her fingers, rolled her shoulders and smiled. If her house had looked warm from the outside, his felt warmer.

From the den came the murmur of voices and music. "Lindsey?" he called out. "I'm home."

"Hi," she called back.

"Did you finish your homework?"

"Yeah."

He shot Susannah a dubious look, as if he didn't believe Lindsey. Tugging open the refrigerator, he surveyed his inventory. "I've got cola, milk, bottled water, beer and some wine left over from last Friday's dinner."

"The wine sounds good," she said, even though wine was not an appropriate refresher after exercise. She remembered drinking a toast with Toby that evening, sipping the wine, asking for a refill and then being so caught up in him she'd had to flee.

She wouldn't flee tonight. She was getting used to the idea that Toby was an attractive man—used to it enough that she could handle the attraction. Maybe she was a little smitten with him, but she was still recovering from her last relationship. She wanted to be on her own, unattached, independent, unbeholden. Fantasizing about a gorgeous neighbor could be entertaining as long as she didn't do anything foolish—like let him know how gorgeous she thought he was.

He pulled the wine from the refrigerator, and a bottle of beer for himself. "The wine's a little cold," he apologized, fetching a goblet from a cabinet. "Let it warm up before you drink it." He poured a glass for her, then twisted off the cap on his beer. "Lindsey?" he hollered into the den. "Susannah and I will be out on the porch."

"Susannah? Susannah's here?" A scramble of footsteps, and Lindsey suddenly appeared in the kitchen doorway, slightly breathless. "Hi!" she said, greeting Susannah with much more enthusiasm than she'd greeted her father.

Susannah smiled. "Hi, Lindsey."

"You were exercising?" Lindsey asked, appraising Susannah's getup. "That's so cool. What kind of exercise do you do?"

"Just walking," Susannah said. "I used to jog when I didn't have as much time to exercise, but walking's actually better for you."

"Yeah," Lindsey said, making no move to return to the den. "So, what's up? You just dropped by?"

"Your father and I ran into each other outside."

Lindsey eyed her father, silently questioning. Then her gaze traveled to the beer and the glass of wine on the counter. "You came over for a drink?"

"Yes."

"Can I join you?"

"I don't think so," Toby broke in. "It's getting close to your bedtime, Hot Stuff. Maybe it's time to turn off the TV and get your school things together for tomorrow."

Lindsey rolled her eyes and curled her lip. "It's *early,* Dad. None of my friends go to bed this early."

"I didn't say you had to go to bed," he elaborated. "I said you should get your stuff together for school. Did you make your lunch yet? Did you take a shower?"

"Jeez." Her eyes rolled again, aiming first at the ceiling and then at Susannah as if hoping to find an ally in her. "He treats me like a baby."

"It's something dads do," Susannah assured her. "It's perfectly normal."

"It's stupid." With a huff, she spun around, her socks whispering on the tile floor, and stomped back into the den. After a moment, the television clicked off.

"Let's go out on the porch," Toby suggested, leading Susannah through a back door off the kitchen into a three-season porch, the jalousie windows shut tight against the cool night. He clicked on the lamp on the glass-topped table between two sling chairs, set Susannah's glass on the table and gestured for her to sit.

She sank into the canvas pouch of the seat, finding it surprisingly comfortable. Through the slatted windows came the muffled chirps of crickets—a peaceful, rural sound. The sky had grown dark, but the glass held the night safely back.

Toby took the other sling chair. He leaned back and closed his eyes for a minute, then let out a slow breath in an uninhibited display of fatigue. It occurred to her that closing one's eyes in front of another person was an act of pure trust. He must feel very comfortable with her.

Well, of course he did. Last night he'd told her things he wouldn't have told her if he didn't.

"So, how was the Daddy School?" she asked him.

He opened his eyes and grinned at her. Tiny creases formed at the outer corners of his eyes, and the curve of his lips etched lines around his mouth. "It was interesting," he said, then added, "it was good."

"Are you going to go back for more classes?"

"Definitely." He took a swig of beer straight from the bottle. "The teacher is a preschool teacher named Molly Saunders-Russo. She's a real dynamo. She works with younger children, mostly, but this class was for fathers of older children.''

''Were they all…single?'' Susannah asked, deciding not to use the word *widowers*. It carried too much sadness.

He shook his head. ''Some were single, but most were married. They'd come because they didn't have the rapport they wanted with their children. Most of them are there for advice in how to communicate with their kids, how to get their kids to listen and how to keep their kids out of trouble. Most of them feel inept when it comes to fathering.''

''You don't feel inept, do you?'' Susannah asked.

Before Toby could offer more of an answer than a self-deprecating snort, Lindsey appeared in the doorway. Although she addressed her father, her gaze zeroed in on Susannah. ''I made my lunch, Dr. Dad. It's too early to go to bed. Can't I watch a little more TV?''

Her wheedling didn't soften him. ''No. It's late. Go upstairs and shower, and if you're still not tired you can read in bed for a while.''

''I don't want to read in bed,'' she said, sending Susannah a pleading look. Susannah gave her nothing more than a sympathetic smile. Frustrated, Lindsey stormed away from the doorway.

''That didn't seem inept at all,'' Susannah murmured.

Toby snorted again. ''It would be nice if I could get her to do the right thing without having her hate me.''

''She doesn't hate you,'' Susannah assured him. ''She's just angry.''

''She lied to me today,'' Toby blurted out, then glanced away, as if shaken by his own statement.

''Lied to you?''

"It scared me," he admitted. "It's not that what she lied about was so significant, but if she can lie to me about nonsense now, what will she be doing when she's fifteen and has a boyfriend and all her friends are drinking or using drugs? What am I going to do if I can't trust her?"

Susannah had no answer for him. "Did you ask the teacher at the Daddy School?"

He took another slug of beer and turned back to her. She could see the worry in his eyes, the fearful, desperate love he felt for Lindsey. "We did talk about lying. Molly—the teacher—said it was important to understand *why* a particular child was lying, so you could deal with the underlying issue. For example, is she lying because she's afraid of how you'd react to the truth? Or is she lying because all her friends are lying about the same thing? Or is she lying to protect a private part of herself from you?"

"Why do you think Lindsey lied to you?" Susannah asked.

He leaned back in his chair and gave a bemused chuckle. "You can't possibly find this interesting. The tedious travails of a frazzled father and his clever daughter. I mean, really."

She laughed, too. She was surprised at how interesting she found Toby's problems. They were so domestic, so wonderfully ordinary. So unlike what she'd had in her own life up to now. "Of course I'm interested," she told him. "Someday, I hope I'll be a mother. Maybe I need to learn what the job entails before I take the plunge."

"No one can ever know exactly what to expect before the fact," he warned her. "Each child is different.'' He regarded her thoughtfully. ''You want to be a mother?''

She felt a twinge low in her belly, in her womb, as she thought about the baby she should have had. ''Yes,'' she said more forcefully than she meant to.

He continued to study her, his eyes dark and assessing, his smile curious but not probing. She wasn't going to tell him about the baby. She felt close to him, but not *that* close.

Or maybe her idea of closeness was for him to open up to her while she refused to open up to him. That didn't seem fair. But she couldn't talk about the baby. Not even to him. It was too painful. ''What did Lindsey lie about?'' she asked, as much to distract herself as because she honestly wanted to know.

He accepted her redirecting the conversation. ''She was in one of her moods this afternoon,'' he said. ''She had friends come over to the house without asking me first, and she said they were doing homework together when they weren't. I know, it's really trivial. Her friends are good girls. I can't imagine that they were doing anything bad—except that Lindsey lied about what they were doing. That makes me suspicious.''

''They were probably doing girl stuff,'' Susannah said. ''Lindsey probably thought you'd laugh at her if you knew what they were doing.''

''Girl stuff?'' He looked intrigued, and relieved that Lindsey's reason for lying to him might be innocuous. ''Tell me, what do three fifth-grade girls do when they get together after school?''

Sipping her wine, Susannah tried to remember what she'd done at that age. In fifth grade, her life hadn't yet veered from the normal. She'd made an occasional commercial, but she'd still been in public school then.

She hadn't started with tutors until high school, when she'd gotten a job on a cable-TV series and had to be on the set every day.

At Lindsey's age, she'd been in school and had girl-friends. "We used to fix each other's hair," she recalled.

"Lindsey would never do that. She's not into hair."

Susannah laughed. "That's what you think. All fifth-grade girls are into hair. And boys."

"Boys? She's not even eleven yet!"

"But she's noticing boys. She and her friends probably sat in a circle and rated all the boys in the school. They argued over who was the cutest and who was the creepiest. Then they complained about their parents."

"As if Lindsey had anything to complain about on that front," Toby said with feigned indignation before succumbing to a wry laugh.

"Maybe they compared figures."

"Figures? What figures? Their grades? Or their bank accounts?"

The man really did seem to need a Daddy School class. "Their bodies," she said delicately. "They might have compared their bosoms."

"They don't have bosoms," he argued, then caught her eye and subsided. "All right. They compared bosoms." He traced a line through the frost dampening the surface of his beer bottle. "She's been so moody lately I've been wondering whether she's started her period yet."

"You'd better have a talk with her."

"I already had a talk with her. I explained everything and told her that she should let me know when it actually started."

Susannah stifled another laugh. "She's not going to tell you. You're her father."

"Well, what am I supposed to do? Buy her supplies and just leave them in her bathroom?"

"That's a good idea."

"I wish she had a woman who could take her shopping. Her friend Cathy's mother helped her buy her first bra. I was willing to do that, but she refused to go with me."

"Much to your relief, I'm sure." Susannah reached across the table to give his hand a comforting pat. "Do you want me to talk to her about her period?"

"I'd love it," he admitted, then grinned sheepishly. "But I can't ask that of you."

"Why not? I don't mind."

"Are you sure?"

She'd offered her help impulsively and realized she ought to give it a little more thought. Could she talk to a ten-year-old girl about menstruation? She might want to be a mother, but she wasn't one yet. Her own mother had been a nonentity, withdrawn and ineffective. As Susannah recalled it, she'd bought her first tampons by herself, because she'd always known she was essentially on her own.

"I'm sure," she said, meaning it. She would have loved having a friendly neighbor to help her buy tampons. Surely she could do that much for Lindsey. Besides, it would draw her closer to the Cole family, which might be a bad idea but which seemed almost inevitable. She felt safe in this house, with Toby and his daughter. No one expected big things of her here. They might ask, but they didn't make demands. They didn't look to her to support them or fulfill their dreams or work her tail off for them.

She'd spent too much of her childhood living for her parents, earning the money that had kept the family housed and fed, accepting the jobs her father had insisted that she take because he'd needed her income. Years later, she'd spent too much of her adulthood accepting what directors wanted, what her agent wanted—anything that could support both her and her parents. She'd spent too much of herself doing what Stephen had wanted, thinking that he would do as much for her. But he hadn't. No one had. Eventually she'd realized that the only way she would ever have anything done for her was if she did it herself.

So she'd left them all and come to Arlington.

"I really don't mind," she said, convinced that she didn't.

"Thank you."

That was another difference. She couldn't remember anyone ever thanking her back in Hollywood. But she wasn't there anymore. This world was different. Toby was different.

She drank a little wine, then decided to see if he might be willing to do something for her. It was scary to have to ask—she was used to not making requests, because the few times she had, her requests had always been denied. But this was different. This was Toby. "I'm wondering if I can ask a favor of you, too," she began tentatively.

"Anything." He actually looked pleased.

His smile gave her courage. She took another drink, then lowered her glass. "I've been writing a script for *Mercy Hospital*. When I left the show, the producer gave me a shot at writing a few scripts. But all I know of hospitals is what I learned by being in the show. Which was fine when I was just an actress, but as a writer I feel kind of ignorant. I was wondering…'' She studied him. He was smiling in encouragement. ''Could I watch you work? I've introduced a character in my script who's a pediatrician—'' *as handsome and gentle and multilayered as you are,* she thought but didn't dare say ''—and it would be really helpful if I could observe a pediatrician on the job for a day.''

''Is that all?'' He laughed. ''No problem. Of course, if a patient objects, you'd have to leave the room, but I don't mind at all.''

''I promise, I wouldn't say a word. I'll just sit quietly and take notes. And I'll wear my eyeglasses and pull my hair back, so maybe people won't realize who I am.''

''Maybe you could wear a pair of Groucho glasses and a wig,'' he teased. ''Seriously, I don't think it will be a problem as long as you stay in the background.''

''I can,'' Susannah assured him. Even when she'd been in front of the camera every day, she'd managed to stay in the background off the set. She did what people asked and hoped they'd appreciate her. She worked and waited for someone to say ''thank you.'' Directors loved working with her because, as they used to say, she had no ego.

She had an ego, but for the chance to observe Toby she'd gladly fade into the scenery.

''We can work out a time when I've got my schedule in front of me,'' he suggested. ''I'll figure out a good day, one where I've got some hospital rounds and some office appointments.''

''Okay.''

He glanced at his watch and winced. ''Can you excuse me for a minute? It's Lindsey's bedtime, and I want to see if she's anywhere close to being ready.''

She twisted her wrist to read her sport watch. It was already after nine-thirty. "It's late," she said. "I really should be going home." Her wineglass was nearly empty, and she drained it in a single sip. Then she stood.

Toby stood, too. He took her glass and his bottle, held the door open so she could enter the kitchen ahead of him, and set the glass and bottle on the counter where she'd left her weights. He carried them with him through the hall to the front door, opened it and let the porch light spill in through the screen door. "Thanks again for agreeing to talk to Lindsey," he said.

"Thanks again for agreeing to let me shadow you at work."

"It'll be fun having you there," he said. He lowered his gaze to his hands, still holding her weights, and she held out her hands to take them. When he placed them into her palms, he let his fingers graze her wrists, then circle around to spread beneath her hands, as if he were helping her hold the weights—or else simply holding her, filling his hands with hers.

His palms were warm and broad. Protective. It was amazing how safe she felt with him—as if he were someone who would help her carry all her burdens, someone willing to give as much as he took, someone who offered support instead of simply demanding it.

She lifted her eyes to his face as he gazed down at her, and suddenly she felt a little less safe. She saw something quite the opposite of protectiveness in his expression, something hot and yearning and insistent.

He bowed and brushed his lips to hers.

Her mind went blank. Her mouth tingled, her breath caught and rationality failed her. Everything they'd discussed earlier that evening—Lindsey? His job? The

Daddy School? Trust? Whatever they'd talked about melted into an irrelevant blur. All that mattered was that she'd just been kissed for the first time since she'd left Stephen, left California, left her old life behind. She'd just been kissed by a man she barely knew, kissed by someone she admired and respected and— damn it—*dreamed* about. Kissed by the father of a moody young girl. Kissed by her next-door neighbor.

Her eyes slowly regained their focus. Toby looked nowhere near as stunned as she felt. His eyes were luminous, searching her face, attempting to read a *yes* in her expression.

She wanted to say yes. She wanted him to wrap his arms around her and cover her mouth with his, to fill it with his tongue. She wanted to feel his body pressed to hers, hard and hungry. She wasn't used to wanting that kind of thing—and certainly not with this kind of man.

Her neighbor, she reminded herself. The father of a vulnerable young girl. A wholesome doctor. Basic and honest and undemanding—except for the blatant demand in his gaze, the subtle demand in his kiss, the promise in his hands cupped around hers.

She shouldn't give in to those demands—but she wanted to. Just for one blissful minute longer, she wanted to be kissed by Toby Cole.

She tilted her mouth up and he took what she offered, releasing her hands not to hug her but instead to slide his own hands up her arms, along her shoulders to her cheeks, digging his fingers into the strands of hair that had unraveled from her braid and holding her head steady for his kiss. His mouth opened over hers, and she tasted beer on his lips, felt passion in his tongue pressing against her teeth and then thrusting deep. She heard a guttural sigh—his or hers, she couldn't say—and moved her tongue against his. The sigh must have come from him, she realized, because she could scarcely breathe—and didn't really care.

Kissing him felt too good. Too heavenly. Too outrageously erotic. So nourishing she didn't need to breathe. So gratifying she felt tears gather along her eyelashes. She closed her eyes and leaned into him, her hands wedged between his body and hers, the weights still tight in her fists. His chest was warm and solid, safe and not safe. If she hadn't been holding the damned weights, she could have slid her fingers up and inside his collar to touch his skin. She could have made him sigh again, made him as breathless as she was.

Instead, he touched her. His thumbs stroked the edge of her jaw and his fingers skimmed underneath her braid to her nape, sending shivers of heat down her spine. She wished he would slide his fingers under the ribbed neckline of her sweatshirt to graze her shoulders, dance across her upper back. She wished he would kiss her harder, deeper. She wished he would touch her all over—

"Daddy? Can't I watch just a little more TV?" The whiny plea floated down the stairs and into the hall.

Susannah would have sprung back if Toby had let her, but he didn't. He continued to hold her close, easing his mouth from hers and tucking her head against his shoulder, where she took desperate gulps of air. "No," he shouted up the stairs in a perfectly calm voice. "No more TV tonight."

"*Mercy Hospital* is on tonight."

"And you've got the VCR set up to tape it. Go to bed, Lindsey. I'll be upstairs to tuck you in in a minute."

"I don't want you to tuck me in!" she hollered, punctuating the sentiment by slamming her door.

Silence resonated in the wake of her outburst. It sank around Susannah, as damp and chilly as the night air. She pulled back and peered up into Toby's face. He looked vexed, a sad smile twisting his lips.

"It's not easy having a sex life when you've got a ten-year-old daughter," he murmured.

Sex life? He'd only kissed her, hadn't he?

But he'd wanted more. He'd wanted to touch her the way she'd wanted to be touched. And maybe it was just as well that Lindsey had interrupted them. Susannah wasn't ready for this.

She'd come to Arlington to get away from relationships, obligations, placing everyone else's needs before her own. And no matter what Toby wanted with her, he had to put his daughter's needs first. He was too good a father not to.

"I should be going," she mumbled, her voice nowhere near as steady as his. She stepped back and lowered her arms, feeling the weights tug down on her elbows. A draft enveloped her as Toby released her. She wanted to tell him that while she had enjoyed the kiss—more than enjoyed it, she'd savored it, adored it, been utterly caught up in it—she didn't think she could handle having a relationship with a man who could use the phrases "sex life" and "ten-year-old daughter" in the same sentence.

But she couldn't bring herself to say that, so she only twisted the knob on the screen door and slipped outside, into the cold night.

A PILE OF PAPERWORK sat on the desk in the study, awaiting his attention, but he ignored it. Armed with another beer, he slumped into the easy chair in the den, pressed the remote control and stared at the television screen. To watch a show at ten o'clock, when he ought to be working, seemed an extreme indulgence, but he didn't care.

He couldn't have concentrated on his work anyway. Not after the evening he'd had with Lindsey, the class he'd taken at the Daddy School and Susannah. Especially Susannah.

Maybe it was masochistic to tune in to her TV show after she'd walked away from him. She regretted the kiss—he knew that. But he didn't. He'd loved every minute of it, and he wanted to kiss her again. He wanted a hell of a lot more than just a kiss.

But she didn't. She hadn't had to spell it out; he could tell. She'd enjoyed the kiss, but it had made her uneasy. Fair enough. There were plenty of good reasons for him to steer clear of an involvement with her, and only one good reason not to: he wanted her.

So he'd have her on the television, a small, two-dimensional view of her. The VCR clicked on as the an announcer's voice said, "Previously on *Mercy Hospital*," and a series of disjointed snippets flashed across the screen. He wondered if he would be unable to follow tonight's episode, not having seen those previous episodes, but he decided it didn't matter. He wasn't watching the show to follow the dramatic narrative. He was watching it because Susannah was in it.

There she was in the opening credits, a glimpse of her darting down an E.R. corridor in a white coat and an improbably short skirt as her name appeared at the bottom of the screen in white block letters. Doctors would never wear miniskirts to work, especially not in an E.R. They'd wear comfortable, machine-washable slacks for E.R. work, and maybe longer skirts if they were making rounds. Patients didn't place their trust in doctors who dressed like flirts.

Her hair was loose, too—another implausible choice. A doctor with long hair would want it out of her face. If she spent a day observing Toby to get a feel for genuine medical practice, he would explain these things to her.

But her hair looked good flowing past her shoulders, and her legs were gorgeous below the hem of her abbreviated skirt. And when she turned to the camera, he remembered how beautiful she'd looked standing before him in the front hall, her eyes so blue he could feel their color as much as see it, her lips so sweet he tasted them still.

He hadn't exaggerated when he'd said it was hard to conduct a sex life when you were the single father of a sensitive daughter. He'd dated over the years, but with extreme caution and more tension than he'd liked. He'd seen one woman for close to a year, but he'd told Lindsey she was only a friend because he hadn't wanted Lindsey to become attached to her before he knew how deeply he felt about her—and she'd resented his telling Lindsey she was only a friend. She'd wanted to be much more, and she'd pushed it, and he'd reacted by ending the relationship.

In the show, Susannah's character found herself cornered in an empty patient room by a polished young man, also in a physician's white coat, a stethoscope looped around his neck. She snapped angrily at him, referring to something that must have happened on an earlier show, and he disputed her, and abruptly they were kissing. Toby should have been thinking how absurd it was for two doctors to have the time to be kissing like that during a tour of duty in the E.R., and how much more absurd it was to find an empty room in a bustling hospital—but his attention was riveted by the kiss. It was a television kiss, openmouthed and juicy and curiously fake looking. Watching Susannah kiss someone else didn't turn him on.

That wasn't Susannah, he reminded himself as he swallowed some beer. That was a character—Lee Something—and the way she was kissing the actor was nothing like the way Susannah had kissed Toby. Their kiss had been hot but not greedy, the desire intensely personal, not played for an audience. What he'd felt during that kiss was deep and profoundly pleasurable, a sip from a magic potion that slaked his thirst while simultaneously making him thirstier.

He wanted another sip. A long, quenching drink. He wanted that potion to flood his body, to drench every cell.

Instead, he was drinking a beer and watching the woman he desired on a television show.

Maybe this was the most he could hope for right now. Lindsey was asleep upstairs, loathing him. Somehow he would raise her. She would grow up, God willing, and forgive him for everything he'd ever done wrong, and she would get on with her own life, liberating him to live his. And then—if he could wait that long—he would be able to pursue a woman freely, without hesitation, without a child shouting down the stairs and slamming doors.

For now, he would have to settle for a television show.

CHAPTER SEVEN

"DOES SHE EVER look out her windows?" Amanda asked. She was kneeling on Lindsey's bed, using Lindsey's *Jurassic Park* binoculars to scrutinize the house next door.

Lindsey had gotten permission from her father for this meeting of the Susannah Dawson Admiration Society. She'd asked him last night, and he'd said that Lindsey could invite two friends over after school, as long as they were Amanda and Meredith and no one else. He'd lectured that he was placing his trust in her, and if she didn't live up to it he would have a hard time trusting her ever again, so he really hoped she and her friends would behave well and not abuse the privilege.

Like anything was going to screw up with Meredith and Amanda visiting. They'd taken Lindsey's bus home from school with her, prepared a bag of popcorn in the microwave, and were now holding their club meeting in Lindsey's bedroom, which offered the best view of Susannah's house. Meredith and Lindsey were eating the popcorn, but Amanda was more interested in viewing Susannah's house through the binoculars than eating.

Not that there was much worth viewing. "I've seen her in Cathy's room sometimes, especially at night," Lindsey told her.

"Which one's Cathy's room?"

"The one with the windows facing ours. She's got her office in there now."

"Her office?" Meredith asked. "Why does she need an office?"

Lindsey shrugged. "She's got a computer in there, and a desk and stuff. I think she's writing something."

"Her memoirs," Meredith guessed. "A book about all her Hollywood affairs."

"I don't think so," Lindsey argued, mostly because she was annoyed that Meredith had come up with such a good theory. "She doesn't like talking about *Mercy Hospital.* I don't see why she'd want to write about it."

"Maybe she doesn't like to talk about it because she is writing about it," Meredith suggested. "You know, like, she doesn't talk about it because she wants you to go out and buy her book."

Amanda swiveled on her knees until she had her back to the window. "She's been in more than just *Mercy Hospital,* you know. It said in *People*—or maybe it was *Entertainment Weekly* or the *Enquirer,* I don't remember, one of those… Anyway, last summer, there was this article about her. It said that she started making commercials when she was thirteen. That's not much older than us."

"What commercials?" Meredith asked.

"I'm trying to remember. My sister reads all those magazines. I woulda stole the magazine from her room if I knew Susannah Dawson was going to move into town and we were going to have a club and every-thing." She crossed her legs, rested her elbows on her knees and propped her chin in her hands. Then she screwed her face into a frown that Lindsey took to mean she was thinking hard. "McDonald's, maybe. Or Burger King."

"We need to know which one," Lindsey said. "Because I think, as the Susannah Dawson Admiration Society, we need to honor Susannah by eating only at the one she made the commercial for. If she was in a McDonald's commercial, I for one don't want to be buying my fries at Burger King."

"Good point," Meredith said, and Lindsey instantly stopped being annoyed with her. "We have an obligation as club members."

"If my sister didn't throw out that magazine, I'll get it," Amanda promised, plucking a single piece of popcorn from the bowl on the edge of the bed and chewing it thoughtfully. "Susannah Dawson did guest roles in some shows, too. And then, before she got the part of Dr. Lee Davis, she had parts in some made-for-TV movies. She was in one where she played this rapist's innocent sister who keeps sticking up for him even though he's way bad, and then she ends up getting killed."

"Wow," Meredith murmured.

Lindsey was pretty impressed, too. When she grew up and left Arlington, she had every intention of playing lots of exciting roles like that in movies. She bet that if she got to play the innocent sister of an evil rapist, she could die just as dramatically as Susannah.

"What else did this article say about her?" Meredith asked, devouring a handful of popcorn and then snatching the binoculars from Amanda. She crawled across the bed to the window and peered out. "Did it say she was planning to move to Connecticut?"

"I don't remember everything," Amanda admitted. "It said she was personally involved with Stephen

Yates, the actor who plays Lucien Roche on *Mercy Hospital*.''

"Really?" Lindsey climbed onto the bed, as well. "Susannah is actually Stephen Yates's girlfriend?"

"There was a picture of them together."

"Oh, wow," Meredith sighed.

"He is so cute," Lindsey added.

"I've gotta find that magazine. I think it was *Entertainment Weekly*. Or maybe the *Star*."

"Yes," Lindsey demanded. "You've got to find that magazine. This stuff is important." Very important, she added. If Susannah was Stephen Yates's girlfriend, was Dr. Dad going to get in trouble for being friendly to her? That was the way he was—friendly and helpful, Mr. Nice Guy. Lindsey had known he would hang Susannah's mirror for her, because that was the way he was. He did stuff for people.

Sometimes Lindsey wished he did less stuff for her. Like visiting her teacher or fussing over her grades. But Susannah, far from home, far from the majorly gorgeous Stephen Yates, needed someone like Lindsey's father to lend her a hand and make her feel at home in the new neighborhood.

That was one of the things Lindsey liked about Susannah—she distracted Dr. Dad from Lindsey a little, so he wasn't spending every waking minute worrying about whether she was working up to her potential in math.

"Omigod. I saw her," Meredith whispered.

"Where?" Amanda squealed, elbowing Meredith to one side of the window so she could look.

"Don't be so obvious," Lindsey warned them, joining them on the bed and pushing down on their shoulders so they weren't as visible through the window.

"She's in the office," Meredith said. "In Cathy's old room."

"I don't believe it!" Amanda's voice rose another octave. "Oh, God, she's so pretty!"

From their vantage point, they could hardly see Susannah's face. Her long blond hair was visible, and her profile, but she was far enough away that even with the binoculars, Meredith would only catch a hint of how beautiful Susannah was. And Amanda would only be able to imagine.

"She really is beautiful," Lindsey confirmed, trying not to sound too superior about the fact that she'd spent so much time with Susannah and Amanda and Meredith had never even seen her in person.

"We need to do something," Meredith decided, relinquishing the binoculars reluctantly when Amanda grabbed for them. "Like take pictures of her or something."

"You'd need one of those big lenses to get a picture of her," Lindsey pointed out. "A tele-something lens."

"Telephoto," Meredith said.

"Maybe we could lure her outside," Amanda suggested. "Like, maybe you could phone her and say her house is on fire or something."

Meredith and Lindsey both gave her contemptuous looks. "Like she'd ever forgive me for doing that," Lindsey muttered.

"Well, you've met her. What could you say to get her to come outside?"

I could tell her my dad's here, Lindsey almost blurted out. Susannah would come over if her father asked her to. She'd come over the other night in those stretchy exercise pants and her wristbands and all, just because Dr. Dad had invited her. They'd gone out to the porch and talked. Lindsey had wanted so badly to join them, but her father had treated her like a baby. "Go to bed," he'd ordered her. He probably wanted Susannah to think of her as a baby, too.

She wasn't a baby. Susannah never treated her like one, especially when her father wasn't around. She treated Lindsey like a pal.

And as her pal, Lindsey understood she shouldn't pester Susannah or trick her into coming outside. Susannah was kind of a private person, not like you'd expect of a showbiz type. She kept a low profile. Out of respect for her, Lindsey shouldn't do anything to lure her out of her house.

But Meredith and Amanda were her pals, also. Now that Cathy was gone, they were as close to best friends as anyone she had. If she didn't do something to get Susannah outside, they might not like her as much. They'd think maybe she'd exaggerated about spending an afternoon inside Susannah's house and talking to her and having dinner with her and stuff.

She needed Amanda and Meredith to believe her. If she could get Susannah outside—or better yet, get her to come over and maybe even meet them—they would be her devoted friends for life.

She was sure she could come up with a way to lure Susannah out of her house. Maybe she could buy a present for MacKenzie, a cat toy or something, and ask if Susannah could bring MacKenzie outside so she could give it to him, and Amanda and Meredith could watch through the window. Or Lindsey could pretend there was a problem in the house—a funny smell, a leaky toilet—and ask Susannah if she could come over and solve the problem.

"I'll think of something," she promised, deciding she wouldn't really be tricking Susannah. She'd just be getting her to show her face for a minute or two. "I'll try to come up with a plan by the time we have our next meeting."

"That would be cool," Meredith said, her eyes glowing with esteem for Lindsey.

"And I'll get hold of that magazine," Amanda promised. Bringing over a magazine with details of Susannah's love life with Stephen Yates would be great. But not as great as Lindsey's getting Susannah to come outside while the society was in session.

Lindsey would do it for the sake of the club. She'd do it because she wanted Amanda and Meredith to recognize how cool she was. Meredith seemed to sort of understand, but Lindsey wanted people to realize how important it was that Susannah Dawson liked her. No matter how her father treated her, Susannah didn't think she was a baby. She talked to Lindsey like an equal.

They were friends. Amanda and Meredith would never be more than Susannah's fans, but Lindsey was truly Susannah's friend, and you couldn't get much cooler than that.

"HEY, ANDY, how are you doing?" Toby asked, peering into Andy Lowenthal's room.

The boy was pale and drawn, his eyes nestled deep into pockets of shadow, and his hair was beginning to thin from his chemotherapy. But when he lifted his gaze from the Game Boy he was playing, he greeted Toby with a huge grin. "Hey, Dr. Cole," he said.

Toby entered the room and smiled at Andy's mother, who sat in a chair near the window with a magazine spread open on her lap. Then he turned back to Andy. "Here's something you might like," he said, presenting the boy with the New York Yankees cap he'd brought. Andy had told him he was a Yankees fan.

"Oh, wow. Cool." Andy sat the hat carefully on his scalp. "Dr. Weiss says I can go home this weekend."

"Really?" Toby glanced at Andy's mother, who confirmed with a nod. "That's great!"

"She says I have to come back for more treatments, but I can at least go home for a while, and see my friends."

"Did she tell you to be very careful with friends who might have a cold or a cough?"

"Yeah, or chicken pox. She said my something was low. What was it, Mommy?"

"Your resistance," his mother supplied.

"Yeah, that was it." He settled back on the pillows. He looked thin, his pajamas swimming on him.

"How's your appetite?" Toby asked.

"I don't like the food here. My mom brought me cookies."

"That's fine. Is your mouth okay? Any sores?"

"Nope."

"Even better." Toby gave Andy's shoulder a squeeze. "You're doing great, Andy. Dr. Weiss is terrific. She really knows how to lick this disease. It looks like the chemo's doing what it has to do."

"If I go home, my mom says I'm going to have to do homework."

"Well, you don't want to fall too far behind the rest of your class. If you continue to do this well, you might be able to return to school before the end of the term."

"You know what?" Andy tipped his head toward Toby, as if to reveal a deep secret. "I miss school."

"I see your class misses you, too," Toby said, waving toward the poster hanging on the wall across from his bed. Andy: Get Well Soon! it said, with classmates' personal messages scribbled all across it in a hodgepodge of third-grade penmanship. "Well, I've got to go check on some other patients. I just wanted to say hi and give you the hat."

"It's cool, Dr. Cole."

"Enjoy it." He nodded to Andy's mother, then strolled out of the room, pleased by the boy's progress.

At least one thing was going right, he thought as he continued down the hall from the pediatrics wing to the neonatal unit. Andy was responding well to his treatment, and his prognosis was excellent. That was no small victory.

Actually, Toby acknowledged, no victory was ever small. He still hadn't achieved a victory with Lindsey, but they'd worked out a truce of sorts; he'd allowed her to invite a couple of friends over to the house in an effort to prove his trust in her. But even though he was going through the motions of trusting her, he wasn't sure he actually did.

The Daddy School teacher had said fathers had to give their children responsibility, let their children make their own mistakes and allow their children to develop competency and independence. So Toby hadn't checked Lindsey's homework in a week—he had only her word that it was getting done—and now he was letting her have friends over after school, when he wasn't present.

He couldn't silence the niggling worry inside him that maybe he was giving trust that hadn't been earned. But his relationship with Lindsey, as rocky as it was, seemed more auspicious than his relationship with the other woman in his life.

He could scarcely claim that Susannah was the other woman in his life, because she seemed to have dropped out of his life the instant she'd escaped from his kiss last week. She'd said she wanted to spend a day observing him at work, but she hadn't gotten in touch with him to set it up. She hadn't contacted him at all.

Had kissing her really been so out of line? She hadn't fought him off; she hadn't said no. They were two healthy adults. And before she'd run away, she'd kissed him back. Enthusiastically. Passionately.

He hadn't stopped thinking about that night, that kiss. He *couldn't* stop thinking about it. He wondered whether his willingness to lighten up with Lindsey was a result of being too distracted by Susannah to give his daughter his full attention. That made him feel guilty. And he knew the drawbacks of becoming involved with his neighbor, which made him wary.

But he couldn't banish Susannah from his mind. When he drove past her house each morning and again on his way home each evening, he glanced at her windows, hoping for a glimpse of her. He'd see the flowering pink impatiens hanging on the porch, and sometimes even her cat sitting on a windowsill, gazing out. But never Susannah.

He ought to forget about her and concentrate on Lindsey. There would be time later for romance in his life—if he could get Lindsey safely through middle school and high school and college....

He swore softly. At Jane, for having died on him, abandoning him to struggle alone with their daughter. At the medical profession, for having failed to save Jane. At himself, for being so damned selfish, wanting sex and love and a woman when he ought to be taking care of business. But hell, he was a human being. He had needs. And kissing Susannah had made him acutely aware of what needs of his weren't being met.

Sighing, he turned the corner and entered Arlington Memorial's neonatal unit. Down the corridor he spotted Allison Winslow at the nurses' station, talking to a familiar-looking man while a toddler hugged her knee. Drawing closer, Toby recognized the man as Allison's husband, whom he'd met at the hospital's Fourth of July barbecue last year. The little girl wrapped around Allison's leg was their daughter.

He slowed his pace, not wanting to interrupt them. Allison's husband said something and she tossed back her head and laughed. Then she saw him and waved. "Hi, Toby."

He guessed he wasn't interrupting after all. He strode over, right hand outstretched, and tried to recollect her husband's name.

"Toby, you remember my husband Jamie, don't you? Jamie this is Toby Cole, one of the pediatricians affiliated with the department. I think I introduced you at the barbecue last summer."

Jamie shook his hand. "Sure I remember you. As I recall, we faced each other on opposite sides of the net during a cutthroat volleyball game."

Toby nodded. "As I recall, your side trounced my side."

"I like this guy," Jamie confided to Allison. "I like his memory." Grinning, he peeled the child off Allison's leg and hoisted her into the air. "Come on, Samantha—let's let Mommy get back to work," he said, straining slightly under her heft.

"I go Mommy," she demanded, reaching for Allison.

"No, sweetheart," Allison said, cuddling in to give her a big kiss. "You're going with Daddy. He's going to take you downtown to buy you new shoes. You want new shoes, don't you?"

"I get chooz!" the girl exclaimed, wriggling in her father's arms until she could grab hold of one of her brightly colored sneakers. "Chooz!"

"That's right. I'll see you at home for dinner." Allison gave the girl another kiss, then signaled Jamie with her eyes and muttered, "Take her while she's still happy."

Jamie winked and heaved the child higher in his arms. "Nice seeing you," he said to Toby before hurrying down the hall to the elevator.

Allison watched them go with a wistful gaze. Toby had known her for a while, and she'd never struck him as particularly sentimental. Yet once the elevator doors slid shut around them and she turned back to Toby, she appeared to be oddly dazed, as if still in a maternal state of mind.

In less than a second, she snapped back, the loving glow fading and her eyes sharp. "So, you picked up a new patient at around two o'clock this morning," she said.

"I'm on my way to meet her. I heard the birth went well."

"Piece of cake. I wasn't here, but it was textbook all the way."

"She did fine on the Apgar, too." He noticed Allison's gaze drifting toward the elevator for a moment and smiled. "You'd rather be taking your daughter shoe shopping, huh."

Allison grinned. "Not a chance. She's horrible in stores. She wants everything, everything, everything. Jamie can handle that better than I can."

"Really? What does he do?"

"He buys her everything, everything, everything." Allison laughed and pulled a strand of hair free from the collar of her white coat. "Not really. I've trained them both."

"How old is she? Around two years?"

"She'll be two in June," Allison confirmed. She must have noticed Toby frowning as he did a mental calculation and the numbers failed to add up. "She was Jamie's baby. I adopted her when I married him."

"Ah." Unbidden, an image of Susannah sprang up in his mind. He recalled asking her to help him with Lindsey. Did she feel he was asking her to step into the role of Lindsey's mother? *Was* he asking her that?

Allison hadn't become her daughter's mother until she'd married Jamie, though. She'd loved Jamie, and adopting his daughter had only been the final step in fulfilling their love.

Toby didn't love Susannah. He liked talking to her, being with her...and he wanted to kiss her again, to feel her hair spill like silk through his fingers, to feel her body pressed tight to his. He wanted to feel her beneath him in that big brass bed of hers—or to have her on top of him, to take her weight as he locked his body to hers.

But that wasn't love. He wasn't sure what it was.

"Who is she?" Allison asked.

Embarrassed, he glanced down. No, his body hadn't given him away. "Who is who?"

"You're thinking about someone."

"Just a friend," he fibbed, and then decided it

wasn't a lie. They were friends. Or they would be, if she ever called him again, if he ever saw her again. "A new neighbor."

"You deserve a romance," Allison said, obviously not believing that Susannah was "just a friend." "I hope she's good enough for you."

Toby dismissed her hunch with a grin. "It's not that way," he insisted. "There's nothing going on between us. My baggage isn't an adorable baby girl. It's a mouthy, sarcastic ten-year-old."

"Your mouthy, sarcastic ten-year-old is going through a stage, Toby. You aren't under any obligation to shut down your life until she grows out of it." Crossing her arms, she appraised him thoughtfully. "Did you go to Molly's Daddy School class last week?"

"Yeah. There's another class tonight. I'll be there."

"You found it worthwhile?"

"Very. But it's one thing to sit in a class and learn the theory, and quite another to put it into practice. Like med school," he recalled with a wry laugh. "Listening to lectures on anatomy was a breeze. Dissecting a cadaver was a whole different thing."

"But with practice, you got good at dissecting cadavers. If you didn't have the talent to apply theory to practice, you'd be doing research in some lab right now instead of healing children. Speaking of which—" she glanced at her watch "—I've got newborns to bathe, and you've got a newborn to introduce yourself to. She's in room 523."

"Right." With a farewell wave, he abandoned the nurses' station for his new patient's room. He knocked lightly on the door, then inched it open. Anne Brewer, the new mother, was sitting up in bed, her baby in her arms.

Anne beamed at Toby. "She's perfect, Dr. Cole," she announced, hugging her swaddled infant to her and bowing to kiss a downy cheek.

Toby recalled when Lindsey had been perfect...and then he decided she still was perfect, in her own exasperating way. Nowhere had it ever been promised that raising a child would be easy. Anyone who wanted easy ought to pass on becoming a parent.

But Toby was a parent, and he loved his daughter, and she was perfect, even when she was perfectly awful. He loved her, and every day, in some symbolic fashion, he felt himself cradling her in his protective arms just as Anne cradled her new daughter.

Children outgrew their parents' arms, but the arms were always there. When a father loved his daughter, his arms were always open, always strong, always ready for her.

LINDSEY HAD LEFT a message for him on his voice mail back at Arlington Pediatrics: "We're out of milk. And also popcorn." He guessed she and her friends had been snacking that afternoon.

Because he had a Daddy School class that evening, he had planned his schedule so he could leave for home by four-thirty. He had time for a quick detour to the supermarket to buy some milk—and popcorn, since Lindsey had specifically requested it.

The sky was bright with sunlight as he cruised down Dudley Road toward the store. Rush-hour traffic hadn't built up yet, and the air held the flavor of spring. A few boys not much older than Lindsey skateboarded along the sidewalk, flexing their legs to steer their boards around hydrants and lampposts. He recalled what Susannah had said about how girls Lindsey's age were already well aware of boys, ranking them on a scale from cute to creepy. Were these boys in Lindsey's school? Did she know them? Did she think they were cute?

They all looked creepy to him. Then again, any boy Lindsey considered cute Toby would hate on principle.

He reached the supermarket and steered into the sprawling parking lot. If Lindsey were with him, she'd demand to be let off in front of the CD store, but he cruised past it, past the drugstore and the dress boutique, and eased into a parking space near the supermarket. Leaving his blazer and briefcase on the back seat, he sprinted across the asphalt to the store and up the dairy aisle. When he'd first taken on the responsibility of grocery shopping, during Jane's final months, he'd been mystified by the supermarket, in awe of all those efficient women who strolled up and down the aisles, buying items in order, sorting their coupons and scanning their lists and always knowing exactly where everything they needed could be found. Now he was as adept as they were. He knew where the milk was, the popcorn, and just about everything else the store had for sale.

He paid for his purchases at the express checkout, then hoisted the bag into the crook of his elbow and headed back outside. A small crowd had gathered near the row of shopping carts. Curious, he wandered toward them, wondering what had drawn them.

"Please give me your autograph!" someone shouted.

"Just sign this bag!"

"Sign my hand, Susannah!"

And then he saw her, standing in the center of the mob, being swarmed as if by bees. She wore sunglasses and a duck-billed cap; her hair was pulled into a ponytail. In old jeans and a white cotton sweater, she looked more like a harried suburban mom than a glamorous actress. She also looked peeved and slightly alarmed.

Without having to think, he elbowed his way through the crowd until he reached her. "We have to go now," he said authoritatively, taking her arm and guiding her through the clinging crowd. Some instinct told him she wanted to be away from these fans, as far away as possible. "Sorry, everyone," he murmured, forging a path through the yammering fans, brushing away a pen-waving hand, a proffered pad. "Sorry, no time now…"

They broke free of the crowd and sprinted across the parking lot toward Toby's car. He released her arm to press the remote button on his key, unlocking the doors before they reached the car. Susannah dove inside and slammed the passenger door. As he circled the car to the driver's side, he glanced behind him. The crowd had followed but halted within a few feet of the car, somehow sensing that to come any closer wouldn't be right.

After wedging his bag of groceries on the floor behind his seat, Toby got in and locked all the doors. He glared at a few stragglers still ogling Susannah through the car's windows, then started the engine. The crowd dispersed as he backed out of the spot and drove away.

He kept going for a few blocks, then turned onto a side street, stopped the car and faced Susannah. She was slouching in the contoured seat, her forehead twisted into a taut scowl. "Are you okay?" he asked.

"I'm fine," she muttered.

It occurred to him that maybe he'd presumed too much, rushing in to rescue her when she might not have wanted to be rescued. "You looked like you needed a little help back there," he explained. "I'm sorry if I—"

"It's all right." She sighed, then pulled off her hat and sunglasses. He saw the tension in her face, the worry. "Actually, I'm grateful."

Relieved, he relaxed and shut off the engine. "They seemed so…leechy," he said. "Are your fans always like that?"

She chuckled grimly and reached under her hair to massage her nape. "Signing autographs for fans used to be a part of my job, and I accepted it. But I don't have that job anymore." She sighed again. "I would have given them autographs if they'd been nice. But they were so demanding, yelling at me. One of them touched me."

"Touched you? You mean, to make sure you were real?" He supposed that as a hormone-driven teenager, if he'd ever met a star—one of Charlie's Angels, for instance—he would have wanted to touch her, and then he would have vowed never to wash his hand again. That pledge would have lasted until dinnertime. His mother had ordained that her children would not be allowed to eat until their hands were clean, and no matter how much he'd lusted after Charlie's Angels, he'd liked food more.

Susannah snorted. "He groped me."

"What?"

"He touched my breast."

"Who did?" He reached for the ignition key, prepared to drive back to the supermarket, grab the offender and beat the crap out of him. "Could you identify him? If you can point him out to me—"

She covered his hand with hers to keep him from turning on the engine. "Forget about it, Toby. It doesn't matter."

"It does! It's a sexual assault! It's—"

"Forget it," she said sharply.

Honoring her request, he let his hand fall from the ignition switch. "Has this happened to you before?"

"Not in Arlington." She shook her head. "That store stays open all night. I've been doing my shopping after ten-thirty. The place is usually dead by then. All the produce is picked over, but at least I'm left alone." She rolled her head back to rest on the cushioned support. "I thought I was acting silly, sneaking around to do my shopping at night. I thought I was being paranoid—or maybe too egotistical, assuming that anyone would even recognize me. So I decided to go shopping at a normal time today. And...I guess I wasn't being egotistical."

"Or paranoid." The thought of some stranger touching her breast made him shudder. "What would you like me to do? Do you want to go back?"

"No. They could still be there. Of course, my car is there," she murmured, thinking out loud. "They'll probably figure out it's mine, too. I still haven't changed the registration from California to Connecticut. The Motor Vehicle Department doesn't stay open twenty-four hours like the supermarket." She muttered a quiet curse. "If they figure out it's my car, they might vandalize it. Tear off a side-view mirror or something."

"Your insurance will cover any damage," he said.

"I'll drive you home. I've got to go out later this evening. I can take you back to get the car then."

"Daddy School?" she guessed.

"How did you know?"

"It's Wednesday. Last week you went on a Wednesday."

Last week he'd come home after Daddy School and found her outside her house, and invited her in, and talked to her, and kissed her. He remembered that Wednesday very well.

He wouldn't make her unpleasant afternoon even more uncomfortable by reminding her of that. Starting the car, he shifted into gear and coasted down the street, deciding to take the meandering back roads home.

Neither of them spoke for a minute. He wanted to ask her how she'd been, why she'd kept her distance, whether she recalled her promise to discuss menstruation with Lindsey. He wanted to invite her to trail him around at work and take notes for her scriptwriting. He wanted to tell her that her absence from his life during the past week hadn't diminished his attraction to her one bit.

"I guess you don't like being famous," he said, instead.

"No." Her voice sounded dull and heavy. "Not at all."

"Most people dream of fame."

"I'm not most people."

He nodded. "Even so...I would think that becoming a successful actress is so hard, the odds are so small that you'll make it—why would anyone do it if they didn't want the glamour part of it?"

"They'd do it because they felt they had to," she

said, and he knew she wasn't talking about "anyone."
She was talking about herself.

"You had to?"

"I was supporting my family."

Her family? She'd told him she had no children.
Maybe she was divorced and she'd had to support her
husband at some point.

She answered the question he hadn't asked. "My
parents and my brothers," she told him. "My father
was an auto mechanic. He wanted to live a better life.
And he thought I was pretty. I had a 'look,' he used
to tell me. One of his clients was the casting director
at an advertising agency, so he made sure I was at the
garage the day that casting director was scheduled to
bring in her Porsche for an oil change. After she saw
me, he told her I was dying to appear in commercials,
so she said I could come in and audition for her. My
father told me I had to do it because the family needed
the money."

"How old were you?"

"Nine." Her voice hadn't lost its drab color. Yet
somehow he knew that beneath the monotone, she was
seething with anger and resentment.

"So you supported your parents?"

"Yes. I made a lot of money, first with commercials
and then with guest shots on TV shows. My father quit
his job to manage my career. I guess you could say he
was my pimp."

The harsh word took Toby aback. When he glanced
at Susannah, though, her face remained emotionless, as
if she'd simply stated a fact.

"You didn't like acting?" he asked carefully.

"I never even thought about whether I liked it. Fame
and glory didn't interest me. I didn't care about being

a star or having fans. It was just something I had to do. If I didn't, my family would lose our home. We wouldn't eat. My brothers wouldn't have basketball sneakers.'' She shrugged. ''I was the breadwinner. It was my duty to the family.''

''But then you grew up. You became an adult. Once you could start making your own decisions—''

''They were so dependent on me,'' she explained. ''They were my family—I couldn't just walk away from them when they had no other money coming in.''

''But they exploited you!''

She mulled over her response, then repeated, ''They were my family,'' as though that was the only answer.

Maybe it was. Maybe family ties could be that strong.

''I finally stopped,'' she added, as if to prove that she truly was an independent adult now. ''My second year on *Mercy Hospital,* I told my parents I was no longer going to support them. I'd bought them a house, a car. I'd paid for my brothers' college educations. And I was done. But for the next few years my father was still after me, constantly asking for loans, begging for extra money. It was a terrible strain.''

Toby could understand why it hadn't been enough for her to quit her acting work. She'd had to move all the way across the country to get away from her money-grubbing parents.

''I'm sorry,'' he said as he turned onto their street.

She glanced at him. ''For what?''

''I'm sorry you went through that.'' He slowed to take a corner. Trees that just a couple of weeks ago had stood barren were now dotted with unfurling leaves. Lilacs bloomed pale lavender, and forsythia flashed its showy yellow blossoms. Arlington in the

spring was a glorious sight. "I became a doctor because I wanted to," he explained. "I loved the work.
I still do. Everyone should have the opportunity to follow his dream. I'm sorry you didn't have that opportunity."

"I did," she said, a shy smile tracing her lips. "Here
I am."

Here she was, he thought. In his town. In his car,
next to him.

What was her dream? he wondered. Had her dream
led her to him?

That was a silly thought. If her dream had led her
to him, she wouldn't have run away when he'd kissed
her.

Reaching her house, he braked and pulled into her
driveway. He briefly considered inviting her to have
dinner with him and Lindsey, but he decided he needed
a little time alone with his daughter. He would be going out again in a couple of hours, and Lindsey deserved his undiluted attention for that time.

So he only said, "I'll stop by around ten past seven,
and we'll go get your car then."

"Thank you," she said. Her eyes were luminous, lit
from within. Was she thanking him for rescuing her
from the autograph seekers? For offering to drive her
back to her car? For listening while she described her
ghastly family and her hostility about her former career? For not reminding her of the last time they'd been
together, not pressing to kiss her again, not telling her
what he was really thinking, really desiring?

Everyone deserved the opportunity to follow his
dream. Why did he feel, when he looked into her eyes,
that she was another dream he wanted to follow?

Given her background, he ought to be leery. She had

a lot of baggage, a lot of emotional scars. If he was going to fall for a woman, it ought to be a woman who was confident and unscathed, a woman strong and whole enough to handle a widower with an occasionally difficult child. A woman who could go shopping in the late afternoon without drawing a crowd.

Susannah wasn't that woman.

But he still wanted to follow this dream.

CHAPTER EIGHT

SHE THOUGHT about him while she poked her fork into the tuna salad she'd fixed for her dinner. Tuna was the closest thing to supper she'd had in her pantry. She would replenish her food supply later, when he brought her back to the supermarket to get her car.

But even if she'd had a well-stocked refrigerator—and even if she'd been a halfway decent cook—she would still have picked at her meal. She wasn't hungry.

She was too busy thinking. About Toby.

She should have called him. But after that night when he'd kissed her and stirred up feelings she'd loved and feared in equal measure, she'd kept her distance. She'd known that if she saw him again, she would wind up involved with him. It would be too easy. Toby was that kind of man.

The last time she'd been involved with a man, it had been easy, too. They'd worked together; they'd been attracted to each other; it had seemed so natural...and easy had proven to be disastrously hard on her emotions. She had learned a lot of lessons from her debacle with Stephen, among them that she needed to look before she leaped, that she mustn't get sucked into a relationship just because it was convenient or because it felt good or because the man had bedroom eyes and persuasive kisses—or because she was used to arranging her life around the needs of others. For the sake of her sanity, she had to declare her independence from *everybody*. She had to live by herself, for herself, without worrying about what everyone else wanted from her.

Maybe it sounded selfish. But she'd been alive for thirty-two years, and in all that time she'd never taken care of herself. Now was the time to start.

She hadn't done a particularly good job taking care of herself at the supermarket that afternoon, she admitted dismally, shoving her plate away and taking a long swallow of iced herbal tea. If Toby hadn't come along...well, she would have survived. She might have had to elbow that sleazy guy a few more times, a bit more imperatively, to get him to stop trying to feel her up, but she would have signed autographs for all the people who'd gathered around her—and for the additional people who would have been attracted by the crowd. She would have stood in the parking lot, courteously signing autographs for a half hour or more, because there was no way she *couldn't* do it.

It wasn't that she disliked her fans. It was just that signing autographs was the same as everything else she'd spent most of her life doing: pleasing others. Putting aside her own needs and desires and satisfying everyone else's demands.

She leaned back in her chair, her tumbler of iced tea cupped in her hands, and gazed through the arched doorway into the dining room, to the window. MacKenzie was seated on the sill, staring out at the Cole residence next door. Susannah couldn't blame him. Just knowing Toby was inside the solid brick house was enough to make her want to stare at it, too. Knowing he was seated with his daughter right now, chatting about his day at work and her day at school, maybe discussing tampons—a smile teased Susannah's lips as she tried to imagine that—made her long to race across the lawn, to plead with them for permission to sit in a corner and observe them. How lucky Lindsey was to have a father like Toby.

Susannah wasn't going to let their family warmth bewitch her. She wanted independence. She wanted to answer to no one but herself. She wanted to stay up late if she felt like it, sleep late, write her scripts in the wee hours, eat when she felt like it and run the laundry when *she* needed clean socks, not when anyone else did. She wanted to spend her money, or save it, according to her own whims. She wanted no one pulling on her.

Toby's nearness pulled on her with all the force of gravity. But she would resist his powerful attraction. Even though she'd tasted his kisses and knew how sweet they were, even though she knew making love with him would be even sweeter...

She wasn't going to fall for him, for the safety and security and suffocation of another relationship. She had MacKenzie and she had herself. That was enough to satisfy her.

DESPITE THE SIDE TRIP to the supermarket to drive Susannah back to her car—which appeared unscathed, no scratches or graffiti added to it and neither side mirror missing—Toby made it to his Daddy School class in the YMCA building in downtown Arlington with a few minutes to spare. Molly Saunders-Russo stood at one end of the room, directing her students to arrange the chairs in a circle. She started pushing one of the chairs, but a father nudged her out of the way. She was at least five months pregnant, her abdomen as round as a bowling ball beneath a blousy shirt. She shouldn't have been dragging chairs across the floor.

One of the other fathers greeted Toby with a nod of recognition as he entered the room. The class was small, only nine fathers, and they all looked familiar from last week.

He hauled a chair over to the circle and settled into it as the other fathers and Molly took their seats. "Okay," she said, gazing around the group with a smile. She already had one child, Toby recalled, and she was expecting another one. Imagine if he'd had more than one child to raise. Imagine if Lindsey had been twins. He'd be in twice as much trouble now.

"Did you all have a good week?" Molly asked. Toby wasn't sure she expected an answer, but a few of the men murmured unintelligibly, and the fellow next to him—Toby recalled that he was the father of an eight-year-old with attention deficit disorder—nodded. Molly's smile seemed to grow. "Did you all practice trusting your kids? Because today we're going to talk about something related to trust—letting go. Giving your children freedom."

Toby arranged himself more comfortably on the folding metal chair. He was curious about what Molly could possibly say that would convince him it was all right to loosen the reins on Lindsey any more than he already had. He'd allowed her to invite her friends over, and he hadn't punished her for telling those white lies about doing a homework project the time her friends had been at the house without his approval. All he'd done about the lying was talk to her. He'd wanted it to be a serious, sincere discussion, but he'd been the only serious, sincere participant. Throughout the entire conversation, Lindsey had squirmed and rolled her eyes and insisted that her misstatements were hardly even lies and shouldn't count, and anyway, he *knew* she wasn't a liar, didn't he?

He wished he knew that, but he didn't. Maybe Molly, the alleged expert on father-child relationships, would explain this evening how a man was supposed to know his daughter wasn't a liar when she'd already lied to him.

Still smiling and looking far too optimistic, Molly tossed out a question: "What's the hardest thing about letting go of your kids?"

"Fear," one of the men shouted out. His response was greeted with knowing chuckles and nods of confirmation.

"Fear," Molly repeated. "What are you afraid of?"

Silence spread around the circle for several seconds. Then one father timidly ventured, "Fear that my son will get hurt."

"Physically or emotionally?" Molly asked.

"Both. You give him the freedom to bike through downtown Arlington with his buddies, and he could get hit by a car. You give him the freedom to hang out with whoever he wants, he might choose the wrong group to hang out with. Maybe they'll be bullies, or they'll be sneaking beer, or…" The father glanced around the circle, looking for support. "I don't know."

"These are legitimate fears," Molly assured him. "What other fears do you have?"

"I'm afraid she'll take advantage of me," another father volunteered. An older man with a silver beard, he'd apparently had his daughter late in life. "I'm already afraid she knows how to manipulate me. If I give her more freedom, she'll manipulate me even more."

Molly nodded. "Anyone else? What are you afraid of, Toby?" she asked, zeroing in on him.

He said the first thing that came to his mind: "I'm afraid of losing my daughter."

"Losing her?" Molly appeared intrigued. "Why?"

Damn. Toby didn't want to spill his guts in front of this group of near strangers. How could they understand his fear of losing Lindsey? Most of them had wives, or at least ex-wives, with whom to share the job of raising their children. Toby had lost his wife. And his daughter was looking more and more like his wife. Every day her face became more like Jane's, her voice echoing Jane's.... Didn't these men realize how easy it was to lose a loved one?

He couldn't say that, though. Baring his soul wasn't his style. He prided himself on his ability to hold his world together throughout ordeals and crises and pain. He was a doctor, a healer. He saved lives. He wasn't going to present himself to this Daddy School class as an incompetent fool who was falling apart inside.

Yet he was at the class, wasn't he? By definition, that pretty well marked him as someone who wasn't holding everything together. Like the other students, he was a father who needed help.

The class was still waiting for him to speak. "I have a friend," he said, shifting in his chair, as if a different posture would make it easier for him to open up to this group. "She had a difficult adolescence with her father. And now she...well, I don't know if *hate* is too strong a word, but..." Closing his eyes briefly, he conjured a vision of Susannah in his car earlier that day, telling him about her tortured relationship with her father. It was nothing like his relationship with Lindsey, but he'd still felt the sorrow of it in a personal way.

"Maybe she does hate her father. She certainly resents him. They're estranged. She moved all the way across the country so there would be three thousand miles between him and her. Losing your child can happen. It isn't just some unrealistic nightmare."

"Is your relationship with your daughter like this friend's relationship with her father?" Molly asked carefully.

"No. Absolutely nothing like it. I'm just saying…" He folded his hands and drew in a deep breath. "Fathers lose their daughters. It happens. That's all."

Molly smiled enigmatically and turned from him. Evidently, she recognized that he didn't want to be the center of attention. She called on someone else, who talked about how his son was always testing limits, and every time he loosened a limit the son pressed harder, trying to push the limit even further. Other members of the class joined in, analyzing how fathers could determine where the lines needed to be drawn. They discussed why it was so often fathers and not mothers who drew the lines, why they felt it was their job to exert discipline, whether too much freedom was as perilous as too little.

Toby listened, gleaning useful nuggets of information from the discussion. But a part of his mind remained mired in the worry he'd admitted to—that he would lose Lindsey, that someday she would loathe him as much as Susannah loathed her father.

He didn't know why he feared such a thing. He didn't exploit Lindsey the way Susannah's father had exploited her. He didn't expect Lindsey to support the family, to take responsibility for anyone else's welfare, to sacrifice her own childhood to a career not of her choosing. He was nothing like Susannah Dawson's father, and he never would be.

Yet he'd heard the bitterness in Susannah's voice even as she'd kept her tone level. He'd sensed the anger seething beneath her placid surface. And God help him, he wondered at the anger that might be seething inside Lindsey, too. Anger about having no mother, perhaps. Anger about floundering into adolescence without a woman to guide her. Anger about all the injustices, both petty and monumental, that she faced every day.

Toby was such a convenient target for that anger. He was her father.

The class wound down, and Toby sorted through what he'd picked up from listening to the others. They seemed to have concluded, thanks to Molly's subtle leadership, that children should have a chance to experiment in the shallow end of the pool before being allowed to dive off the high board. "Start slow. Give them five dollars and ask them to buy you a newspaper. See if they come back with the right change. Or tell them they have to be home from a friend's house by four o'clock, and see if they persistently come home at four-fifteen, armed with a different excuse each time. These are ways you can safely measure their level of responsibility. Do they live up to your expectations, or do they constantly cross the line? If they can't swim safely in the shallow end, they aren't ready for the deep end."

Useful advice, if a bit general. Some of his classmates' comments had been useful, too, or at least reassuring. Some of them had children far more aggressive than Lindsey. Maybe a truly awful kid would make discipline easier—it was a snap to say no to

someone who kept making unreasonable demands—
but such a child would certainly be more exhausting.
Compared with those fathers, Toby felt lucky to have
a daughter like Lindsey.

Yet he still feared losing her, giving her so much
freedom that she floated away from him like a balloon
on a breeze, while he frantically, futilely, tried to grab
the string that had slipped out of his fist.

"Toby?" Molly approached him as he and the other
fathers stood and stretched and started moving toward
the door.

He glanced at his fellow classmates, then turned
back to Molly. She wasn't asking anyone else to stay
after class. He felt almost like a naughty schoolchild
about to be handed a detention slip.

She looked toward one of the fathers as he shouted
a farewell, then smiled and waved at a few others,
waiting for the room to empty out. She was at least
six inches shorter than Toby, her hands tiny, her body
petite except for her swollen abdomen. The only thing
huge about her was her smile.

"Allison's told me about you," she began. "She's
my best friend, and she's a big fan of yours."

"Allison Winslow?" He nodded, relaxing slightly.
Maybe he wasn't going to get detention after all. "I'm
a big fan of hers, too."

Still smiling, Molly assessed him with a long gaze,
one hand rubbing her belly. "She told me you lost your
wife to cancer a few years ago, and you're raising your
daughter single-handedly."

"That's right." He stopped relaxing. Was she going
to tell him how sorry she was? He hoped not.

"She also told me you're a perfectionist. You're terrific with your patients, exacting with your colleagues and very hard on yourself.''

''No, I'm not,'' he argued, even less relaxed as his defenses started massing protectively around him. ''I'm good with my patients, and I'm professional with my colleagues—''

''And you're very hard on yourself.'' Molly seemed to consider her options for a moment, then chose to reach up and pat his shoulder. ''You can't be perfect, Toby. You need to stop worrying so much about falling short.''

''Meaning…?''

''Meaning, I'll bet you're a wonderful father. You're not going to lose your daughter. You love her, and I'm sure she loves you. So stop being so afraid of messing up with her.''

''I'm not—'' He cut himself off. He'd already admitted his fear in front of the entire class.

''You need to take care of yourself a little, Toby. Worry a little less about your daughter and spend a little time on yourself. Can you do that?''

''I'm the only parent she has,'' he answered automatically. It was the truth, after all. Lindsey had no one else to worry about her, to raise her properly, to keep her on track at school and to help her weather the turbulent journey of growing up.

''Maybe you'd be a better parent if you didn't try so hard,'' Molly suggested, her voice soft and tender, as if that would take the sting out of her criticism. ''Do you ever worry about yourself?''

''No, I…'' He sighed. ''I'm fine.''

''You're tense. You're stressed out. You think you're losing you're daughter.'' Her smile could melt a polar cap. ''You're not fine, Toby. You need a life.''

"I have a life."

"And her name is Lindsey." Molly gave his shoulder another pat. "You probably resent my talking to you this way. But I'm just trying to help. It's my job as the teacher of this Daddy School class. No father can be a good father if he isn't happy with himself. What do *you* need? What would make *your* life better? You don't have to tell me—just think about it. And try to come up with answers that don't include the word Lindsey."

What he needed—besides a healthy, lovely daughter who lived up to her potential and didn't wallow in sarcasm—was...

Yes, damn it. Molly was right. He needed a life. He needed friends he could talk to about something other than Lindsey or work. He needed someone he could laugh with. He needed sex. He needed human warmth and companionship.

He needed Susannah Dawson.

Staggered by a rush of emotions—gratitude and amazement mixed in with his usual quota of panic and frustration—he smiled down at Molly Saunders-Russo. "Thanks," he murmured. "You've given me something to think about."

He was still thinking about it as he pulled out of the parking lot behind the YMCA and eased into the light evening traffic. Across the street loomed the massive *Arlington Gazette* building, its windows lit as staffers labored to put together tomorrow morning's edition. The luncheonette next door to the *Gazette* building was still open for business, but most of the other stores and offices along the street were dark for the night.

He glanced at his watch: eight-forty. He really ought to get home.

The supermarket was on his way. He could take a quick spin around the parking lot and make sure Susannah had gotten her shopping done and was safely out of there. All he'd do was check to see that her car was gone, and then he'd go home.

The parking lot in front of the supermarket was illuminated by the floodlights on towering poles planted in the asphalt. The supermarket itself looked bright and welcoming; so did the discount drugstore at the far end of the lot. Lindsey's favorite CD store was closed, as were most of the other stores in the shopping center. But people needed food and medicine at all hours, so those stores stayed open late.

The parking lot was nearly empty, and he spotted Susannah's Volkswagen beetle almost immediately. It was parked where she'd abandoned it that afternoon, where he'd dropped her an hour and a half ago. Its pea-green color and turtle shape were so distinctive, he didn't even have to see the California license plate to know it was hers.

Why was it still in the lot? Had she even made it into the supermarket, or had a mad horde of fans swept her off? He knew she was an adult, fully capable of taking care of herself, but he couldn't shake his picture of her under siege that afternoon, with some son of a bitch pawing at her breast.

Why was her car still here? What if she wasn't all right?

He slid his car into the vacant spot next to hers, yanked the parking brake and bolted from the car, pressing the remote lock button as he jogged toward the supermarket. The automatic glass door swung open and he hurried inside.

The store was nearly empty. Two cashiers stood idle

at their checkout counters, chatting. A middle-aged man hovered in the produce section near the door, a basket hooked over his arm and a rapt expression on his face as he inspected tomatoes. Céline Dion's rendition of the *Titanic* theme song poured from ceiling speakers. The light was glaring enough to hurt his eyes.

He sprinted past the produce displays and along the aisles, peering down each one. A few stray shoppers with carts were making their way through the store, but the place seemed almost desolate compared with the crush of customers he usually encountered on weekends. He didn't care how many shoppers were there tonight, though. All he cared about was one shopper. If she wasn't in the supermarket, or in the drugstore at the other end of the lot, he didn't know what he'd do.

Three-quarters of the way through the store, in the bread aisle, he finally located her. She had tied a colorful silk scarf pirate-style around her hair, and she had a pair of owl-round horn-rimmed eyeglasses perched on her nose, but Toby recognized her. He knew her posture, her slender physique. He knew the way she tilted her head, the graceful length of her fingers as she lifted a package of English muffins from a shelf and tossed it into her cart, which was already crammed with groceries—far more than he bought for both him and Lindsey every week.

Maybe she was hoarding supplies so she wouldn't have to shop as often. Or maybe she ate a lot.

The mere sight of her filled him with relief. That she was all by herself, not being hounded and harassed by fans, brought his pulse rate down to normal and made his breath come easier. Perhaps Lindsey wasn't the only person he ought to stop worrying about. Susannah was doing fine.

He almost considered sneaking away, leaving her to the privacy she craved. At home, Lindsey might be wondering where he was. Or worse, she might be watching some brain-numbing show on TV instead of doing her homework. Reassured that Susannah was all right, he could go home and take care of his daughter.

But he didn't want to. Molly's advice resounded in his mind: he needed a life. He needed to think about what he wanted—not just what was best for Lindsey, but what was best for him.

Maybe Susannah wasn't best for him. But at that moment, spending a few minutes talking to her seemed more important to him than shutting down the part of himself that wasn't about Lindsey.

With a resolute shrug, he strode down the aisle until he was close behind Susannah. "Hey," he murmured.

She flinched and spun around. Regret filled him for having startled her. She must be tense to the point of near paranoia about being approached by strangers in public places.

But he wasn't a stranger, and when she saw him she relaxed and smiled. "Toby! What are you doing here?"

He refrained from answering that he'd been checking up on her. "My Daddy School class just let out," he said. To keep her from questioning him further, he went on, "Are you really buying all this stuff? This cereal has got a lot of sugar in it." He lifted a box from the mountain of food in her cart. "It'll rot your teeth."

"I know, Dr. Cole," Susannah said with feigned

solemnity. "I was hoping to get some tooth decay. I thought that cereal might do the trick."

He laughed. "Then you chose wisely. Have you really been shopping all this time?"

"I went to the drugstore first," she told him. "I needed shampoo and aspirin. The two greatest necessities of my life." She picked a jar of all-natural peanut butter from the shelf across from the bread and added it to her cart. Then she glanced up at him. "You had no trouble recognizing me," she conceded, sounding vexed.

"I know you." He studied her. He didn't like the scarf, which hid her beautiful hair. But the eyeglasses weren't bad. "These are cute," he said, gesturing toward the frames. "You should wear them more often."

"I don't need them. They're just plain glass," she said, then sighed. "Well, if anyone else recognized me this evening, they were tactful about it. I haven't been asked to give any autographs." She scrutinized the array of jams. "So, how was your class?" she asked before selecting a jar of raspberry preserves.

"Enlightening," he said, falling into step beside her as she continued down the aisle. "We talked about freedom."

"Freedom?"

"Giving our children freedom. Trusting them enough to let them fly." And he and Molly had talked about Toby's giving himself some freedom—freedom to remain at the store with Susannah because watching her fill a small paper sack with gourmet coffee beans brought him pleasure. He observed as she rolled down the top of the sack and folded the wire tabs to seal it. Her hands were more than graceful, he admitted. They were sensual, the skin pale and smooth, the fingers

tapered, the nails perfect ovals. He wanted to feel those
hands on him, moving across his skin, learning his
body as he learned hers. He wanted to kiss her, not
just her lips but everywhere. He wanted to untie the
scarf and watch her hair tumble loose.

She placed the sack of coffee beans in her cart and
started up the next aisle. A few steps in from the end,
Toby closed his hand over one of hers, halting the cart.
She turned to him, curiosity glimmering in her eyes.

"I'd like to see you," he said, then cursed silently.
It had been a while since he'd asked a woman out—
and he'd never asked out a woman like Susannah. He
felt awkward all of a sudden. Conversation with her
had always been a comfortable thing, but this wasn't
conversation. It was something more. "I mean, I'd like
to have dinner with you Saturday night."

"Spaghetti and shrimp at your house?"

"No."

She took a minute to absorb what he was actually
saying. He left his hand on hers, savoring the delicacy
of her bones and the silkiness of her skin against his
palm. She didn't pull away, which was a good sign.

"No," she said, which was a bad sign.

He stared at their hands for a moment, wondering
why, if that physical contact felt so right to him, their
having dinner together Saturday night should seem
wrong to her. "No? Just no?"

She sighed, and her smile struck him as sad. "I like
you, Toby. I don't want to ruin that."

"You think having dinner with me would ruin it?"

"I don't know." She slid her gaze to the jars of jam
and marmalade. They were translucent, red and amber,
like garnets and topaz in the fluorescent light.

He wondered what she was afraid of. He wasn't a

gaga fan; he'd never even heard of her before Lindsey
had told him about her TV show. Nor did he have any
intention of exploiting her the way her family had. All
he wanted was to take her out to dinner, and to kiss
her again, and to see where a kiss might lead. All he
wanted was to spend time with her, talk to her and
give the passion that flared between them a chance to
burn brighter.

Since she still hadn't withdrawn her hand from his,
he risked lifting his other hand to her chin and steering
her face back to him. "Why not give it a try?" he
suggested, his voice low and gentle. "What's the worst
that could happen? It wouldn't work out, and we'd go
back to being neighbors."

"That's not the worst that could happen," she said,
meeting his gaze now, her eyes crystalline through the
flat lenses of her glasses.

She was right. Lots of worse things could happen:
someone's heart could get broken. Or they'd have a
terrible fight and find themselves unable to remain amiable neighbors. Or Lindsey could become attached to
Susannah, more attached than she already was. Lindsey
was obviously infatuated with the idea of Susannah.
She was enthralled by Susannah's past, her fame, her
alleged glamour. If she and Toby had a falling out, it
would upset Lindsey terribly.

Damn. He was supposed to be putting his own needs
ahead of Lindsey's for once. That was what Molly
Saunders-Russo had instructed him.

"All I'm asking for is one dinner," he said. "Not
a lifetime commitment. Not a love affair. Just a table
for two at a nice restaurant."

The skin beneath her chin was even smoother than
her hand. He remembered the way she'd kissed him,

the velvet softness of her lips, and the memory nagged at him, reminding him that he wanted much more than he was asking for.

"One dinner," she murmured, flickering a glance at the mountain of food in her shopping cart, enough food for many, many dinners.

He risked a smile. "Come on, Susannah. Be brave. Take a chance."

She smiled back. "All right. Dinner Saturday."

He could let her go now. He had her promise. He had Saturday to look forward to, a night when he would do something that qualified as getting a life. They would eat dinner, they would talk, they would be not a widowed father and a burned-out actress but a man and a woman, enjoying a good meal and each other's company. They would talk and smile and get to know each other even better.

And maybe, just maybe, they would do more than talk and smile and eat. Maybe they would discover just how far passion could take them if they let it.

CHAPTER NINE

IT WAS A PERFECT Saturday afternoon for a soccer game—warm but not hot, sunny and dry. Seated in the passenger seat next to her father, Lindsey decided she was looking forward to playing. The practices had been kind of boring this season, but she really thought she was going to enjoy herself today, even though soccer had stopped being fun for her after Cathy moved away. They'd always been on the same team, ever since they were seven and spent every game running up and down the field, giggling and chasing the ball like a couple of goofs.

Cathy had played on Lindsey's team last summer. But then she'd moved. Lindsey's father couldn't seem to understand why she'd lost her enthusiasm for the sport. It should have been obvious.

Well, she wasn't going to complain about her father. He'd been so nice lately, not arguing with her, not nagging her about her bedtime or going over her homework and pointing out every little punctuation error. It was like he'd decided to become cool, all of a sudden.

He hadn't even made a big fuss about sunscreen before they'd left the house. He'd simply handed her the bottle and walked away, not bothering to check whether she'd covered every square inch of her face with the stuff. Without him bugging her, she'd probably done a more careful job than usual, slathering the lotion not just on her face and arms but down her neck, into the V of her jersey.

It was an ugly jersey, dark-red polyester with black trim on the neckline and sleeves, but the shorts were great, black and shiny like satin. The shin guards and socks made her legs look fat, but all the other girls' legs looked fat in the shin guards, too, so it didn't matter. And the socks went all the way up to her knees, so no one would notice how hairy her legs were.

She was going to have to start shaving. Meredith shaved her legs, and she probably didn't even need to, since she was blond. But eleven wasn't too young to start, and she was only three months away from turning eleven. She would have to talk to Dr. Dad about it.

Like that would be easy. "Hey, Daddy, would you buy me a razor? I've got to do something about my gorilla legs." Yeah, right.

Maybe she could ask Susannah to talk to him about it.

They were going to have dinner together tonight, just the two of them. Lindsey wasn't sure what to make of that—except that she thought it was probably not a good thing. Her father and Susannah were a lousy match. Susannah was rich and famous and beautiful, and her father was just a guy, about as ordinary as an Arlington, Connecticut, father could be. And then there was the matter of Susannah's general love life. Amanda was supposedly getting hold of her sister's magazine that explained about Susannah's relationship with Stephen Yates. Lindsey's father couldn't hope to compete with a famous actor like Stephen Yates.

Susannah was probably just stringing him along, using him to pass the time until she and Stephen Yates had a flashy million-dollar Hollywood wedding, with tabloid photographers taking pictures through the trees and helicopters spying on them from above. She did seem to like being with Lindsey's father, but not in a Saturday-night-dinner-out sort of way. Their friendship was more like what he'd had with Cathy's mom—a next-door-neighbor, I'll-hang-your-mirror kind of friendship. Lindsey hoped her father didn't expect more than that from Susannah, because if he did, he was going to get his heart broken. He was so naive about things. He hadn't dated much since breaking up with that icky lady he'd been with a couple of years ago. Lindsey hadn't liked her. She'd seemed like a phony.

There was nothing phony about Susannah. She was perfect—but not perfect for Lindsey's father. If he was looking for true love, he wasn't going to find it with a Hollywood star. He didn't even watch TV.

"Which team are you playing today?" he asked as he braked for a red light.

"The Hurricanes."

"The dreaded Hurricanes," he said with exaggerated horror.

She decided to play along. "They don't scare me," she boasted. "We're gonna blow them right off the field."

Her father laughed. He was in such a good mood it was really nice. "You said it, Hot Stuff."

"How's that kid?" she asked. "The one with leukemia."

Her father seemed surprised that she'd asked. Turning the corner, he grinned. "He's home. Dr. Weiss— that's his oncologist—decided he could spend a little time at home before his next round of chemo. He's responding well."

"Is he bald?"

"His hair is just beginning to fall out, but it'll grow back."

Her mother's never had. Lindsey vaguely remembered her mother when she wasn't wearing her wig. She'd looked like a baby, with downy strands fuzzing her scalp.

Lindsey shut that image out of her mind. She only wanted to think about today, the sun so bright in the cloudless sky, the azaleas in bloom, the dogwoods thick with blossoms. The Hurricanes were from the southern part of town, mostly kids from Clampitt Hill School. Next year Lindsey would be going to the middle school with Clampitt Hill kids and sixth-graders from the four other primary schools in town. They'd all be classmates then. But right now the Clampitt Hill kids were her soccer enemies, and she had every intention of beating the pants off those wusses on the field.

"So, where are you taking Susannah tonight?" she asked casually, trying to make it sound like just a part of the conversation.

Her father didn't answer right away. "I was thinking of Dominic's."

"That Italian restaurant?" Lindsey rolled her eyes. He was such a dork. "Why don't you take her to Reynaud?" Reynaud was the fanciest, most expensive restaurant in town. Susannah was probably used to dining at establishments like that.

Her father shot her a glance, then returned his gaze to the road. "You think so? I doubt I'll be able to get a reservation there. I think you've got to book a table weeks in advance."

"You should have thought of that earlier." She sighed and shook her head.

"Actually, I thought she'd like something a little less pretentious. Do you know what 'pretentious' means?"

"Fancy?"

"More than fancy. Fancy for the sake of showing off and intimidating people."

"A restaurant can't intimidate someone like her," Lindsey argued. "She's a fancy lady."

"No, she isn't. You've seen her, Lindsey. She's always wearing exercise clothes or jeans, and she doesn't bother with makeup or lots of jewelry. There's nothing fancy about her."

"You've never taken her out to dinner. You know what those restaurants are like in Hollywood? You have to go to the right one or people think your career is down the tubes. And you have to sit at the right table. If you don't, people assume you're washed up."

He sent her another glance. "How do you know so much about Hollywood restaurants?"

"I read."

They'd reached the community park where the soccer fields were located. Lindsey spotted several girls in burgundy jerseys identical to hers. "There's my team," she said. "Drop me off, okay? They're starting to warm up."

Her father stopped the car near the grass and she shoved open the door. Her cleats hit the ground, and then she turned back. "So—about tonight? I mean, you can take her to Dominic's. It's probably okay. Just don't expect too much."

"Too much what?" he asked, looking puzzled.

She gazed skyward for a minute. He was *such* a

dork. "The thing is…" She tried to think of a tactful way to put it. "Susannah's a little out of your league, you know?"

He looked like he was wrestling against a grin. "Do you think so?"

"I know so, Dr. Dad. I mean, she's very, very cool. But kind of from a different planet."

"Planet Hollywood," he joked.

She wished he would take her seriously. She was trying to protect his ego, trying to spare him a major hurt. "I know you'll have a good time," she said, figuring that would get him to listen to her. "Susannah's a terrific lady. But she's…" *She's involved with Stephen Yates, one of the hottest, sexiest stars on TV.* "I just don't think this is going to lead to anything big, you know?"

"We're having dinner together," her father insisted. "It's not supposed to lead to anything at all. It's just dinner."

"Okay." His words reassured her. As long as he knew going in that he wasn't embarking on a great romance, he wouldn't be disappointed. She started to back away from the car, then leaned back in. "Oh, and Dad? If you're gonna cheer, don't say my name. Just cheer for the Pumas." She hated when he shouted, "Go, Lindsey," singling her out like that. "Okay?"

He nodded solemnly. "Okay."

"See ya!" She straightened up, slammed the door and raced across the lawn to her teammates, deciding she wasn't going to think about her father's dinner date anymore—at least not until after the game.

SUSANNAH STUDIED herself in the mirror on the back of her closet door—the mirror Toby had hung. She owned jeans and casual clothes, and she owned designer ensembles. But a simple, attractive, modest dress for dinner at a restaurant with Toby?

The skirt she had on had cost eighteen hundred dollars in a Beverly Hills boutique, but despite its price it looked pretty simple, a swirl of gauzy linen that flowed gently around her hips and legs. If Toby didn't know it was a designer original, he wouldn't guess. It would have to do.

She wasn't concerned about her appearance; it was Toby's reaction she was worried about. She didn't want him to think she was a show-off—and she certainly didn't want people at the restaurant to gawk at her and Toby while they ate. She just wanted to be a quiet, private Arlington homeowner having a meal with a friend.

A *friend,* she emphasized to herself. She and Toby were friends. She wouldn't let him kiss her. She couldn't. If he kissed her, she'd want more. She'd want to give more. She'd want to become his lover, and once she was his lover she'd want to rearrange her life around him. She knew the way she was. She had to protect herself from her own foolishness.

The short-sleeved sweater she paired with the skirt was also deceptively plain, a textured weave of unbleached cotton. She fastened pearl studs to her ears and added a gold necklace with a cluster of pearls gathered into a pendant.

She resembled a member of the Junior League, she thought grimly. But that was better than looking like Dr. Lee Davis of *Mercy Hospital.*

Downstairs, the doorbell rang. She sighed, layered her lips with a slick of rose-tinted gloss and stepped into low-heeled sandals with leather straps crisscross-

ing her insteps. Another peal of the bell, and she
snatched her purse from the dresser and left the bedroom, trying to forget the way Toby had looked standing beside her in the mirror the night he'd hung it—
the night she'd been smacked hard in the soul with the
recognition that he was an incredibly attractive man.

He stood on the front porch, fresh and casual in
beige slacks, a pale-blue shirt and a navy blazer. His
dark hair was still damp from a shower, and his eyes
glowed with a warmth that put her at ease even as it
reminded her of how much she liked him, how much
more she could like him if she let herself.

"You look great," he said. Nothing flowery or fake
in his attitude, nothing scripted or plotted. He was the
opposite of everything she'd loathed in Los Angeles—
the empty values, the fake attitudes, the sense that
everyone had a hidden agenda.

Toby might have an agenda, too, she thought as she
thanked him for the compliment and locked the front
door behind her. She still remembered his kiss—every
moment of it, every movement, every sweet nuance.
That kiss had probably reflected his agenda—and there
was nothing hidden about it.

She shouldn't have said yes to this invitation. Too
late, though—she was already down the front walk,
letting him help her into his car. He wasn't a beast,
she reassured herself. He was arguably the most responsible man she'd ever met. Whatever his agenda
was, she had nothing to fear, at least not from him. It
was herself she ought to be worried about.

"I thought we'd go to Dominic's," he said as he
backed out of her driveway. "I know you like Italian
food—you ate a reasonable facsimile of it at my
house."

"Italian sounds fine." Within the confines of his car, she could smell his aftershave, a faint, tangy fragrance. She could admire the motions of his hands on the wheel. He had a light, sure touch, his fingers thick but nimble, his nails clean and short. She deliberately turned her gaze to the road ahead.

"Lindsey said I should have taken you to Reynaud," he added, apparently much more relaxed than she was. "It's an elegant French restaurant, one of those places where they have one waiter to serve your bread and another to serve your butter. I think it's a bit much, but if you'd like, we could go there another time."

Did he feel he had to impress her? "It sounds like a bit much to me, too. Have you ever eaten there?"

"I took my wife there for our tenth anniversary," he said. "We had a good laugh trying to remember which fork was which."

His wife. His wife, to whom he'd been married for more than ten years. His wife, who'd given him a daughter and died tragically young, making a mockery of his training and his trust in medicine. Why had he mentioned her? The only reason Susannah could think of was that he wanted to set the tone for the evening: friendly. Not romantic. Love would not be on the menu.

This was good, she decided, determined to shed her tension. It was fine. It was exactly what she wanted.

They reached the restaurant a few minutes later, and she debated whether to don her eyeglasses. Toby was already out of the car and circling to her side before she'd removed them from her purse, so she decided to leave them off. He knew how she felt about attracting attention; he'd seen how awkward it could be. Surely he wouldn't have taken her to this restaurant if he'd thought there would be a problem.

If the maître d' recognized her, he gave no indication. He did, however, greet Toby by name: "Dr. Cole! Good to see you. Please follow me."

He led them to a secluded table in a dark corner. Susannah wondered whether Toby had arranged in advance to be seated in the most private area of the room, so they wouldn't be bothered by fans.

They busied themselves with their menus for a few minutes. The entrées were more elaborate than the store-bought spaghetti with jarred sauce and rubbery shrimp that Toby had served the last time they'd had dinner together. She ordered a veal dish. He chose seafood, an antipasto platter for them to share and a bottle of Chianti Classico. The waiter took their menus and vanished, leaving Susannah with nothing to look at but Toby's handsome face.

Did he know she was anxious? Could he guess that she was pathetically inexperienced when it came to dating? She'd never had time to socialize as a teenager, when normal kids were learning how to mingle with the opposite sex. Once she'd turned twenty, her father had hired a public-relations firm to promote her career. The firm had set her up with assorted celebrities with whom she was supposed to be "seen." That had been the whole point of the exercise; Susannah Dawson would be seen here or there, escorted by this star or that, as if mere proximity to stardom would turn her into a star, as well. She'd struggled through stilted dinners with B-list actors, second-tier rock stars, men on their way up or on their way down. At best, they'd have a few pleasant outings, both of them aware of the artificiality of the arrangement. At worst, photographers would capture them on film, and she'd find herself in one or another tabloid, the picture carrying a caption insinuating that true love was just around the corner for up-and-coming actress Susannah Dawson.

The fact was, she didn't know how to date.

Toby seemed completely comfortable, however. His face was tanned, his posture relaxed as he sipped his wine. "I spent this afternoon at a soccer game," he told her. "Lindsey's team won big. She plays midfield. She got two assists."

Susannah smiled. Surely no man who intended to get romantic would talk about his daughter.

"I don't know much about soccer," she admitted.

"I didn't know anything about it until Lindsey started playing a few years ago." He proceeded to explain the game to her, what it meant to play midfield, how until last year Lindsey had played on six-person teams, but once she'd turned ten she'd moved up to the older league, where the children played on larger fields and each team had eleven players.

If the evening continued in this vein, with the conversation centering on Lindsey and sports, Susannah would be fine.

The antipasto arrived, a platter heaped with prosciutto, plum tomatoes, sprigs of basil, slabs of fresh mozzarella, olives and herbs drizzled with balsamic vinegar. Toby solicitously advised her on what to try and how to soak the cheese in the dark vinegar before she ate it. He was definitely in a fatherly mood, she acknowledged, feeling more of her tension drain away. She could imagine him counseling Lindsey on how to get the most out of the antipasto, too.

"So," Susannah said, transferring a strip of prosciutto to her plate, "tell me how you wound up becoming a pediatrician."

The question caught him unprepared. "I thought you were going to come and observe me at work."

"I intend to." She truly did, once she was sure she could avoid a dangerously intimate involvement with him—and once she had him clearly separated in her mind from the pediatrician character she'd created for her script. "Maybe next week, if that would be all right with you. But meantime, tell me about your work. Did you always want to be a pediatrician?"

He laughed. She noticed his dimples, the tiny laugh lines extending from the outer edges of his eyes, the even white of his teeth. "I don't think anyone grows up dreaming of becoming a pediatrician. A doctor, maybe, but choosing a pediatrics specialty isn't what little kids set their sights on."

"Why not?"

"It's not dramatic. As far as I can tell, people become doctors because they want to save the world, they want to get rich or they're good in science and can't think of anything better to do with that ability. Of course, nowadays, with managed care, only a fool would become a doctor because he wanted to get rich."

"So which are you? Do you want to save the world or did you have an aptitude for science?"

"A little of both, I guess." Their entrees arrived. Toby waited until the waiter was gone before he elaborated. "My older brother was a golden boy. A triple-threat athlete—football, basketball, lacrosse—and a straight-A student. Officer on the student council. Winner of the oratory competition. Recruited by colleges from coast to coast. I guess I figured there was nothing left for me to do but save the world.''

She detected no jealousy in his tone. ''What does your brother do now?''

''He sells insurance,'' Toby said without a trace of irony. ''And he's damned good at it. I wish I saw more of him, but he lives out in Minnesota, near my parents.''

''Were you an athlete, too?''

''I did some sports, but I was never as good as he was.'' Toby shrugged. ''I followed my own path. Sciences, college, med school.'' As they ate, he told her about his years in college and then at Yale Medical School. He'd met his wife in college, and they'd gotten married and moved to New Haven when he'd started medical school. She'd taken a job with a local television station, selling advertising. She'd been good at her job, he said, but once she'd become pregnant her commitment to her career had faltered. And he'd decided not to pursue one of the more time-consuming specializations, because he'd wanted to have time for his daughter.

He told Susannah that once he and his wife had settled in Arlington, she'd decided to return to work, designing ads for the *Arlington Gazette* on a part-time basis. Lindsey had adjusted well to preschool. Toby had begun to pursue a subspecialization in pediatric cardiology. He loved working with children, knowing his patients practically from the moment they were born, watching them grow and thrive. He thought kids were fantastic. In fact, he'd pretty much thought his life was perfect until Jane had been diagnosed and everything changed.

''You must miss her,'' Susannah murmured, sym-

pathetic and also gratified that Toby kept sending her
signals that this meal wasn't a romantic adventure. He
wouldn't have kept discussing his wife with her if it
was.

"Yes and no," he admitted, nudging his plate away
and lifting his refilled wineglass. He swirled the ruby
fluid in the bowl, then took a sip. "I miss her sometimes. But on a day-to-day basis… I have a life. Maybe
not enough of one yet, but I'm working on it. And it's
mine."

"How do you build a new life?" Susannah asked,
genuinely curious. She was trying to build a new life
for herself, but she'd barely started, and she didn't
know if she was doing it right.

"My Daddy School teacher tells me I need to put
my own needs first. That's not something I'm used to
doing. But I'm trying."

Susannah would bet he wasn't used to it. He lived
for Lindsey, and he'd doted on his wife through her
illness, and his patients were always on his mind.

She wasn't used to putting her own needs first, either. But like him, she was trying. How odd that she
and Toby were going through the same thing, in their
own ways.

"What's so funny?" he asked.

She hadn't realized she was grinning. "Just that
we're both trying to learn how to be selfish."

"It's a whole new thing, huh? Maybe we ought to
start a movement—'All me, all the time.'"

"God, no! There are more than enough selfish people in the world. They don't need encouragement."

"Just you and me, then. We'll make our own movement. We can be completely egotistical and self-
serving."

"Sure. Why not?"

He laughed. "You can't have anymore wine. I want it all for myself," he teased before refilling her glass.

"That was the most unconvincing acting I've ever seen," she criticized. His smile was contagious. It warmed her from the inside out, like the wine.

"Maybe after I teach you everything about being a pediatrician, you can teach me about acting."

"No," she said swiftly, her smile fading. "That part of my life is behind me."

"You don't think you'll ever go back to it?"

She started to say no again, then rethought her answer. She'd actually enjoyed acting. It had been everything else about her career she'd hated—the pressures and demands, the lack of choices, the control everyone had exerted over her. The fact that she'd sacrificed such a large part of her life to it, and been taken advantage of by her family.

"Maybe," she allowed, "I'll join a community theater. Is there one in Arlington?"

He nodded. "In the summer, when all the city people spend their weekends in the area. I guess you'd call it summer stock. They'd be thrilled to have you."

The waiter returned to their table to clear away their plates and inquire about dessert. Susannah declined with a shake of her head. She wasn't used to eating big, heavy dinners. If not for Toby's invitations, she'd be eating tuna fish or salad for supper every night.

He asked for the check, handed the waiter his credit card and settled the bill. Susannah watched him, envying his poise. She'd started to unwind during dinner, but now her anxiety returned. What would happen when they left the restaurant? When they got back to her house, what would he expect?

His hair looked nearly black in the dimly lit corner of the dining room. His hands looked strong wielding the pen, flipping open his wallet, separating his receipt from the restaurant's. She knew his hands would feel as strong as they looked—strong but graceful. Talented. Hands that healed babies, she thought. Hands that comforted sick children. Hands that applauded for his daughter on the soccer field.

Hands that could hold a woman, caress her, arouse her. Hands that could touch her the way Susannah hadn't been touched since she'd kicked Stephen out of her life.

She blinked and glanced away. She wasn't going to let Toby touch her tonight.

They left the restaurant for the mild, moonlit night. It was only nine-thirty, early enough to take a walk or a drive, to catch a late movie—except that he had an unsupervised daughter at home. Which was just as well, Susannah told herself. If she spent more time with him, she'd feel closer to him, and if she felt closer, she'd grow more vulnerable to him and to her own troublesome yearnings. But that threat wouldn't materialize. He wouldn't prolong their evening with a movie or a walk...or anything else. He would have to go straight home to Lindsey.

He helped her into the car, then climbed in behind the wheel. "See?" he said, apparently pleased. "You got through a few hours in a restaurant without any fans pestering you."

"I know." She shared his smile. "What a pleasure."

"Did people pester you in Hollywood? When you went out to dinner, I mean."

"Sometimes." She smoothed her skirt over her

knees. "There was always jockeying for a table. You'd want to sit at the right table in the right restaurant at the right time, so the right people would see you."

"You're kidding. Really?" He appeared astonished.

"Yes, really. Do you find that shocking?"

He laughed and shook his head. "I'm not shocked by what you said. I'm shocked that Lindsey knew about this. She warned me today that I needed to know about sitting at the right table in the right restaurant and all. She knows more about showbiz than I do."

"She's young. I'm sure it seems exciting to her."

"She wants to be a star when she grows up," he said, starting the engine and backing out of the parking space. "I'm hoping she'll outgrow that."

"I'd be happy to tell her all about the dark side of showbiz life," Susannah offered.

He shook his head again, this time serious. "Don't. It's her dream. Nobody should ever skewer a kid's dream. Let her enjoy it."

Susannah blinked again. She didn't want to think Toby was wonderful. She didn't want to be so aware of everything about him—not just his long legs and chiseled features and those big male hands, but also his kindness and sensitivity to his daughter. *Please,* she implored him silently, *do something awful. Be obnoxious. Belch or launch into a boring monologue about sports. Do something offensive so I can stop liking you so much.*

But he didn't belch, didn't comment on the way the baseball season was shaping up, didn't say he hoped Lindsey would stop daydreaming, didn't say he thought Susannah was actually quite selfish and ought to have continued supporting her family. He simply drove home through the quiet streets of Arlington, an enigmatic smile curving his lips.

As she'd predicted, he walked her to her front door. They climbed the steps to the porch, and she noticed MacKenzie's silhouette filling one of the windows in the living room, where she'd left a lamp on. The impatiens she'd hung on the porch looked nearly white in the silver moonlight. The porch lamp spilled a cone of brighter light in front of the door.

"This was lovely," she said, her heart thumping in anticipation, in dread. She wanted him to kiss her good-night, but not a real kiss, not a kiss that would entrance her. Not a kiss that would make her careless and mindless and eager to give too much. Just a peck on the cheek, because they were friends.

"We should do it again."

"I'd like that." She turned from him and inserted her key in the lock. Her pulse drummed in her ears. He stood so close behind her she could feel his warmth along her back, his breath against her hair.

She fumbled with the key. He reached around her and closed his hand over hers. His touch, just a brush of warmth, fingers against fingers, nearly undid her. He eased the key from her trembling fingers and unlocked the door for her.

"Thank you," she whispered, feeling the way she imagined a typical sixteen-year-old would feel coming home from her first date with an awesome guy. Edgy, panicked and seized by a treacherous longing.

She could have sworn a million times that she didn't want him to take her in his arms. But he circled them around her, and her heart told her she truly wanted this, wanted it more than she should. Wanted it more than she could remember wanting anything in a long time.

For just one moment she would ignore the danger.

CHAPTER TEN

IF ASKING SUSANNAH out had been a significant step in Toby's living his own life, kissing her seemed the most essential step of all. When his lips touched hers, he felt more alive than he'd ever felt before.

Dinner had been terrific. He'd enjoyed talking to her, listening to her, laughing with her. But this… This was unbelievable.

She tasted of wine and warmth, her mouth opening eagerly beneath his, her tongue darting out to touch his. As he pulled her closer she ringed his waist with her arms and nestled against him, as if seeking sex and safety at the same time.

He didn't want to offer her safety.

He moved his hands up and down her back, feeling the delicate angles of her shoulder blades, the narrow ridge of her spine, the weight of her hair against his knuckles. He roamed to her nape, then reversed direction, sliding down to the small of her back, to the swell of her hips. All the while he kissed her, deep, hungry, greedy kisses, drinking her in, absorbing her sighs.

His body hummed with energy. He felt hard all over, not just in his groin but in his chest, his thighs, his arms. His muscles tensed in delicious agony. If he and Susannah hadn't been standing on her front porch in full view of anyone who might come along, he would have lifted her skirt and moved his hand between her legs, making her as ready as he was.

But they *were* on her front porch, and even though he had his back to the street, he was not in the sort of condition a man ought to be in while standing where his neighbors could see him. Behind her, the door was open. He'd unlocked it himself. All she had to do was invite him in.

She sighed again, then gasped as he tightened his hold and angled her hips to his. "Toby," she whispered, her lips rubbing erotically against his as she spoke his name.

"Yes." His voice sounded as breathless as hers.

She touched her mouth to his chin, then tucked her head into the hollow of his neck.

Ask me in, he pleaded silently. *Tell me you want this as much as I do.*

He felt her lips brush his throat. His fingers flexed against the soft curves of her bottom, rocking her to him.

"We can't..." She let out a broken breath, her body so snug against him he could feel the contours of her breasts pressing into his chest.

"We're outside. I know," he murmured, his voice surprisingly calm given his anything-but-calm state.

She hugged him, her head nestled in the curve of his shoulder. She said nothing for a minute, and he willed himself to relax, to lower his expectations. But then she thrilled him by saying, "Would you like a cup of coffee?"

"Yes." He had no interest in coffee, but he wanted to go inside with her. And that was what she was really talking about—not coffee but going inside.

Reluctantly, she eased out of his arms. She avoided

making eye contact with him as she turned away and twisted the doorknob. The door swung inward and Toby followed her into the front hall, closing the door behind him.

She still didn't look at him. He wondered why. Certainly, she couldn't have developed a sudden case of bashfulness. Her kisses out on the porch had hardly been bashful. What had changed between those kisses and now—other than their having moved indoors, where kisses could lead to something much more intimate?

Intimacy was impossible if Susannah wouldn't even look at him. He restrained himself from hauling her back into his arms, and instead watched her cautiously, remaining where he was while she started toward the kitchen. "I have both regular and decaf," she said, her tone artificially bright.

"I don't really want coffee," he told her.

She paused and glanced over her shoulder at him, though she didn't lift her eyes all the way to his face. "I do," she finally said, and headed down the hall.

Lacking a better idea, he followed her. He couldn't stay too long—Lindsey was home alone, after all—and Susannah might use up what time they had by lingering over her damned coffee. What he wanted so much his body nearly shook from the wanting was not going to happen. Not unless she was teasing him right now, pretending not to be aroused when she was actually in the same crazed state he was in.

But he didn't like games. One of the things about Susannah that appealed to him was that she didn't seem to be the game-playing type.

Her kitchen was brightly lit. The cat trailed them in, leaped onto a chair and eyed Toby arrogantly. Susannah opened and slammed cabinet doors, searching for a mug, then filters, then a can of coffee. The noise was jarring—and her silence was even more jarring.

"Did I do something wrong?" he asked. He'd never been a slick operator; he'd never learned any smooth moves. Maybe she'd wanted to be seduced more emphatically. Maybe she'd expected him to sweep her off her feet and carry her up the stairs like Rhett Butler in *Gone With the Wind*.

"No." Her hands trembled as she attempted to scoop coffee into the filter-lined basket.

"Then what's going on here? Why are you so nervous?" he asked. He heard impatience in his tone, reflecting the impatience that nibbled at the edges of his mind.

She pressed the button to start the coffeemaker, then spun around to confront him, her face set in a benign smile that he didn't believe for a minute. When her gaze locked with his, the smile faded slightly, becoming more genuine. "I like you, Toby," she said. "But I'm just…" She sighed. He saw anguish in her eyes. "I'm trying to hold on to my independence, okay?"

Her independence? Did she think that making love with him would steal her independence away? Did she think he intended to enslave her?

She must have sensed his doubt. Even the cat seemed to sense it. He leaped onto the table and walked to the edge closest to Susannah, silently imploring her to pick him up. Susannah obeyed, gathering the cat into her arms and combing her fingers through his fur. "I'm not ready to get involved with anyone right now," she explained.

He still didn't believe her, but he wasn't going to

argue. Her kisses had said yes, but her words were saying no, and he couldn't ignore her words.

"All right," he said quietly, hiding his frustration behind a stoic facade. He stared for a minute at her fingers plowing deep into her cat's fur. They were slender yet strong, and it irked him that her cat was getting the caresses he wanted for himself. He took a step backward, as if a few more feet of distance between Susannah and himself might make him desire her a little less.

"It's not just me," she went on, as though aware that he needed persuading. "There's Lindsey to think about. I mean, if we were to...well, whatever it was we were going to do—"

"Make love," he said deliberately. Stoicism didn't suit him. He was seething, and he wanted Susannah to feel as uncomfortable as he did.

He didn't rattle her as much as he'd hoped. "Make love," she agreed, still stroking the cat, her eyes crystalline as she lifted them to meet his. His anger only seemed to strengthen her resolve. "How would it affect Lindsey if we were to do that?"

"I've been trying really hard to stop basing all my decisions on how they'd affect Lindsey."

A smile flitted across her lips. "Well, then...I guess this decision is going to be based on how it would affect me." The hint of a smile vanished, and she returned her attention to the coffeemaker. "I'm not looking for a romance."

"Just a friendship," he deduced, his anger cooled by a splash of irony. "Isn't that what they say in Hollywood? 'We're just friends.'"

"Do you mind being just friends with me?" she asked in a small, hesitant voice.

A dry laugh escaped him. "I think I can handle it."

She turned back to him. "Because I treasure this friendship, Toby. I want us to stay friends. I want to come and observe you while you work. And I want to help you out with Lindsey if you need it. We can make a good friendship here, don't you think?"

A good friendship. He supposed he could use one of those. He would have preferred to have that good friendship with someone he hadn't kissed the way he'd kissed Susannah, someone who didn't turn him on simply by existing. Someone who didn't keep him up at night, in every possible interpretation of the phrase.

But if he couldn't have anything more than a friendship with Susannah, so be it. As his friend, she would still be his sounding board when he had concerns about Lindsey. And he'd still be able to help her with tasks that required a man, whether they entailed hanging a mirror or rescuing her from an avid crowd of fans. He could do that for her.

In the meantime, he'd better talk to Molly, his Daddy School teacher, and see if she had any good ideas about how he could live his own life—specifically, how he could live it without Susannah's guest-starring in it.

"Sure," he conceded, feeling the last hot embers inside him die and fade to gray, feeling his disappointment chill to grudging resignation. "We can be friends."

AMANDA'S BEDROOM was pink. Really pink. The walls were light pink, her bedspread was Barbie pink and the carpet was a kind of purplish pink, the color of raspberry sherbet. Her furniture was white with pink roses

painted on the drawers and pink scrolling on the headboard.

The funny thing was that the pink sort of clashed
with Amanda. She had brown hair and tan skin. Meredith matched the room much better.

Lindsey had darker hair than Amanda, and lighter
skin, so she wasn't sure whether she matched or not.
It didn't matter. This was an emergency meeting of the
Susannah Dawson Admiration Society, and she was
glad that it was being held in someone else's house
instead of hers.

Actually, she'd hoped they could have their meeting
at the mall, so they could have bought stuff and treated
themselves to ice-cream cones after the meeting was
over, but Dr. Dad had vetoed that plan. So had
Amanda's and Meredith's parents. None of the adults
had felt like driving them all the way to the mall and
then sitting around for an hour or two while the girls
hung out.

But it was just as well that they were meeting at
Amanda's house, because Amanda had her sister's
magazine. It was one of those tabloids, the kind they
sold at checkout counters in supermarkets, usually with
an ugly picture of a famous person on the cover and a
headline about some famous person's breast implants
or mysterious pregnancy or heartbreak. Almost always,
a famous person's heartbreak was featured on the
cover: the famous person's heartbreaking final days, or
the heartbreak of the famous person getting a divorce,
or the famous person's heartbreak over drugs or bank-
ruptcy or the childhood secret no one knew about. Except the tabloid knew about it, of course, and published
it so the whole world would know about it, too.

Amanda had brought a bag of chocolate-chip cookies up to her room for them to munch on as they had their meeting. "So tell us about their date," she said.

"It wasn't really a date," Lindsey said. She was a little uneasy about telling the club about her father's dinner date with Susannah. Judging from Dr. Dad's mood when he came home Saturday night, she didn't think it had gone well.

He'd told her that he and Susannah had had a good time. At Lindsey's insistence, he'd described the food they'd ordered—"Yes, we had wine," he'd said—and then he'd driven Susannah home and come home himself. Lindsey had still been awake, watching TV in the den, when he'd arrived. "We had a very nice meal, and we talked" was his summation of the evening.

Well, of course that was all they'd done: talk. Susannah Dawson could have her pick of any single man in the country, maybe the world. Lindsey bet *Mercy Hospital* was broadcast all around the planet. They probably aired the show in Italy and France and Japan, and Susannah would appear on the screen with Italian or French or Japanese coming out of her mouth in someone else's voice. Lindsey would bet lots of Italian and French and Japanese guys had big crushes on Susannah.

So there was no way she'd fall for Lindsey's father. He should have known that going in. If he had, he might not have been wearing such an expression of disappointment when he'd gotten home.

He'd definitely looked disappointed. Even when he smiled. Even when he told her he'd had a good time. Even the following morning, just hours ago, when Lindsey had found him in the kitchen, brooding over a cup of coffee and staring out the window at nothing.

"Where did they go?" Meredith asked.

"Dominic's."

"Dominic's?" Amanda sneered. "He should have taken her someplace classy, like Reynaud."

"I told him that," Lindsey said.

"Well, it probably wouldn't do him any good," Amanda said, flipping through her sister's magazine. "Because if this is anything to go by, she's in love with Stephen Yates." She found the page she was looking for and flung it toward Lindsey.

Meredith crowded behind Lindsey to read over her shoulder. There was a big color photo of Susannah and Stephen Yates, both of them dressed to kill. Susannah wore a designer gown, sleek and slinky, with spaghetti straps that showed off her shoulders and throat. Her hair was piled on top of her head and she had humongous diamonds dangling from her ears. Stephen Yates was in a tuxedo—one of those Hollywood tuxedos, way too stylish, with a black shirt with a banded collar underneath. They were holding hands, looking in opposite directions and smiling, as if they were greeting fans who surrounded them on all sides.

"She is *so* pretty," Meredith murmured.

"He's *so* cute," Amanda added, coming around Lindsey to read over her other shoulder. "They look perfect together, don't they?"

"Well, they looked perfect together on *Mercy Hospital*," Meredith pointed out. "I don't know what Lucien Roche is going to do now that Dr. Davis is gone."

"They'll find someone else for him," Lindsey predicted. "They'll hire a new actress."

"She won't be as perfect for him as Susannah was," Meredith complained. "See how perfect they are?"

Lindsey studied the picture. She had to admit Stephen Yates looked a lot more right with Susannah than her father did. Her dad was so just plain normal. If he ever wore a tuxedo, it would be the usual kind, with a pleated white shirt, a satin sash and one of those dippy little bow ties. Dressed to kill, Stephen and Susannah were like high-style royalty.

"Read the article," Amanda urged her. "You'll see how perfect they really are for each other."

"Read it out loud," Meredith requested, crawling around Lindsey to sit facing her, her legs extended across the pink carpet and her back resting against Amanda's pink bed.

Lindsey lifted the magazine and read:

"'Oh, Susannah! In the Life Imitates Art department, romance is sizzling both on-screen and off-screen between *Mercy Hospital* stars Susannah Dawson and Stephen Yates. According to friends, the handsome actor known as Lucien Roche on the medical drama moved into Susannah's cozy canyon abode months ago. "They're inseparable," this friend says. "They live together and they work together. They're completely and totally in love." Any chance of wedding bells in the couple's future? A reliable source says marriage is the only way this relationship can go. "Susannah's an old-fashioned kind of girl," this source insists. "Now that she's expecting, she'll want Stephen to marry the mother of his child."'"

Lindsey dropped the magazine to her knees and scowled. *The mother of his child?* "This whole thing's a crock," she declared. "Susannah doesn't have a child."

"How do you know that?" Amanda asked. "Maybe she had the child and left it back in California with Stephen."

"Oh, come on! I've been watching *Mercy Hospital* every week. The shows that are on now would have been taped when she was pregnant. She doesn't look pregnant on them."

"They have ways of hiding pregnancies," Amanda claimed. "It's showbiz. They can do special effects. They can design her costume to hide a pregnancy. In any case, this magazine is from last June, which means she would have had the baby in December or January. The shows we're watching now could have been taped after she had the baby, couldn't they?"

"If she had a baby, she would have it here in Arlington with her. You think she left it with Stephen Yates? No way. She wouldn't do that," Lindsey argued.

"How do you know? It says right here—" Amanda jabbed her index finger at the magazine "—that she's expecting."

"Maybe it meant she was expecting him to marry her." Lindsey simply couldn't believe Susannah had a baby. She turned to Meredith, searching for support.

Meredith shook her head. "Expecting is expecting, Lindsey. And it says she's the mother of Stephen's child."

"She doesn't look pregnant." Lindsey scrutinized the photo. "She looks skinny in that dress."

"She was probably just a little pregnant when the picture was taken," Amanda explained. "Or maybe it's a file photo taken earlier and printed because they wanted a picture of her and Stephen to go along with the article about how she was expecting."

"I still don't believe it." Lindsey tossed the magazine aside. "You know these tabloids are always full of lies."

"I don't think it's a lie," Amanda declared.

Lindsey turned once more to Meredith, who suggested, "Maybe you could ask Susannah."

"Oh, sure. Like, I can just go up to her and say, 'So, is it true you've got a baby? And if so, where might the little one be? Did you just, like, leave him behind when you moved to Arlington?'"

"Well, you could be more subtle," Meredith advised.

"Or get her someplace where we can meet her, and I'll ask her," Amanda said, almost boasting. "She doesn't scare me."

"That would be so rude." Lindsey stared at the magazine with a combination of disgust and dread. "She's a very nice lady. She wants her privacy. I can't ask her such a personal question. I mean, we're an admiration society. We admire her. We have to show some respect."

"Especially if she's dating your dad," Meredith added.

"She's not. They just had dinner, that's all." If Susannah had a baby, there was no way Lindsey was going to let her date Dr. Dad. He might be a pain in the butt, but he was her father and she loved him. She couldn't let him get tangled up with some woman who had heartlessly abandoned her own baby.

Besides which, if Susannah and Stephen Yates were destined for marriage, she was probably going to go back to California to be with him sooner or later. Lindsey wasn't going to let her father get involved with a woman who was going to be leaving town. If Susannah

hurt him, it would be awful—not just for him but for
Lindsey. When Dr. Dad was miserable, he wasn't fun
to be with.

"We need to investigate this more," she resolved.
"As a society, we need to know the truth. I can't ask
her flat-out, but maybe I can get her talking or something. And we'll find out about this baby, one way or
the other."

"Okay." Amanda nodded her approval, then pulled
out a cookie from the bag and bit into it. A real bite,
not just one of her little crumbly nibbles.

Lindsey had sort of lost her appetite, but she took a
cookie anyway. She bit off a crescent and let it dissolve
on her tongue while she tried to sort her thoughts.

Magazines lied. Tacky tabloids in particular lied.

Yet Susannah and Stephen Yates did look perfect
together. And what Amanda said about how actresses
could disguise their pregnancies with carefully designed outfits and special effects was true. And if this
story about the pregnancy wasn't factual, wouldn't Susannah have sued the magazine for printing falsehoods
about her?

Lindsey didn't want to believe any of it, but she had
to admit Susannah was awfully private. She hated talking about her life back in Los Angeles. She might just
be hiding something.

Lindsey was appalled by the idea, but she couldn't
deny its plausibility. And maybe there was something
exciting about it—maybe Susannah had had to abandon her baby for a reason. Maybe she was planning to
return to Stephen and their child as soon as whatever
it was that had driven her away was resolved. Maybe
there was a deep, dark mystery behind the whole cir-
cumstance.

As the founder of the Susannah Dawson Admiration Society, Lindsey acknowledged that it was her responsibility to find out the truth.

SUSANNAH ALMOST DIDN'T call him Sunday. She was embarrassed about the way things had gone Saturday night, embarrassed by the mixed signals she'd sent him. When he kissed her, she seemed unable to do anything but kiss him back. But when he stopped kissing her long enough for her to restart her brain, she had to force herself to bring things to a halt. She couldn't give up what she'd fought so hard to attain— her independence—and she knew that if she kept kissing Toby, if she let him insinuate himself deeper and deeper into her heart, she would lose her independence.

It wasn't his fault. It was hers, and admitting that added a hefty dose of guilt to her embarrassment.

She'd sat at her desk late into the wee hours of Sunday morning, hoping that she might be able to get some writing done, since she couldn't sleep. But after struggling over the script, she'd acknowledged that she was going to have to observe Toby at work. Not just because she wanted to get the technical details right but because the pediatrician character she'd created seemed stagnant to her. She'd concocted a few crises for him in the story arc and developed some nice interaction between him and the series regulars, but she needed to see him at work to nail him down. Which meant she needed to see Toby at work.

Screwing her courage, she dialed his number at around six Sunday evening. His phone rang four times, and then his answering machine came on. She left a message for him to call her back, her voice smooth and amiable, without a hint of her ambivalence or her anguish. Then she hung up and groaned.

MacKenzie gave her a disgusted look. He knew her too well. He knew she was a wimp, too spineless to trust her emotions around a man she could fall in love with. "Well, I'm trying to develop my spine," she told him, wondering if she should let him walk on the kitchen table. Even though she sponged the table clean before she ate, having a cat stroll across the tabletop wasn't exactly sanitary.

MacKenzie licked his lips and puckered his little pink nose.

"I can't develop my spine if I start leaning on Toby," she justified herself to the judgmental beast. "I know he's nothing like Stephen. He's nothing like anyone I ever knew in my life. But I'm really trying to be my own person for a change. Not Daddy's wage earner, not Lee Davis, not Stephen's arm candy. Just me, myself. And your slave, of course," she added, scooping MacKenzie off the table and giving him a hug, which he coolly tolerated.

She set him down on the floor and he glided silently away. Too restless to remain indoors, she went upstairs to her bedroom and changed into a pair of athletic shorts, a sweatshirt, thick cotton socks and her sneakers. She pulled her hair back into a barrette, donned her eyeglasses, strapped on her wrist weights and headed out for a brisk, aerobic walk. She pumped her hands and pushed her feet, block after block, until a film of sweat coated her face and her wrists and biceps ached. Would there be a message from Toby on her machine when she got home? Or would he ignore her call, dismissing her as a bitch, a tease, someone he couldn't trust?

Lights were on in his house when she concluded her three-mile loop through the neighborhood and returned to their block. The last of the sun had faded, making the glowing gold light spilling through his windows terribly inviting. Did he know how lucky he was to have a daughter who loved him, a house that was a home, a sense of himself and his strength? All the power walks and wrist weights in the world couldn't make Susannah as strong as he was.

Sighing, she accelerated to a jog, passing his house and springing up the porch steps to her own front door. She entered the house and listened for the rhythmic beep that would indicate she had a phone message. She heard nothing.

All right. She couldn't blame him for wanting nothing to do with her, despite his insistence that they could still be friends. She would have to write her scripts without his input. Maybe she'd scrap the pediatrician character altogether. She had several other story arcs she could work with. She'd telephone her editor back in Los Angeles on Monday and describe the new direction she was taking her scripts. He'd been keen on the story line she'd faxed him, but if she couldn't execute it, she couldn't. If he told her he wasn't going to buy her other scripts, she'd deal with that. She could manage her finances comfortably until another opportunity arose. In the meantime, she could get rid of her sexy pediatrician and—

The phone rang.

Plucking off her eyeglasses, she hurried down the hall to the kitchen and answered the phone. "Susannah?" Toby's voice came through the line. "It's Toby."

"Oh." All right, she wouldn't get rid of the sexy

pediatrician. She groped for the paper towels, tore off a sheet and mopped the perspiration from her face. "Hi."

"Are you okay? You sound out of breath."

"I just got in from an aerobic walk," she told him, wondering if he'd been watching for her to return home before he called.

"We just got home a few minutes ago ourselves," he told her, chatting affably as if Saturday night had never happened. "I took Lindsey to Paganini's. It's an ice-cream place."

She sighed again, fighting off another twinge of envy. Perhaps if she'd kept kissing Toby last night, if she'd let the kissing lead to lovemaking, she could have accompanied him and his daughter to Paganini's tonight. She could have been a part of their loving little family.

Which was exactly why she hadn't let the kissing lead anywhere. She didn't want to be part of a family, not even his.

"The reason I called," she said, no longer out of breath from her walk, "is that I was wondering if you'd mind my observing you at work. You said it would be okay, but that was before…" She bit her lip, not wanting to revive unpleasant memories of last night for him.

"Before what?" he asked. His tone was benign, but she sensed that he was goading her.

She inhaled and straightened her shoulders, pretending she had more spine than she did. "Before last night," she said bravely.

He didn't speak for a moment. He was letting her stew in her words, she realized, letting her remember how badly last night had ended. Just as his silence threatened to make her crazy, he said, "If you want to observe me at work, you're going to be bored to tears. But it's okay with me."

She hadn't realized how anxious she was until she digested his answer. Slowly her body unwound, her hands unfisted around the receiver and her breath came evenly. "Are you sure?"

"I'm sure you'll be bored to tears, yes."

She smiled and felt a few tears fill her eyes—not from boredom but from a fresh flood of guilt. She didn't deserve his generosity. "Would tomorrow be all right?" she asked.

"Sure. I'll be starting my rounds at Arlington Memorial Hospital at nine. Do you want to meet me there or drive in with me?"

She didn't want to impose even more on him, but she also didn't want to have to wend her way through a hospital, asking directions of people who might recognize her and make a fuss. "If you wouldn't mind giving me a lift—"

"I wouldn't mind," he said. "Be ready at eight-thirty."

"Okay."

"See you tomorrow." She heard a click as he hung up.

Not the warmest of farewells, but she couldn't expect warm from him. She'd extinguished his warmth quite effectively last night.

But she had his friendship. His neighborliness. His willingness to let her accompany him tomorrow. She should be grateful for that—and even more grateful that he wasn't trying to give her anything more.

Because she honestly wanted nothing more than

that, she swore to herself, even though a rebellious voice inside her denied it. She swore that all she wanted from Toby Cole was the kind of relationship that ended with a "see you tomorrow" and a click.

CHAPTER ELEVEN

HE COULD HANDLE THIS, he thought as she emerged from her house Monday morning just seconds after he pulled into her driveway. She must have been watching for him.

He was secretly relieved that he hadn't had to walk up to her front door and ring her bell. He wasn't sure how he'd feel about standing on her porch. The last time he'd stood there, he'd had her in his arms. He'd had her mouth beneath his, and he'd been hard and hungry—and hopeful. More than hopeful. He'd been positive she'd wanted him. He'd honestly believed they were on the same wavelength, feeling the same feelings, desiring each other equally.

What an idiot he was. She was a showbiz star, a glamorous icon. They might share the same street, but they didn't really share the same universe.

That was the message Lindsey had more or less imparted to him over pizza and ice cream last night. When he'd picked her up from her friend Amanda's house, she'd been subdued, thoughtful, neither bubbly nor snide. "What did you girls do?" he'd asked, trying to strike up a conversation.

"Nothing," she'd answered with a shrug. But over pizza—just plain cheese, the only way she would eat it—she'd suddenly embarked on a lecture about Susannah. "I know you took her out last night, Daddy, but it doesn't mean a thing," she'd said. "You hardly know her, and what you know doesn't really count, because as long as she's living next door to us she's, like, different from her usual self. Her usual self is an actress in Hollywood, not a lady in Arlington."

"I think she's trying to change from the Hollywood actress to the Arlington lady," Toby had pointed out.

"Don't let her fool you, Dr. Dad. She's lived a whole other life. She's dated famous, gorgeous actors. I mean, nothing personal, but she's not like you and me."

Lindsey had been so earnest he'd accepted her assertion without argument. He'd actually been touched that she cared enough to advise him on his social life, such as it was. She'd never commented on the other women he'd dated.

But then, the other women he'd dated hadn't been Susannah. Not that he was bewitched by her alleged fame—a fame she seemed determined to escape, no matter what Lindsey thought—but she was unique. She projected strength, yet he sensed a genuine vulnerability inside her. Her kindness toward Lindsey, her lack of pretense, her refusal to pull rank or put on airs…and that vulnerability, that bruised soul in desperate need of healing…

He wanted to heal her. Like the doctor he was, he wanted to make her all better. Even if they never wound up having sex, he wanted to make her well.

It was a remarkably arrogant attitude, he thought as she strolled across the lawn to the driveway. She looked perfectly healthy, not at all in need of medical—or any other—rescue. Lindsey might be wrong about Susannah's protecting her other life in Los Angeles, but she was right that he and Susannah were

barely one step removed from strangers. For all he
knew, she didn't like sex. Or maybe she didn't like sex
with single fathers who lived next door.

She got into the car and smiled hesitantly at him.
She was wearing her phony eyeglasses, and she carried
a leather handbag the size of a grocery sack. Her hair
was pulled straight back from her face in a severe
braid, and her outfit—a cream-colored cotton sweater
and a long paisley skirt—was simple and unobtrusive.
She probably wanted to look bland enough to go un-
noticed, and he supposed she'd achieved that effect.
But even if people didn't recognize her, they would
still be taken by her striking beauty. Even if she were
as anonymous as he was, she'd attract attention.

"I really appreciate your letting me do this," she
said as he backed down the driveway.

"You won't bother me," he assured her, wondering
whether that was the complete truth. Her nearness
would distract him if he let it. Every time he glimpsed
her he would think of how spectacularly he'd struck
out with her Saturday night, how mercilessly she'd
shut him down. But he would try his best to ignore her
and remain focused on his work. "If my patients complain, though, I'll have to ask you to respect their
wishes and wait outside the examining room."

"I understand."

He swore silently. They were talking like strangers,
two professionals establishing a working relationship.
He wondered what she'd do if he reminded her of the
fact that not too long ago, they'd come quite close to
embarking on a very different kind of relationship.

She'd probably flee from him and find some other
pediatrician to observe.

"My routine is to do my hospital rounds first thing,

then head over to my office to see patients,'' he explained to her. ''Again, if any of the patients has an objection to your being in the room with us, you'll have to make yourself scarce.''

''Of course,'' she said. Her voice was as silky as her hair had been when he'd sifted it through his fingers Saturday night.

Another curse teased his tongue. He didn't want to talk about his workday. He wanted to talk about what had gone wrong the last time they'd been together, how he'd managed to misread her completely, why the mere hint of her fragrance—something light and spicy—made his hands fist on the steering wheel in frustration.

But perhaps Lindsey was right. Perhaps he and Susannah were so far apart in so many ways there was no point in talking about anything personal.

He pulled into the staff parking lot of the hospital, took a deep breath to stifle that frustration and shaped a smile for Susannah. ''Ready?'' he asked.

''Ready.'' The smile she sent back to him was both warm and shy, and it did nothing to silence his powerful attraction to her.

''Then let's do it.'' He got out of the car, started around to her side to help her out, then reversed himself when she got out on her own. He doffed his blazer, donned the white coat he'd left in the back seat, lifted his bag from the floor and led the way into the hospital, determined to pretend he didn't care about the woman spending the day with him.

SHE HADN'T REALIZED how gentle he was.

She should have, of course. Toby Cole had a more tender heart than anyone she'd ever met before. She should have assumed his kindness would color everything he did, including his work.

He had only two patients in the hospital's pediatrics wing. One was a forty-hour-old baby about to be discharged, along with his bleary but ecstatic mother. Toby introduced Susannah to the mother as Sue Dawson and explained that she was observing him work. The mother voiced no objections.

She questioned Toby about her baby's belly button—Toby assured her it was healing just fine—and about whether it was normal for the baby to soil his diaper six times in one day—Toby informed her it was indeed quite normal. As he answered her questions he examined the baby, warming his stethoscope with his palm before he touched the metal disk to the baby's chest, sliding his pinkie against the baby's tiny palms to test his reflexes, talking to the baby in a soft, soothing patter. "This one's a keeper," he announced, handing the baby back to his mother. "How are you feeling?"

"Tired. A little sore."

"Did the midwife talk to you about postpartum depression?"

As the mother discussed her tumultuous emotions, Susannah stood quietly in a corner of the room, taking it all in. Toby was the boy's doctor, yet he treated the mother as if she was his patient, too, listening to her concerns and offering suggestions. "Remember, you can call anytime with any questions. If it's after office hours, your call will be transferred over to the hospital emergency line. There are nurses here who can answer your questions, and if it's essential that you talk to me, they'll contact me and I'll call you right back. Okay?"

"I wouldn't want to bother you at home."

"What would bother me is if little Matthew has a problem and you don't know how to solve it. He's your first child, and you and he are going to do a lot of on-the-job training. But you're not all alone in this. You've got the midwife, the nurses here and me. Right?"

"Right."

"So you're all set to go home today. You have a crib or a cradle for him?"

"Yes."

"And a baby seat in the car?"

"Yes."

"Great. I want to see Matthew in my office in two weeks. I'll have my nurse call you tomorrow to set up an appointment."

"Okay."

"Relax. And trust me, as exhausted as you are, you're going to be fine. I can tell Matthew is crazy about you."

"I'm crazy about him, too," the mother said, tears filling her eyes.

Susannah felt the sting of tears in her own eyes. Seeing the mother cradle little Matthew in her arms forced Susannah to think about the baby she'd lost. If fate had spun in another direction, she might have found herself four months ago in a hospital bed like the one across the room from her, with her own baby nestled into the curve of her arm, peering up at her with curiosity and trust.

But fate was what it was, and Susannah was only a witness to another woman's bliss. As they left the room, she had to resist the urge to run back in and plead with the woman for a chance merely to hold her newborn son. "He's so small," she murmured, allowing herself one glance backward.

"Actually, he's kind of big," Toby disputed her, pulling a clipboard from a plastic bracket fastened to the wall by the door. He skimmed the papers fastened to the clipboard, then extracted a pen from the chest pocket of his white coat. "He tipped the scales at eight pounds, two ounces at birth. That's bigger than average." He jotted a note on one of the sheets of paper, then tucked the clipboard back into its bracket. "I've got one more patient here," he told her, striding down the hall at a brisk gait.

He was all business, and she ought to have been glad. But she felt a twinge of disappointment over his crisp professional demeanor that mingled with the disappointment she felt about her own baby, amplifying it until fresh tears sprang to her eyes.

She hastily blinked them away. She hadn't imposed on Toby to wallow in all her defeats. She'd done it to get a sense of a real-life pediatrician's workday.

This real-life pediatrician's workday brought them to a semiprivate room in which a thin girl of about six sat propped up in a bed, a plastic mask covering her nose and mouth and connected by a tube to a machine on the wall. Toby pulled up the chair next to the girl, who was reading a Dr. Seuss book. Once again he was soft-spoken and comforting, asking the girl how her breathing was, how she'd slept last night, where her mommy was.

"Getting coffee," the girl told him. "When can I go home?"

"Soon," Toby promised. "I'm thinking maybe tomorrow. How does that sound?"

"Okay."

He listened to her heart and her lungs, asked her if she was still swimming on a regular basis and told her he was going to try her on a different inhalator that would probably work better than the one she was using now.

"She has asthma," he told Susannah once they'd left the room. "She was admitted last night. There's been a huge increase in pediatric asthma over the past decade. It's really troubling."

"What do you think is causing it?" Susannah asked.

Jotting notes on the clipboard outside the girl's room, Toby didn't answer right away. Once he'd slid the clipboard back into place and pocketed his pen, he said, "My guess would be pollution. What do you think?"

She shrugged. She'd never thought about it at all. "I'm not a doctor," she reminded him.

"But they got pretty technical on your television show. I figured you actors would have had to learn a little about what you were talking about."

"You've seen *Mercy Hospital*?" She was surprised. He hadn't known who she was when they'd met. If he'd seen the show, he would have to have recognized her.

He smiled sheepishly. "After you moved in next door, I watched an episode."

"Did we get it right?" she asked, strolling down the hall with him. "The medical stuff, I mean."

"The technical jargon, yes. The actual job of doctoring?" He considered his reply. "Not quite."

She grinned. "What did we get wrong?"

"For one thing, there's a lot more paperwork in real doctoring." He paused at the nurses' station and signed a few more papers. "Hey, Allison," he greeted one of the nurses behind the counter, a tall, pretty woman with curly red hair tumbling down her back.

"Hey, yourself," she responded, then turned her friendly smile to Susannah.

"Allison, this is my neighbor, Sue Dawson. Sue, this is Allison Winslow, the woman who steered me in the direction of the Daddy School."

"Hi." Susannah smiled impassively. Allison was studying her, as if she recognized her. Susannah braced herself.

"You're Toby's new neighbor?" she asked.

"Yes."

Allison scrutinized her for a moment longer, then nodded. "Welcome to Arlington," she said, her grin taking on a teasing quality as she turned back to Toby.

He nudged the papers he'd been writing on across the counter to her. "No," he said.

"Hmm," Allison grunted skeptically.

Intrigued, Susannah waited until they were on the elevator, traveling down to the lobby, before she questioned him about the cryptic exchange. "Why did you say no?" she asked. "I wouldn't have minded if she'd identified me."

"You wouldn't?" He gazed at her. The elevator was large, with green walls and glaring light. Although Toby was a doctor, he looked out of place in such stark surroundings. He was too warm, too alive.

"It wasn't like there was a huge crowd of people there," she pointed out. "And she's a friend of yours."

He shrugged. "I don't think she was thinking about your TV show," he said.

"Then why did you say no?"

"She can get a little personal with me sometimes. I

wasn't in the mood for it this morning, so I stopped her before she could start.''

His answer intrigued her even more, but his tone implied that he didn't wish to discuss it further. She wondered whether he'd been more than friends with Allison—but his laconic reply didn't translate that way. A man wouldn't describe a former lover as getting a little personal with him sometimes.

Yet she wondered. Why was Toby still single? How had a man as good-natured and sexy as he was remained unclaimed all this time? Years had passed since his wife's death. Surely Lindsey wasn't enough to scare off potential girlfriends.

Susannah wished she could ask him. But they'd lost their ability to talk about such personal things when she'd sent him home Saturday night. It was her fault, too. She was the one refusing to open up to him. She couldn't expect him to open up to her.

His office was located in a two-story brick building that housed several other medical practices a five-minute drive from the hospital. Entering the suite that housed Arlington Pediatric Associates, Susannah was assailed by a cacophony of giggly young voices. The waiting area looked more like a preschool than a doctor's office. A wide chalkboard hung on one wall, a huge aquarium filled with fish occupied another, push toys and building blocks littered the floor and a carved wooden rocking horse stood in a corner. The noise came from a half-dozen toddlers who were busily engaged in marking up the chalkboard with big white squiggles and pushing plastic trucks around the floor. One small child sat solemnly on the rocking horse, her father hovering over her, pushing the horse gently back and forth.

The entire mood was so cheerful Susannah might not have realized she'd entered a doctor's office. Shouldn't toddlers be panicking about having to see the doctor? Shouldn't they be clinging to their parents and whining that they didn't want to get a shot?

Evidently, they weren't afraid of Toby and his partners. Or they were so distracted by the array of playthings in the bright, bustling waiting area, they forgot what would be happening to them once they were taken to an examining room.

The nurse and the receptionist behind the broad desk across from the fish tank gave Susannah a long, hard stare. They recognized her; she knew the look. She squared her shoulders and smiled at them, determined not to rattle or be rattled by them.

Toby ushered her through the waiting area, deftly avoiding scampering children and crawling toddlers as he steered her toward the receptionist desk. "Nan, Serena, this is Sue Dawson. She's going to be observing me at work today."

Serena, the nurse, gaped openly at Susannah. "I've got to ask—you're that actress from *Mercy Hospital,* aren't you."

"Yes," Susannah said softly, not wanting everyone in the waiting area to hear—not that her voice would have carried above the din of giggling, chattering children.

"I told you," Serena boasted, elbowing Nan. "When you walked in, I said, 'Nan, that lady with Toby looks just like Dr. Lee Davis on *Mercy Hospital,*' and lo and behold! Toby, since when did you start hanging around with actresses?"

"Since this actress retired and moved into the house next to mine," he said.

The discomfort Susannah had braced herself for didn't come. That Toby's colleagues recognized her didn't unnerve her—maybe because they seemed so friendly and good-natured. They weren't pushy, demanding anything from her. They were simply acknowledging her.

She acknowledged them right back. "Toby has graciously let me come and watch how a real doctor works. On the show I was just faking it. But people like him—and you—are the real thing."

Nan seemed to think this was hilarious. She laughed so hard she struck a few errant keys on her computer keyboard. "The real thing, huh? What do you think, Serena? Are we the real thing?"

"We're the real *something*," Serena allowed. "I'm not sure what. Listen, Toby, you've got a pretty full schedule today. Your first appointment's at eleven, so you'd better get your butt in gear."

"Yes, ma'am." He saluted her with a nod, then led Susannah past the desk and through the door to the examining rooms and offices in back.

His office was small, occupied by a broad desk, a few shelves bracketed to the walls, a framed diploma from Yale Medical School, several potted plants lining the windowsill. There was less personality in the room than she would have expected—except that Toby's personality was devoted to his patients. She understood that it was with them, not in this cubicle, where he was most fully himself.

Over the next few hours, she and Toby spent little time in that office. Mostly they were in one or another of the examining rooms. She watched as he examined each patient, talking, asking questions, listening, bringing the child out as he checked the child's heart, peered into the child's ears, grilled the child's parent on symptoms and explained therapies. His office, she learned, was only for writing notes in files and telephoning prescriptions to the pharmacy.

She lurked in the corner of whichever examining room they were in while he diagnosed an ear infection, took a throat culture for strep, removed the sutures from a cut on a boy's forehead, described the difference between a croup cough and a bronchitis cough to a worried father. Several of the parents who brought their children in to see him recognized Susannah—and she discovered that it didn't matter. One mother asked politely for her autograph and explained to her chicken-pox-spotted daughter that Susannah was a famous actress. Toby offered a sheet from his prescription pad, and Susannah wrote, "Get well soon!" to the little girl.

At one-thirty he took ten minutes to wolf down a sandwich from a deli across the street. He told Susannah she should take her time with her own lunch, but she wanted to stay with him, to experience the hectic pace of his workday. Unable to finish her sandwich as quickly as he'd finished his, she rewrapped half of it, stashed it in her tote bag and accompanied him back to an examining room, where a boy in his early teens, dressed in an Arlington Middle School baseball uniform, sat on the table, with one foot elevated and packed in ice. The boy explained, in exuberant detail, how he'd been stealing second when his foot got caught on the bag and his ankle twisted.

Toby nodded in understanding. "Did you feel anything pop?" he asked as he unwrapped the bandage that held the ice pack in place. "Did you hear a crack?"

"Uh-uh. I didn't feel anything. But then my foot swolled up something wicked."

"We're going to need some X rays," he said as he examined the boy's foot. "The lab is down at the other end of the hall. We'll get you a wheelchair. I'm guessing it's just a sprain, but we'll need some pictures to be sure. Just tell me this, Mike—were you safe, or did they tag you out?"

"I was safe," the kid boasted, his grin glittering with the silver wires of orthodontia.

By the time Mike was settled in the wheelchair and his harried-looking mother was pushing him back through the waiting area, a gray-haired woman in a white coat like Toby's approached him in the back hall. "Can I bother you for a minute, Toby?" she asked, ignoring Susannah. "I've got a patient I want you check. I'm hearing a heart murmur. I think it's just an innocuous noise, but I'd like your opinion."

"Sure." Toby shot Susannah a quick smile. "You can wait in my office," he said before hurrying after his colleague.

Susannah returned to his office, almost grateful for a moment's break. On *Mercy Hospital,* the doctors ran around a lot, but they were always driven by emergencies contrived to propel the drama—accidents, shootings, stabbings, women going into labor at inopportune times. Toby ran around as much as those fictional doctors did, yet he didn't seem frantic or rushed. He didn't shout orders like the doctors on the show. No matter how tight his time was, he remained friendly and unhurried with his patients, talking and listening to them. There was a tranquillity about him, a sense of purpose and utter confidence.

His office was a peaceful refuge, its uncluttered

space relaxing her. She noted his blazer hanging from a hook on the back of his door, the neat pile of files sitting squarely on his blotter, the thick somber reference books arranged on one shelf. A large framed photo of Lindsey stood prominently on a corner of his desk. A school photo, Susannah guessed, given the bland background and the stiff pose. In spite of Lindsey's rigid smile and her too-neat hair, she looked lovely.

On a shelf above his desk was a smaller photo. Susannah lifted it and angled it to the light. Taken in what appeared to be a park, it featured Toby, an adorable toddler and a woman who resembled Lindsey uncannily.

His wife. The toddler was Lindsey, and the beautiful woman with the dark hair and creamy skin was Toby's wife.

She seemed so happy in the picture. So did Toby. His hair was shorter, his smile brighter. Susannah saw no sign of tension in him, no edge of wistfulness, no hint of doubt. He looked secure and satisfied—and extraordinarily handsome, although not as sexy as he looked now. There was no urgency in his gaze, no need burning inside him. He'd been content then.

He wasn't anymore. He'd suffered a loss; he harbored doubts now. He lived with anger and fear and desperate yearning. She'd sensed it in his kisses; she'd seen it in his smiles. She remembered the evening he'd hung her mirror, when he'd admitted that he had lost his faith in the discipline he'd devoted himself to. He wasn't the same man he'd been the sunny afternoon that photo had been taken.

Somehow, the shadow that darkened his soul, that tempered his smile and gave his eyes an enigmatic glow, made him more fascinating. More trustworthy. More approachable. People as certain of the world as the man in the photo scared her. She related much more easily to people who wrestled with demons, as she did.

"Hi." Toby's voice came from behind her.

He must have already seen her studying the picture, so there was no need to pretend she hadn't. She set it back on the shelf, then turned to him. "Your wife was beautiful," she said.

He smiled—that poignant smile she found so alluring.

"Lindsey takes after her."

"A lot," he agreed.

She gazed at him, filling his office door, his shirt slightly rumpled beneath his white coat, his tie loosened, his hair mussed, his chin bristly, his stethoscope peeking out of a pocket. The day's labor showed in his face—he appeared not so much weary as full, as if each patient he'd seen had satisfied a hunger inside him.

Toby was a man who needed to heal others, to make them well and whole. As hard as he worked, his job wasn't a habit. It was a source of joy.

She wanted her independence, but she wanted him, too.

"There was a man in California...." she said.

She saw movement in his neck as he swallowed. He stepped farther into the office and closed the door. Then, digging his hands into his trouser pockets, he leaned against the door and nodded slightly, an invitation for her to elaborate.

"It ended badly."

Again a slight nod. She wondered how much detail

she would have to go into. She didn't want to recite
the entire miserable story of her relationship with Stephen, but Toby deserved some sort of explanation for
why she'd pushed him away Saturday night, why she
was so afraid to stop pushing him away.

"It wasn't as if I wouldn't have quit the series and
left Los Angeles anyway. But that was just the final
straw."

"You don't have to explain," he said.

"I do." She wished he would step away from the
door, move toward her, open his arms. She wanted his
forgiveness. She wanted him to swear to her that she
would be safe with him, that he would never try to
bend her to his will. He seemed so far away from her,
as if waiting for her to make the first move.

She'd made the first move by talking, hadn't she?
Obviously, it wasn't enough.

"I worked with him. He was one of the other stars
on the show," she said. "I thought I loved him. I
wanted a marriage. I wanted to create a family with
him. But as far as he was concerned, it was all showbiz. We looked good together. We helped each other
on the show. We were good for each other's careers.
He didn't want what I wanted."

"Then you were smart to break up with him," Toby
said, a trace of a smile teasing his lips.

That mere flicker of a smile gave her courage. She
pushed away from his desk and walked toward him,
not too close but closer than they'd been. "I'm sorry
about Saturday night. I should have told you then. Instead, I acted like a jerk."

"It would have been nice to know what was
wrong," he admitted, although his careless shrug im-

plied that he considered the matter closed. "If you're still working things out with him—"

"I'm not," she insisted. "There's nothing to work out."

"Well, so you need some time to recover. That makes sense."

"I'm all recovered," she argued. "I just don't want to let anyone have that kind of control over me again. I don't want to get swallowed up by another intense relationship. I don't want to be thinking about someone else all the time." A pointless wish, since she seemed to be spending an awful lot of time thinking about Toby.

Another sly smile flickered across his face. "So we'll skip the intense relationship. Any chance you'd be open to a totally meaningless, no-strings-attached fling?"

She laughed. His joke made her desire him even more. She would love a fling with him—but she was the one who would attach strings to it. She wasn't cut out for casual affairs, and even if she was, she couldn't have one with Toby. She already liked him too much.

"I'm open to a lot of things," she conceded. "I just want to take it slow. I know it sounds silly for a thirty-two-year-old woman to be trying to find herself, but that's where I am right now."

He extended his hand to capture hers and tugged her across the few feet of space that still separated them. Tenderly, he brushed his lips over hers. "We can take it as slow as you want," he murmured.

The promise of a real kiss from him was almost enough to make her want to take it fast. The warmth of his body so close to hers, the whisper of his breath against her cheek, the possessive clasp of his hand around hers made her want to lose herself, not find herself.

But that was a mistake she wouldn't let herself make. So she resisted the urge to throw her arms around him, pull his mouth back to hers and press her body to his. She would take it slow because she had to—and she would thank her lucky stars that she'd met a man like Toby, generous enough to let her do what she had to do.

CHAPTER TWELVE

"Hi, Susannah?" Lindsey cupped the phone to her ear. She was in the kitchen, Amanda and Meredith hovering next to her as if they were dying to snatch the phone away from her so they could hear Susannah's voice themselves.

Well, they'd hear it soon enough. Lindsey had promised them she'd figure out a way for them to see Susannah, and she'd come up with a great plan. Assuming Susannah fell for it, which was a big assumption. But Lindsey believed it would work.

"Yes?" Susannah's voice sounded exactly the same on the phone as it did on TV.

"It's Lindsey."

"Hi, Lindsey."

Lindsey tried to measure Susannah's mood by her tone. She didn't sound annoyed, as though Lindsey was the last person she wanted to hear from. So she took a deep breath, turned away from her friends' eager faces and said, "I was wondering if I could, like, borrow MacKenzie."

"Borrow him?" Susannah sounded surprised and amused.

"Yeah. See, like, I've got this friend, and her cousin is really into cats, and she wanted to send a photo of her and a cat to her cousin, only she doesn't have a cat. And I was like telling her about how wonderful

MacKenzie is, and we just sort of thought maybe we could take a picture of her with MacKenzie to send her cousin.''

"Sure," Susannah said so automatically Lindsey wasn't certain she'd heard right.

"Sure?"

"Sure. When does your friend want to borrow him?''

Lindsey grinned at Meredith and Amanda. ''Well, she's here now.''

"At your house?''

"Yeah. It's okay with my dad. He lets me have friends over when he's not home.''

"Well…okay. Why don't I bring MacKenzie over and your friend can have her picture taken.''

Lindsey gave Meredith and Amanda a thumbs-up. They squealed and gave each other a high five. "Okay," Lindsey remembered to answer Susannah. ''That'd be great.''

"I'll be right over," Susannah said. "'Bye.''

Lindsey hung up the phone and announced, ''She'll be right over.''

Amanda and Meredith squealed some more and hugged her, which was a bit much although Lindsey relished having them so in love with her. After about ten seconds of being hugged, she wriggled out of their arms. "Come on, guys. We've got to get organized. Meredith, is your camera ready?''

"Yeah.'' Meredith had gotten a camera for her eleventh birthday. It wasn't too fancy—it focused all by itself and had a built-in flash, and Meredith had already taught Lindsey how to use it. Lindsey had phoned her last night and told her to bring the camera to school with her so they could try this scheme out at their weekly Susannah Dawson Admiration Society meeting.

That the plan seemed to have worked and her friends adored her gave Lindsey a huge boost. She'd had another really awful day at school. Ms. Hathaway had chewed her out in front of the whole class because her math homework was wrinkled. "This looks like something you might have pulled out of a trash can," she'd said. "And what a shame, because you probably got all the answers right. But when you have no regard for your work, why should I have any regard for it?"

Lindsey had had to sit at her desk, saying nothing, staring at her hands, as Ms. Hathaway lectured her in front of everybody on having no regard. She had only a few weeks more school and then she'd be done with Ms. Hathaway forever. The question was, could she survive those few weeks without going nuts?

At the moment, with Meredith double-checking her camera and Amanda standing by the window, watching for Susannah, Lindsey believed she might survive after all. It was a clear, summery afternoon, finally hot enough for sandals. More important than the warm weather was the fact that Lindsey's father seemed to be in better spirits than he'd been on Sunday after his date with Susannah, and when he was in good spirits, Lindsey's life was a lot easier. She figured he had cheered up because he'd abandoned the idea of actually dating Susannah, which was a good thing, given Susannah's secret baby back in California.

And now Susannah was coming over with MacKenzie. Except for school, Lindsey's life was definitely looking up.

"Here she comes!" Amanda shrieked from the window. "Oh, my God!"

"Listen, you guys—be cool, okay? Don't make a fuss over her or she'll leave. Okay?"

"Okay," Meredith promised.

"I'm just screaming now. I'll stop when she comes in," Amanda assured Lindsey. "She's going around to the front door."

The doorbell rang, as if to prove Amanda's report had been accurate.

"Remember—be cool," Lindsey warned them one final time before hurrying down the hall to answer the door.

Susannah looked anything but glamorous in her jeans and a clean white T-shirt. Her hair was held back with a tortoiseshell headband, and she had no makeup or anything on. Even so, she was gorgeous. Lindsey wished she could be half as gorgeous.

"Hi," she said, beckoning Susannah inside. MacKenzie sat in the crook of Susannah's arm and eyed Lindsey suspiciously. "Hey, MacKenzie, remember me?"

He seemed as if he might.

Susannah stared past Lindsey, and she turned to see Amanda and Meredith lurking in the hall behind her, gawking at Susannah. "These are my friends, Meredith and Amanda. Meredith's the one with the cousin," she said.

"Your dad knows you have *two* friends over?" Susannah asked.

"Yeah. It's okay with him."

"Well," Susannah said. "This is MacKenzie." She extended the cat toward Meredith, who flinched back to life and reached to take him. "He's kind of heavy, but he's very sweet."

"He's a great cat," Lindsey said, leading the group

back down the hall to the kitchen, where the lighting was better for shooting photographs.

"He's beautiful," Meredith agreed, standing in the sunlit corner of the room and stroking MacKenzie. "He's so soft."

"Okay, move a little to the left so the light hits your face," Lindsey ordered, lifting the camera. Then the picture taking began. First Meredith and MacKenzie. Then Meredith, Amanda and MacKenzie. Then all three girls and MacKenzie, with Susannah taking the picture. Then—with very little goading—a picture of Amanda, Meredith and MacKenzie with Susannah.

She was so relaxed, as if she didn't even care that Lindsey's friends knew she was a famous actress. When Amanda said, "I watch your show all the time," Susannah only laughed and said, "It's not my show anymore." When Meredith asked if acting was fun, Susannah actually admitted that there were definitely some fun aspects to it, even though it was also a lot of hard work. When Amanda asked why Susannah had moved to Arlington, of all places, Susannah said, "Maybe because I wanted to have a next-door neighbor like Lindsey."

It was all Lindsey could do not to kiss her for saying such a nice thing. Whatever might have gone wrong with Lindsey's father Saturday night, Susannah still liked her. Dr. Dad hadn't spoiled things for his daughter.

They used up all twelve exposures on the roll of film. If Lindsey didn't come up with an idea fast, Susannah would leave—but they were all getting along so well, and Amanda and Meredith were really enjoying being with Susannah, and Lindsey knew they'd be

her slaves forever if she could figure out a way to get
Susannah to stick around a little longer.

"Why don't we bake cookies," she suggested. "Susannah thinks she isn't a good cook, but she really is.
Would you stay and help us, Susannah?"

Susannah hesitated for a minute and then said,
"Okay. You girls shouldn't be using an oven without
an adult around, anyway. But don't listen to Lindsey—
I *am* a lousy cook. I'll just watch while you bake."

Meredith and Amanda seemed excited about baking.
They clearly saw Lindsey as their leader, which
pleased her enormously. Meredith was more of a leader
type than Lindsey, and Amanda was the one who'd
supplied the information about Stephen Yates and the
baby, so she might have stepped into a leadership role,
too. But they both seemed willing to let Lindsey be
the star. Well, Susannah was the *real* star, but Lindsey
was the star of the fifth-graders.

Rummaging through the kitchen cabinets, she found
enough ingredients to make chocolate-chip cookies if
they skipped the walnuts, which everyone agreed
would be acceptable. MacKenzie curled up in a pool
of sunlight on the floor and licked himself, ignoring
the rest of them as they banged around the kitchen,
smashing butter into a soft mush with a fork, measuring white and brown sugar, spilling flour on the
counter. Susannah helped by wiping the spills, breaking eggs and making sure they were using the right
measuring spoons.

She also amazed Lindsey by keeping the conversation going. Lindsey and her friends couldn't talk much
beyond "How much baking soda am I supposed to
use?" or "Do we have to grease the cookie sheets?"
But Susannah kept talking about other stuff. "Are you

all in the same class?'' she asked. ''I bet you can't wait till summer vacation. What are you going to do this summer?''

Meredith was going to a sleep-away camp in New Hampshire. ''We do boating and tennis,'' she said. ''My mother went there when she was a girl.''

Amanda's mother had signed her up for an art program at the Arlington Museum. ''It's kind of boring, but it's okay,'' she said. ''It's just mornings. Hey, Lindsey, maybe your dad could sign you up for it, too. Then we could do it together.''

Lindsey perked up. She was so bored by school in general and Ms. Hathaway in particular that she hadn't gotten around to worrying about whether she'd be bored all summer, too. Last summer she'd had Cathy to hang out with, and they'd had a great time, biking to the community pool, swimming and buying soft-serve ice cream at the snack bar there, or planning picnics in their backyards. They'd played soccer and they'd slept over at each other's houses a lot. But Cathy wasn't going to be around this summer, and Lindsey hadn't given much thought to how she was going to fill that void.

Amanda wasn't Cathy, but Lindsey could hang out with her. Maybe she could get her to eat a little more. ''Here, have some chocolate chips,'' she said, tearing open the bag and shaking a few chips into Amanda's hand.

Meredith stirred the rest of the chips into the batter while Lindsey and Amanda smeared butter over the cookie sheets. ''What are you going to do this summer?'' she asked Susannah.

''Write. Fix up the house a little more. And I'd like

to drive around the area, do some exploring. I haven't seen much of New England.''

"You should go to Tanglewood," Meredith said. "You just drive straight north across the Massachusetts border. My parents go every summer while I'm at camp. The Boston Symphony Orchestra plays there.''

"That sounds like fun. Maybe I'll do that." Susannah smiled at Lindsey. "Maybe you could come with me.''

Lindsey took a deep breath to conceal her amazement. Classical music didn't do much for her, but to spend a day in the Berkshires with Susannah was worth sitting through all of Beethoven's symphonies at once. "Are you really going to spend the whole summer in New England?'' she asked, putting aside her excitement about Susannah's invitation and remembering that there were certain things she needed to know about Susannah. "I mean, don't you want to go back to Hollywood?''

Susannah laughed. "No.''

What about her baby, though? Didn't she want to see her child? "Haven't you got family there?'' Lindsey asked carefully.

Amanda and Meredith fell silent, spooning the batter onto the cookie sheets and waiting for Susannah to answer.

"I do have family there," Susannah told them. "But I'm not sure I'll be visiting them over the summer.''

"Why not?'' Lindsey was pushing, but she needed to know. Not just for the sake of the club but for her father's sake, as well, just in case he had any lingering dreams of asking Susannah out for dinner again. If she had a baby, Dr. Dad ought to know about it before he got any complicated ideas.

Susannah didn't seem disturbed by the question. "I think I need a break from my family," she said. "I'm sure I'll visit eventually, but I only just moved here a few weeks ago. I'm not ready to go back yet."

Not ready. Not ready to be a mother to her child? Or not ready to work out whatever had gone wrong between her and Stephen Yates? Something must have gone wrong, or Susannah wouldn't have left.

Lindsey wasn't going to let her father be the guy Susannah passed the time with until she decided she was ready to go home. As dazzled as she was by Susannah, her father was the one she lived with, the one she was going to be stuck dealing with if Susannah led him on and then dumped him. Lindsey didn't want to believe Susannah would do such a thing, but she *was* a Hollywood star, after all, in the habit of being doted on and worshiped like a goddess. And there was the baby, too. It couldn't be denied. Susannah was a fantastic neighbor, but as Dr. Dad's girlfriend she'd be bad news.

"I'd love to go to California," Amanda said as Lindsey slid the cookie sheets into the oven. "It's sunny all the time, and I bet the beaches are much nicer than our beaches in Connecticut."

"It isn't sunny all the time," Susannah corrected her with a smile. "Sometimes we get so much rain there are mud slides. And there's never any snow. I can't wait until my first winter here in Connecticut. I think snow is beautiful."

"Yeah, unless you have to shovel the driveway," Meredith joked, and they all laughed. Lindsey knew Susannah would never have to shovel her driveway. One reason Lindsey wanted to be a Hollywood star when she grew up was so she'd never have to shovel the driveway—or collect the garbage or rake leaves or do any of those other tedious chores—again. She would be as gracious as Susannah was with her fans, but she'd expect them to adore her. It would be like the way Amanda and Meredith were her friends but also were kind of in awe of her at the moment—only multiplied by millions. That was what Lindsey wanted.

"I'm going to go to California someday," Lindsey announced. She didn't add that she was going to become a star like Susannah. Things were going so well Lindsey didn't want to wreck them by saying something wrong.

The kitchen began to smell from the cookies—a rich, warm fragrance that made her stomach growl with hunger. MacKenzie must have noticed the smell, because he stirred from his sunny spot and wandered over to the table. He leaped onto Susannah's lap and sniffed the air, turning his head left and right as if was trying to figure out where the aroma was coming from.

When Lindsey became a star, she was going to get a cat like MacKenzie, too. And she'd bake chocolate-chip cookies and let him eat a few.

The first batch was done. Meredith pulled the sheets out of the oven while Lindsey got a couple of plates and a spatula. The cookies were soft and steamy and kind of weird-shaped—not one of them was a perfect circle—but they smelled even better out of the oven than in it. MacKenzie stretched toward the table as Meredith and Amanda moved the cookies onto the plates to cool, but Susannah held him tightly so he couldn't jump off her lap.

Amanda's mother arrived just minutes after they slid the second batch into the oven. She remained in her minivan, beeping the horn, and Lindsey was glad. She

didn't want Amanda's mother to come in and meet
Susannah. The more people who met Susannah, the
less special meeting her would be. She'd actually turn
into a regular Arlington resident, and then Amanda and
Meredith wouldn't think Lindsey was so important
anymore.

Lindsey wrapped some of the cookies in foil for
Amanda and Meredith to take with them and walked
them to the door. She was glad when they were gone.
Having Susannah all to herself meant maybe she could
find out some more about Susannah's family in California.

Susannah was pulling the second batch of cookies
from the oven when Lindsey got back to the kitchen.
She set the two sheets on the stove top and shut the
oven door. "That's it," she said with a grin. "You've
just seen the extent of my culinary ability. I can take
things out of an oven."

Lindsey smiled. Susannah was treating her like a pal,
someone to share jokes with. Lindsey liked that.

She sat at the table and Susannah resumed her seat
across from Lindsey. They each helped themselves to
a cookie from the first batch. "You want some milk?"
Lindsey asked. Chocolate-chip cookies tasted much
better with milk.

"No, thanks."

If Susannah wasn't going to have milk, Lindsey
wouldn't have any, either. She bit into her cookie. It
might not have looked perfect, but it tasted great, warm
and soft with the chips practically liquid.

"Your friends are nice," Susannah commented
lightly.

"Yeah."

"The blond one—Meredith?" Lindsey nodded, and

Susannah continued. "She looks a little older. Is she a fifth-grader, too?"

"Yeah. She turned eleven in January. Amanda's older than me, too, but she's so skinny she looks younger."

"Girls your age change a lot," Susannah remarked, her tone still light and casual, although Lindsey sensed a serious intent behind her words. She remained silent, and Susannah went on. "You're all hitting puberty. I guess they've talked to you about that in school, haven't they?"

Lindsey licked the melted chocolate from her lips. "In health class," she said. "Daddy talked to me about it, also."

"I think he's a little worried that you might prefer to talk to a woman about it," Susannah said, and Lindsey understood then what her intention was. Dr. Dad must have asked her to speak to Lindsey about this stuff. The idea didn't exactly bother Lindsey, but it was sort of weird, his going to Susannah about it. She would have thought that if they were on a date or something, they'd discuss more romantic things than Lindsey's puberty.

Then again, their date hadn't been romantic. Susannah's romance was waiting for her back in California. "So my dad wants you to speak to me?" she asked.

"Actually—" Susannah leaned forward, as though she was going to confide a deep, dark secret to Lindsey "—he wants me to ask you if you need tampons."

Lindsey was so startled she laughed. Susannah laughed, too. And then Lindsey laughed again, less in surprise than in what could only be called sisterhood. Poor Dad! He was just a guy. Guys couldn't handle things like tampons, could they? They just didn't have what it took.

"I don't," she said, still giggling.

"Well, when you do, if you can't tell your father, you can tell me," Susannah assured her.

This was interesting. Lindsey helped herself to another cookie and nibbled it slowly, giving herself time to think. If Dr. Dad was asking Susannah to speak to her about puberty, did that mean he wanted Susannah to act kind of like a role model or something? Having Susannah as a role model suited Lindsey fine, so far as Lindsey wanting to be a star when she grew up. But this other stuff, tampons and all...that was more like what you'd talk about with your mother.

Did Lindsey's father want her to think of Susannah as a mother?

If he did, did that mean he was planning to keep dating her, to build a real relationship with her?

But what about Stephen Yates and the baby? Lindsey had to know. She couldn't come right out and ask, though. She couldn't just say, "So, that pregnancy of yours the magazine wrote about last summer—what's the deal with that?"

She had to find a subtler way to approach the subject. "What's it like, having magazine articles written about you?" she asked.

Susannah sat back in her chair and eyed Lindsey. She obviously hadn't been expecting the change of topic. "Fame looks like more fun than it is," she finally answered. "If I'd done something worthwhile, I wouldn't have minded having magazine articles written about me. But being written about just because of who I was, rather than what I'd done, was annoying."

"You did do worthwhile things. You starred in the best show on TV. That's worthwhile."

Susannah snorted.

Lindsey knew what Susannah meant. The article in Amanda's sister's magazine was basically about who Susannah was dating and not important stuff like her acting. The article was really kind of pointless. Who Susannah was dating and whether she was expecting shouldn't have been anyone's business but hers.

But it was everyone's business now, because the magazine had published that story. "Do magazines ever lie about you?" she asked.

Susannah shrugged. "I never read articles about me. But there were people at the production company who oversaw the publicity I got. I'm sure if any of the magazine articles had included serious lies, they would have told me."

"I mean...'cause I read an article about you that was in a magazine last summer. And I didn't know if it was true or not."

"What did it say?"

Lindsey suddenly felt like a snoop, poking around in Susannah's private life. She had the right to protect her father, but did she have the right to question Susannah about her love life back in California? "I dunno," she mumbled. "It said you were dating the guy who played Lucien Roche on *Mercy Hospital*."

"I did date him," Susannah admitted.

Then the article was true. Which meant Susannah had a child. "Do you still date him now?" Lindsey asked.

Susannah smiled. "Well, I'm here and he's there. So it would be kind of hard to date him."

In other words, Lindsey thought, if Susannah *wasn't*

here and Stephen Yates *wasn't* there, they'd still be dating. Which meant she shouldn't be dating Dr. Dad.

She heard a rattle coming from the mudroom. MacKenzie must have heard it, as well, because he leaped down from Susannah's lap and started toward the mudroom door. When it opened, he froze, staring at Lindsey's father, who stood in the doorway, his briefcase in one hand and his jacket in the other. "Hello," he said, clearly surprised to find Susannah at the table with Lindsey.

"We baked cookies," Lindsey told him, as if that explained why Susannah was there.

"Lindsey and her friends baked them," Susannah corrected her. "All I did was wipe up the spills."

"She did more than that," Lindsey argued. "And the cookies are really good, even though they look kind of funny. Have one."

Her father exchanged a gaze with Susannah before smiling at Lindsey. "We're going to be eating supper soon, but…" He swiped a cookie from the plate. "One cookie won't spoil my appetite. And they don't look funny," he added before biting into it. "Mmm. Delicious."

"Well, I guess I should be on my way." Susannah pushed away from the table and bent over to lift MacKenzie. When she straightened, she and Lindsey's father exchanged another glance. Lindsey wondered what they were trying to tell each other. Something private, something between just the two of them. Lindsey hoped it wasn't about dating, because Susannah's answers assured her that her father shouldn't be viewing Susannah as a woman to date.

"I'd ask you to stay for dinner, but I've got a class tonight," Lindsey's father said.

"Daddy School?" Susannah smiled. Lindsey tried not to frown. If Susannah knew where Dr. Dad was going at night, they were too close. "That's all right. I've got things to do, anyway."

"It was nice of you to stay with the girls," he said, tossing his jacket onto one of the chairs. "Did your friends have a good time?" he asked Lindsey.

Nice of him to even notice she was there, she thought sullenly. "Yeah."

His attention lingered on her, and his so-happy-to-see-Susannah smile faltered. He must have sensed that she was getting grouchy. Great. He'd probably lecture her about her attitude all through supper. He might even ask her how school went, and she'd have to tell him about Mrs. Hathaway throwing a fit over her wrinkled math homework.

He turned from her and walked Susannah to the door. Lindsey heard their muted voices drifting down the hall, but she couldn't make out the words. Like she cared. Let Dr. Dad make a fool of himself over Susannah. Lindsey wouldn't interfere. No way. She'd just back off and let him make a total ass of himself.

He returned to the kitchen alone. He studied her for a minute as he loosened his tie. Then he gave her a crooked smile. "So, how was your day?"

This must be something he learned at the Daddy School—to be nice to your kid even when you and the kid were on the verge of a blowup. He knew Lindsey well enough to sense when something was bugging her, and before he'd started the Daddy School classes he would have made her tell him what it was. And they would have had a big fight, or he would have given her a hard time for being in a mood. Now, when she was in a mood, he let it go. He smiled at her and kept his distance.

Maybe the change had nothing to do with the Daddy School. Maybe he just didn't care about her moods anymore. Maybe he was so focused on Susannah Lindsey didn't matter to him.

Susannah was *her* friend, though. He thought she was his friend, but she could do a serious number on him. She couldn't hurt Lindsey, because Lindsey understood what it meant to be a high-flying TV star who didn't live the way normal people did.

"My day was fine," she muttered, reaching for another cookie.

"Why don't you save that till after dinner," he suggested, sweeping the plate off the table before she could grab a cookie. "I'm going to cook up some burgers."

They always had burgers on the nights he had Daddy School. Burgers were quick and easy.

She didn't care. She'd rather just eat chocolate-chip cookies, or nothing at all.

She sat at the table, moping while he slapped the burgers into a pan, slid the rolls into the toaster oven and sliced up a tomato and a pickle. The meat sizzled, overtaking the aroma of the cookies. She could have helped her father, but she was too glum to do anything more than pluck two napkins from the dispenser on the table and fold them.

He put a plate in front of her and then circled the table to sit facing her. "How was school?" he asked.

"Okay," she mumbled before taking a bite of her burger.

"All right, I give up." He forced another crooked smile. "What's bothering you?"

Did he really want to know? Fine. She'd tell him. "I don't think you should date Susannah."

He made a face that she interpreted to mean, *Fair enough. I'll hear you out.* "It's not as if I'm actually dating her," he claimed, "but for the sake of argument, why don't you think I should?"

As reasonable as he sounded, she believed he was mocking her. "You like her a lot, don't you?"

"Yes, I do. Don't you?"

"It's different. I like her like this really cool lady who's kind of a special friend. You like her like a man liking a woman."

He couldn't deny that. "All right. That's how I like her."

"Well, she's got a boyfriend back in Hollywood."

He narrowed his eyes on her. "How do you know that?"

"It was in a magazine, with a lot of other stuff about her. She and Stephen Yates are like this big, heavy couple."

"She told me about him," he said. "They used to be a couple, but they aren't anymore."

"Maybe that's what she told you, but the magazine…" She set down her burger. She'd thought it would be easy to tell Dr. Dad because she was angry with him, but the more she considered it, the more she realized she *wasn't* angry. She wanted to be angry, but she couldn't be. Not when she knew he was going to get hurt.

"What about the magazine?"

"It said she was pregnant."

That got his attention. He put down his burger, too, and scowled. "What magazine was this?"

"It came out last summer. So she was pregnant then,

which means she would have had the baby by now. And Stephen Yates is the father. I asked her, and she said it was true.''

''That she had a baby?''

''She didn't exactly say that, but she said the magazine didn't lie.''

He drew in a deep breath and let it out slowly. He was upset. Really upset. Lindsey hoped it wasn't with her for having told him about the magazine article. But someone had had to tell him before he got in too deep with Susannah. Someone had had to open his eyes.

''I don't think she has a baby,'' he said slowly. ''She's told me she wants to have children.''

''Well, she's got a child back in California. I'm guessing the baby's with Stephen Yates, since he's the father.''

''And you think she just left that baby behind and moved here?'' He shook his head. ''I don't believe it. She wouldn't do something like that.''

''But she said the magazine told the truth. And the magazine said she was pregnant. 'Expecting,' it said, and that she and Stephen Yates were going to get married and have the baby.''

''I'll talk to her about it,'' he said carefully. He lifted his burger and took a bite, but she could tell his heart wasn't in it. Chewing seemed to be a struggle for him. He stared past Lindsey as if he could see his thoughts in the air around her, like a silent movie.

Lindsey felt bad for him. He'd had enough sadness in his life when her mother had died. He didn't deserve more. ''It's just that you don't know her really well,'' she said sympathetically. She wished she hadn't had to break the news to him, but telling him was better than not telling him. He would have been much sadder if he'd found out later, after he was madly in love with Susannah.

"I'll talk to her," he said again, managing one more bite before he put his burger down for good.

She didn't have much appetite, either. Since he'd cooked dinner, she rose and cleared the table while he continued to stare into space. "You want a cookie?" she asked.

"No, thanks." He got up from his chair, crossed to the sink where she was standing and wrapped her in a hug. She was surprised. He hadn't hugged her in a while, and it felt good. "Thank you for telling me," he said, his chin resting on her head and bouncing against her skull with each word. "I'm sure there's an explanation. I'll work things out with her."

"I just—I don't want you falling in love with her, Daddy," Lindsey explained. Even though he'd been wearing his shirt all day, it smelled fresh, like him. Clean and fresh and safe. She'd really missed hugging him.

"Why not?"

"She's not right for you," Lindsey said. "She's a star. You don't understand about stars, Daddy. They're different."

"You're the only star I care about," he murmured. "Susannah isn't a star anymore. And I'm not in love with her. Okay?"

She was reassured. "Okay."

"Do you want me to skip class tonight? I'll stay home if you want me to," he said, loosening his hold on her.

"No, that's all right. I've got homework to do, anyway." She didn't want to do her homework, but she figured saying it would cheer him up.

It did. He stepped back and gave her a real, full-fledged smile. "Okay, Hot Stuff. You do your homework and I'll go to class. And don't worry about Susannah."

"I'm not worried about her. She's cool. She's terrific. She's just..." *More than you can handle,* Lindsey wanted to say. "She's different."

"Yeah," he said, and Lindsey was sure he didn't mean it the way she did. "Susannah is different."

CHAPTER THIRTEEN

MOLLY SAUNDERS-RUSSO was leading a discussion on setting limits for children. Toby absently noted her warm voice, her dark, blunt-cut hair, the expanding roundness of her abdomen. He ought to have been paying close attention to her words, but they drifted past him, a string of indecipherable syllables and sounds.

How could he concentrate on Molly's lecture after Lindsey had told him Susannah had a child?

He knew Lindsey lied, but only when she had to, when her own neck was on the block. There was nothing sophisticated about her dishonesty, nothing subversive in it. She lied to stay out of trouble or to avoid having to do something she didn't want to do.

She wouldn't lie about something like Susannah's pregnancy being written about in a magazine a year ago.

The Daddy School class blurred out of focus as he dug through his memory, searching for evidence that such a thing might be true. Susannah had said she wanted to be a mother. Why would she have abandoned her child if she wanted to be a mother?

And another thing: why had he told Lindsey he wasn't in love with Susannah? He was pretty sure that statement wasn't true—but he didn't know whether it would still be true tomorrow, or the next day. Until an hour ago, he wouldn't have been surprised to find himself in love with her. But Lindsey had said he didn't understand the way it was with stars, and maybe she was right. Maybe he was clueless when it came to a whole hell of a lot about Susannah.

Nor did he understand why Lindsey didn't want him to fall in love with Susannah. She adored Susannah. He would have thought she'd be thrilled that her father was in a relationship with an actress she idolized.

None of it made sense. Not Lindsey's concerns, not his own jumbled feelings, not the baby. Certainly not the baby.

"So, I want you to try some of these techniques with your kids and see what works," Molly said. "Remember, every child is unique. What's effective with one child might bomb with another. Be creative and flexible. Any questions?"

Toby glanced at his watch. He couldn't believe he'd sat in the small community room at the YMCA for a full hour without having absorbed a single word Molly said. Fortunately, setting limits was not a big problem for him with Lindsey. She presented her share of challenges, but she didn't break many rules.

His classmates were rising to their feet, talking among themselves. Molly conferred with one of them privately. Good, Toby thought—she wasn't going to grill him about having zoned out during class.

He'd nearly reached the door when his luck failed. "Toby?" she called to him.

For a moment, he felt a keen empathy for Lindsey, who was chronically being singled out by her teacher for her lapses and shortcomings. Of course, he liked Molly a lot more than Lindsey liked Ms. Hathaway. And he did want to do well in Daddy School. He regretted having been distracted during tonight's class.

Maybe Lindsey regretted being distracted in class. Maybe the reason she couldn't do better in school was that she was too preoccupied with other things in her life—the absence of her mother, compounded by the loss of her best friend, augmented by the physical changes she was undergoing.

"Are you going to give me detention?" he asked Molly, smiling sheepishly.

She smiled back. "I worry about you, Toby. You always seem to have so much on your mind."

"And it isn't my class work," he admitted. "I'm sorry. It's no reflection on you. Your lectures are wonderful."

Her smile evolved into a laugh. "They're not wonderful. I'd like to think they're useful, but wonderful?" Her laugher waned. "Is it your daughter, Toby? Does she have you worried?"

"My daughter is fine," he said. "It's me. My life has gotten a little too complicated all of a sudden."

"Complications can be fun," she assured him. "Dive in and see what happens."

That sounded a lot more foolhardy than Toby could afford to be. If he were single, with no dependents, he'd be a lot more reckless. But he was a father—and a mother—to Lindsey, a homeowner, a professional. Complications were the last thing he needed.

He gazed down at the petite teacher, who was still smiling encouragingly as she rubbed her hand over her swollen belly. "How are you feeling?" he asked.

"Tired. Unfortunately, my baby is never tired. It's constantly moving."

"That's a sign of good health," he said. "Take it easy. And make sure you're eating a sensible, well-rounded diet."

"Yes, Dr. Cole," she teased. "You seem to forget, I'm Allison Winslow's best friend. She nags me all the time."

"I'll leave you in her hands, then. She's very good at nagging." With a grin, he turned back to the door.

"You take care of yourself, too," Molly called after him.

He left the YMCA building, strolled around to the parking lot in back and climbed into his car. Molly's parting words haunted him. She instructed all the other fathers in the class to take care of their children, but not him. Did she think he cared about Lindsey at his own expense? Or did she simply sense the restlessness in him, that deeply buried ache of loneliness? Did she recognize that he wanted more?

He reached his street at a quarter to nine. The block was quiet, the trees dense with leaves and the moon as round and silver as a new dime glued to the sky. He noticed the den and living-room lights still on in his house. Lindsey wouldn't be getting ready for bed for at least a half hour. He wondered if she'd finished her homework, or if she'd spent the entire evening planted in front of the television, watching a videotape of last week's episode of *Mercy Hospital*.

It was early. He was edgy. The only way he would ever find out the truth about Susannah's alleged pregnancy was if he asked her himself. And the only way he would know whether he loved her was if he found out the truth.

He pulled into her driveway, crossed the lawn to the porch, climbed the steps and rang the bell. The air was scented with the fresh smells of grass and the flowers drizzling down from the hanging porch basket. He

waited a minute, rang again, and then the door swung
open.

Seeing her made him want to believe everything
good about her and nothing bad. Her face was open,
as sweet as the night air, and radiant with delight at
the mere sight of him. God, yes, he could love this
woman...but only if Lindsey was wrong about her.

"Do you have a minute?" he asked.

"Sure. Come in." She stepped back, welcoming him
into her house. "Would you like something to drink?
I've got an open bottle of Chablis."

"No, thanks." He headed for the living room. The
lamps were on, the drapes pulled back and the windows open to let in the cool evening breeze. That
morning's copy of the *Arlington Gazette* lay scattered
across the coffee table. The cat sat on the brick hearth
of the fireplace, meticulously grooming himself.

Susannah followed Toby into the living room. If she
was aware of his tension, she didn't show it. Her hair
fell loose down her back, her shirt hung untucked from
her jeans and she was barefoot. She looked utterly
comfortable and relaxed.

"I need to ask you something," he said bluntly. He
wasn't good at smooth talk or easing into a difficult
conversation. He could be diplomatic, he could be optimistic, but he couldn't edge in sideways.

Susannah gazed at him expectantly.

"Do you have a child?"

She blinked, and her smile vanished. Her face lost
its glow; the color drained from her cheeks. "No," she
said, turning from him and stalking to the side window,
where the breeze was strongest.

"I'm sorry I'm asking. You probably think this is
none of my business."

"I don't know whose business it's none of," she said, her voice uncharacteristically cold. "I don't have a child."

"Lindsey told me about a magazine article from last summer. She said the article claimed you were expecting." He watched her. He didn't like playing the part of interrogator, but he had to know. His question had obviously touched a nerve, which convinced him Susannah had an answer. "Lindsey also told me you said magazines didn't lie about you, or something like that. Maybe she got it wrong—"

"She didn't get it wrong," Susannah said wearily. "The magazine didn't lie. Last summer I was expecting. But I miscarried. I lost the baby."

That made much more sense than her having left a baby behind when she moved from California to Connecticut. "I'm sorry," he said—sorry for her loss, and sorry for having grilled her this way. Perhaps sorry, as well, that he'd experienced a twinge of relief at the news that she hadn't concealed a baby from him.

"I wanted the baby." She addressed the window more than him. Some emotion crept back into her voice. "I wanted it so much, Toby. I thought that at last I'd have a normal life. I could be a mother, and this baby would love me for myself, not because I was famous or making a lot of money. It would love me just because I was its mother and I loved it."

"I'm sorry," he said again, this time because of her pain.

"I was so thrilled when I became pregnant. It was the happiest day of my life. It hadn't been planned, but I didn't care. I was ecstatic."

He wished he could think of something to say besides "I'm sorry." He was a doctor, and he knew about miscarriages. But he'd never experienced one. He was only a man. The science of medicine couldn't define a woman's sorrow.

"Stephen had told me to get an abortion," she said.

Toby crossed the room to her. Her voice had changed from sad to bitter, and he wanted to be closer to her, in case she fell apart.

"He said we weren't ready to have a baby yet, and it would screw up my career, and my career was so damned important, the most important thing about me. My father said the same thing. He said if I had the baby I'd want to take time off from work, and my career would go down the toilet. It wasn't as if I was some top-dollar marquee name, he said. I couldn't afford to take a break right now, while I was still on the rise. They both told me to get rid of the baby."

"But you didn't," Toby said, reminding her that she'd stood up to all the pressure her supposed loved ones had placed on her. She hadn't given in to them.

"No. Mother Nature took care of it. That was the worst," she said, her voice cracking. "I miscarried, and they were so happy. They were celebrating, because their problem was solved."

He understood now—understood why she'd left California, why she'd turned her back on that life, on her acting, on everything that had defined her world for so many years. "So you moved to Arlington," he concluded.

"As soon as I could. I fulfilled my contract and then quit. I—" Her voice crumbled a little more. "I wanted that baby so much, Toby...."

A low sob escaped her, and he took her in his arms. She wept against his shoulder, her body trembling in his embrace, her tears soaking through his shirt. He held her tight, absorbing her grief, wishing he could do something to erase the hurting parts of her past. Doctors could heal only so much. He couldn't heal Susannah's anguish.

After a minute she sniffled and pulled back. "I have no right to be crying like this," she apologized. "You've lost so much more than me. You must think I'm such a wimp. All I lost was the promise of something—"

"You lost much more than a pregnancy," he told her. "You lost your faith in the people you loved. That must have been agonizing."

She sniffled again, and brushed her fingertips against her tear-stained cheeks. He pulled a handkerchief from his trouser pocket and handed it to her. She studied it as if it were a precious gift, then patted it against her face. "Thank you."

"No problem."

"No—not just for the handkerchief but for putting up with me."

"Putting up with you?" He laughed. Did she think taking her in his arms was such an ordeal?

"Well..." Her voice sounded watery, and she dabbed the handkerchief to her eyes again. "You spend your working life taking care of your patients, then you come home and take of your daughter. And here you are, taking care of me as if I were another helpless little child."

"You're not a helpless little child," he murmured, using his thumb to catch a tear that had escaped her and skittered down her cheek. "You're a woman, Susannah. A woman strong enough to walk away from the life that made you miserable." He dropped his hand back to her waist, not wanting to let go of her.

"I'm not taking care of you. I'm just letting you borrow a handkerchief."

She gave him a lopsided smile, wiped her cheeks one last time and returned the square of linen to him.

"I take care of my patients because it's my job," he explained. "I take care of Lindsey because she's my daughter. I'm not taking care of you."

"Yes, you are." She sighed and lowered her eyes. "And it scares me, Toby. I want to take care of myself, but there are times…" She sighed again and lifted her gaze back to him. "There are times I need you. I don't want to, but I do." Her eyes looked bluer than ever, their color magnified by the sheen of moisture. "When I cried in California, I needed to be held. But no one held me."

"I'll hold you," he vowed. "Whenever you need to be held, I'm here."

She stared into his face, searching. "You're the best thing that's ever happened to me." Her voice was hoarse from crying, low but certain.

He gazed down into her eyes and saw only honesty, trust, a mixture of generosity and yearning and need that felt an awful lot like love. And he realized that if ever Susannah needed anything, he wanted to be the one she turned to, the one who gave it to her.

He lowered his mouth to hers.

Her lips were salty from her tears. They were soft yet firm, accepting his kiss, welcoming it. Before he could catch a breath she opened to him, and then he didn't want to breathe anymore. He wanted only to take her.

His tongue slid deep, needing her as much as she needed him. She parried each eager thrust, reaching up to hold his head steady, threading her fingers into his hair. She tasted hot and rich and wild, and alive. Unbearably alive.

The kiss so intoxicated him that he wasn't at first aware of her hands moving through his hair, around to his neck, forward over his shoulders. Only when she reached the buttons at the front of his shirt and plucked the first one open did he break from her. "Susannah…"

"Yes."

"You said you wanted to go slow."

"Not anymore."

He wanted her, wanted her the way a dying man wanted one more breath. But he didn't want her like this, when she was emotionally overloaded, when she still had tearstains on her cheeks, when she was seeking comfort more than passion. "I don't think—"

"Make love to me, Toby," she whispered, and his protest died in his throat. Maybe the timing could have been better, the context, the circumstances. But he didn't care. She wanted him to make love to her, and he couldn't say no.

He brought his mouth down to hers again, in joy and resignation, in acknowledgment that he needed this, needed her, needed to be held at least as much as she did. As her tongue tangled with his, her hands slid down the front of his shirt, opening the buttons and pushing back the cloth. Her fingers were cool against his skin. He felt as if he were burning up inside, and he was grateful when she skimmed her hands up to his shoulders and shoved the shirt off him.

But the light friction of her palms against his chest only made him hotter. The gentle scrape of her fingernails along his sides sent his temperature soaring.

He raised his hands to the buttons of her shirt. It was

a man-tailored shirt, almost identical in styling to his, and he could unbutton it blind. But his hands froze when she pressed her lips to his sternum. He groaned— a soft, desperate sound in the quiet house. She grazed across his chest to his shoulder and his hands fisted around the fabric of her blouse.

"Susannah…"

She lifted her face and he had to kiss her again, had to take those full, rosy lips with his. Just once, though. His rationality was battling not to go up in smoke along with his willpower.

He pulled back from her and inhaled sharply, ordering his mind to remain clear. "I don't have anything with me. We can't—"

"I have protection," she whispered. "Upstairs." She ducked her head shyly and added, "I bought it after I met you."

The implied compliment touched him—and the knowledge that there was nothing left to stop them caused him to surrender—to her, to himself, to his heart and his soul and the fire raging inside him.

Her shirt gaped as she stepped back and slid her hand into his. One glimpse of the cream-colored lace cupping the swells of her breasts and he had to summon all his self-control to keep from dragging her onto the floor and making love to her right there. He felt like the starving survivor of a tragedy—and maybe he was one. He'd been without sex a long time, without a woman's love a lot longer.

Her hand felt small and delicate in his, but he couldn't deny its power as she led him through the living room to the stairs and up. He remembered his first time in her bedroom, when he'd stared longingly at her bed and entertained the remote fantasy of making love to her there. When they reached the doorway and he once again saw the broad brass bed, heaped with pillows and blanketed with its plush beige quilt, he realized that the bed didn't do a thing for him. It was only the thought of Susannah sprawled out across the bed that turned him on.

She clicked the lamp to a low setting, then drew him to her. Her hands roamed over his back while he slid his under the loose tails of her shirt and touched her skin. It felt like silk, smooth and sleek. He wanted to kiss it, to kiss her everywhere, to know if she tasted as heavenly as she felt.

He brought his hands forward to finish unbuttoning her shirt. She writhed out of it and let it drop to the floor. Her breasts were full and round, straining against her bra. He flicked open the clasp and drew the straps down her arms.

She was beautiful. Not TV-star beautiful but real and solid and robust. For a brief, shameful moment he thought about the only other woman he'd ever loved, a woman whose final days had left her frail and wasted. Having known illness too intimately, he couldn't keep from responding to Susannah's strength, the healthy flush of her skin as he skimmed his hands up to her breasts, the stiffening of her nipples as he brushed his thumbs over them. Her vitality aroused him as much as her beauty.

She moaned as he caressed her, and moaned again when he lowered his mouth to one breast, moving his lips over the warm, pliant flesh and then flicking his tongue over the hardened tip. She settled back across the bed, bringing him with her. He was surrounded by her, his hands caught in her hair, her left leg wrapped around his right.

He freed himself so he could remove her jeans and his slacks. As beautiful as he'd found her just minutes ago, she was even more magnificent stripped naked, her body slim yet well muscled, softly curving in some places and taut in others. He explored the taut places and the curves, trailing his hands over her thighs, her bottom, the flat surface of her belly, the exotic boniness of her shoulders.

She explored him just as eagerly, her hands and lips electrifying him wherever they touched. She stroked his back, his chest, tugged teasingly on the hair of his thighs and followed the ridge of his hipbone. When at last she ran her hand experimentally along his erection, he bit his lip and held his breath. One more caress like that and he would explode.

He leaned away from her, fighting for self-control, and rolled onto his side. He slid his hand between her thighs and played his fingers over the damp folds. She was as ready for him as he was for her, but she sighed and arched to him and he couldn't stop touching her. Her skin was tawny in the dim lamplight, her breath shallow, her hair a spill of gold across the pillows. He entered her with his finger, and she cried out, her eyes closed and her hand squeezing his arm.

He waited until she started breathing again, until her eyes fluttered open and an abashed smile curved her lips. "Oh, Toby," she said, more a sigh than a sound.

"Where are the condoms?" he asked, tension mixing with pleasure at the sight of her dazed smile.

"Oh…" She gestured vaguely toward the night table beside the bed.

He reached over her, opened the drawer and found the box, still sealed in plastic. He tore it open, readied himself and then sank into her arms, into her heat.

If ever they were going to go slow, he thought, this would be the time. He wanted to savor each instant, each heartbeat of it. But she brought her hands to his hips and urged him deeper, and his restraint slipped away. She felt too good, too right. Need and want and love fused inside him, turning into something physical, something fierce and demanding and implacable.

He surged into her again and again, hard and fast. She stayed with him, wrapping her legs around his waist, twining her fingers into his hair. Her hips rose to meet each thrust and he felt her strain beneath him, flexing, reaching.

She let out another cry, soft and helpless, and her body contracted around him. He let go, releasing himself in a rush so powerful it exhausted and rejuvenated him at the same time.

An endless moment passed, and his lungs begged for air. He barely had the energy to breathe, but once he managed that, he found the strength to roll off her, keeping his arms around her so when he landed on his back she wound up on top of him. She was surprisingly light, her skin smooth and damp, her hair splaying across his shoulder and chest.

After another long moment, she stirred against him. She traced a meandering line across his chest with her index finger, and it was enough to turn him on all over again. If he made love to her a second time, maybe he could slow it down, take his time, make it last.

But he couldn't make love to her again. He wasn't sure what time it was, but Lindsey was home alone, waiting for him. "I wish I could stay," he murmured, hating himself for resenting his daughter.

Her fingers fell still, then came back to life, journeying across his shoulder and down his arm to capture his hand. He closed it tightly around hers, and lifted their twined hands to his mouth so he could kiss her fingertips.

"Toby." She propped herself up high enough to look at him. He couldn't read her expression—wistful? Replete? Disappointed? Sympathetic? Enormously frustrated?

He was frustrated, too. But he was a father. "It's Lindsey," he explained. "She's probably wondering where I am right now."

"Would it upset her if you were here?"

"I don't know." He absorbed the contours of her hand within his. He didn't want to let go. "It doesn't matter. I've got to go home."

"Maybe I could come with you," she suggested.

He shook his head. It was a Wednesday night. Lindsey was right now stuffing her homework into her backpack, waiting for him to return from Daddy School. Maybe she'd noticed the time and started wondering why he was late. If he walked in with Susannah, who knew how Lindsey would react?

He wasn't ready to find out. Not yet. "I've got to go alone."

She turned away. "Fine."

He'd hurt her feelings, choosing his daughter over her. But it wasn't a choice; it was an obligation. And he loved Lindsey, would love her no matter what, would always love her. With Susannah, love was new, exciting—but unpredictable. He didn't know what was going to happen next.

She was right: they should have gone slow. At least until Toby could prepare Lindsey for what was blossoming between him and their next-door neighbor.

He allowed himself one last, lingering kiss before

he pushed himself up to sit. Stupidly, he glanced at Susannah as he swung his legs over the side of the bed, and it was all he could do not to turn around, to gather her into his arms and put Lindsey out of his mind for another few minutes.

He was a father, though. And he had to leave.

SHE'D BEEN DIDDLING around with her homework in front of the TV when she'd heard her father's car cruising up the street. She'd turned the volume down way low so she could listen for him. As soon as he pulled into the garage, she would turn off the TV and move her homework into the kitchen, so she'd look as though she'd really been concentrating hard on it.

But she didn't hear him pull into the garage. She raced across the hall to his office and peered out the window. He had parked in Susannah's driveway.

He must have gone to her house to have it out with her, to tell her to go back to Stephen Yates and her baby in California. Dr. Dad was into parental responsibility in a major way. He had patients whose parents didn't take good care of them, and it ate at him. He was always telling Lindsey how important it was for parents to give as much love and attention as they could to their children.

She saw him standing on Susannah's front porch, ringing the bell. She couldn't really see *him*—she saw just his shadow. She needed the binoculars.

She hurried up the stairs to her bedroom, grabbed the binoculars and climbed onto her bed. Her father must have gone into Susannah's house, because there was no one on the porch anymore. The light was on in Susannah's living room, and Lindsey saw Susannah

standing by the window on the side of the house facing
her bedroom.

With the binoculars, Lindsey could see Susannah really clearly. Her face was kind of downcast, and she
was dressed in an old, baggy, man-tailored shirt. She
looked to be staring out through the window at the
hedge separating their properties.

Dr. Dad must be talking to her, Lindsey thought. He
must be telling Susannah he knew about her baby.
Maybe he was telling her he understood that famous
stars did things differently from normal people, and he
wasn't standing in judgment of her. But he knew they
could never be anything but neighbors and friends, because even though he understood about famous stars,
he didn't think it was a good idea to date someone so
completely different from him.

He joined Susannah at the window—two silhouettes
with the light behind them. They were facing each
other; Lindsey could see their profiles, their noses and
chins pointing at each other. Her father put his arms
around Susannah, and she buried her face against him.

Was she crying? Surely she wouldn't fall apart just
because Dr. Dad had told her he wasn't going to date
her anymore. Heck, he hadn't even taken her to a
classy restaurant Saturday night. She'd be better off
dating a guy who knew how to treat a star the way she
was used to being treated. She ought to be relieved
that Lindsey's father wasn't going to get all mushy and
romantic about her.

Then she lifted her face. Apparently, she was done
bawling her eyes out. They were talking again—Lindsey wished she could hear them, but she couldn't. She
could only see them through the binoculars.

Dr. Dad bent his head. He kissed Susannah.

Lindsey gasped. She knew she shouldn't watch this. She should put the binoculars away, close her curtains and forget she'd ever seen her father kiss Susannah Dawson. But she couldn't turn her head, couldn't lower the binoculars. She knelt on her bed, transfixed and horrified as Susannah twined her arms around Lindsey's father and locked lips with him.

It was a long kiss. A very long kiss. Longer than the kisses Dr. Lee Davis used to share with Lucien Roche on *Mercy Hospital*. This kiss was big, massive, epic. It was sickening.

And then Lindsey saw Susannah's arms moving. She couldn't tell exactly what Susannah was doing at first... Oh, God. She was taking off his shirt. Opening it, shoving it back from his shoulders, kissing his naked chest.

Lindsey felt queasy. She should have stopped watching before, but she hadn't, and now it was too late. She wanted to scream, or throw up, or break the damned binoculars. She wanted to charge across the lawn to Susannah's house, storm through the open window and yell at them to stop.

But they weren't going to stop. In the last instant, before she hurled the binoculars down onto the mattress, she glimpsed her father's face. She could barely make out his features, but what she saw was scary. He looked changed. He looked sad and happy at once, angry and pleased, tired and full of energy. He looked like a man she hardly knew.

Susannah was taking him away from Lindsey. She was transforming him, turning him into a strange creature, someone who couldn't even stop and tell her she was a bad mother to abandon her child. Susannah had sucked the soul right out of Dr. Dad, and he was never going to be the same.

Nothing was ever going to be the same.

CHAPTER FOURTEEN

SHE TRIED NOT TO think about him, but that was like trying not to breathe. Knowing he was right next door, a ten-second sprint away, both soothed and unsettled her. She liked having him near, but she wanted him nearer. She wanted him with her.

But that was not a simple matter, not when a ten-year-old girl was a part of the package.

He telephoned her several hours after leaving her bed—undoubtedly waiting until Lindsey was asleep before he called. "I wish I hadn't had to leave like that," he murmured.

Hearing his voice through a telephone receiver at 11:00 p.m. frustrated her—yet his concern for his daughter was one of the things she loved about him. He was a good father, a magnificent father. As much as she would have liked him to stay the night with her, she understood his need to leave.

"It's all right."

"I was thinking...maybe we could spend all day Saturday together. The three of us, I mean. I know Lindsey is crazy about you. I'm just not sure she's going to be crazy about *us*. If we had a whole day together, maybe she'd grow accustomed to the idea."

"If you feel that would help, okay."

"Lindsey has a soccer game in the afternoon. Afterward, we could all go out someplace for dinner and a movie.''

''Whatever you'd like.'' The plan sounded great. It was what ordinary families did, families where parents and children loved one another. It was what Susannah had imagined a real family would be like that first night she'd had dinner with Toby and Lindsey and envied their lives.

''I'll be dreaming about you,'' Toby whispered before hanging up.

She didn't dream at all that night. She was too restless to sleep, her body still tingling from him, her mind still reeling from how it had felt to make love with him. And her heart pounding the pulse of dread when she thought about how readily she'd agreed to do what she could to make the relationship palatable to Lindsey.

Once again, she was doing what other people needed. She'd made love with Toby. She'd rushed when she should have gone slow. She'd fallen headlong, and now she was eager to do whatever she could to make the relationship work.

It was what she'd done in California—tried to make things right for everyone else. It was what she'd promised herself she wouldn't do again. But Toby... Lord help her, she didn't want to go slow with him.

He phoned her again from work the next day. He told her he'd like to have her over for dinner, but Lindsey was in a really bad mood. ''I don't know what's bugging her,'' he said. ''I've never seen her this gloomy.''

''I don't think it's PMS,'' Susannah told him. Lindsey had only laughed when Susannah had asked her whether she needed tampons.

"Well, whatever it is, it's driving me crazy. I don't want to subject you to her when she's like this. I'll call you later."

He did, late that evening, after Lindsey's bedtime again. And Friday they talked again. But she didn't see him until Saturday.

When he opened his door to her that bright, sunny morning, she felt reborn. She hadn't realized how much she'd missed him until she was gazing into his dark, expressive eyes, until she could slide her hand into his and accept a discreet kiss on the cheek. His touch reawakened sensations that had never really fallen dormant inside her. The brush of his lips against her cheek made her want to press herself to him, kiss him for real, open her body and her heart to him.

She'd spent more time than usual choosing an outfit, as if she were extra eager to impress him. Maybe she was. She wanted him to see her and remember the night they'd spent together. She wanted him to take one look at her and realize that Lindsey's moods shouldn't determine what he and Susannah did.

Lindsey was in the kitchen, dressed in a soccer uniform of burgundy and black. She glanced up when Susannah entered, then muttered, "Hello," and busied herself strapping on her shin guards.

"There's time for a quick cup of coffee, if you'd like one," Toby offered.

"No, thanks." Susannah was disturbed by Lindsey's chilliness toward her. The last time she'd seen Lindsey—just hours before making love with Toby—they'd talked so easily together. They'd posed for photos and baked cookies. Now Lindsey wouldn't even glance at her.

"I'm looking forward to seeing you play," she said.

Lindsey grunted.

"It's a perfect day for a game. Sunny but not too hot."

Lindsey pulled dark-red knee socks up over her shin guards.

Susannah turned to Toby, who was standing behind Lindsey's chair. He shrugged and shook his head, as if to say, *Don't bother. Nothing you do will make a difference in her mood.*

They headed for the park where the game was to be played. Lindsey immediately abandoned Susannah and Toby for her teammates. Susannah felt a knot of pain in her chest, a sense of failure. She and Lindsey had gotten along so well until now. What had Susannah done wrong?

Toby touched the small of her back—a subtle, almost unnoticeable gesture that meant far too much to her. "Don't worry about it," he murmured. "It's not your fault."

"Whose fault is it?" She watched Lindsey line up with her teammates for warm-up drills. Lindsey dribbled the ball up toward the goal, then gave it a hard kick, trying to send it past the goalie and into the net. Her face was set in a frown of concentration. The mild breeze tugged at her dark hair, which was held back from her face in a ponytail.

"I don't know. I thought she'd be glad we were getting close," he said. Although Lindsey obviously took after his wife, Susannah saw a similarity between their frowns. The tight focus of his eyes, the angle of his chin, the taut line of his mouth mirrored her expression.

"Do you think it's because of her mother?" Susannah asked, remembering the photo she'd seen in

Toby's office. They'd been an ideal family once and that ideal had been destroyed, and now Susannah was trespassing in the wreckage.

"No. I honestly don't." He strummed his fingers against her waist, but he kept his eyes on Lindsey. "I've dated women before. It never threw her into a tailspin. I'm really stumped. I thought she was crazy about you."

"I think she idolizes me," Susannah pointed out. "That's not the same as liking me."

"I want her to be happy," he said. Such a simple wish, yet so enormous. His hand lingered on her for a moment longer, then fell. "The Daddy School teacher says I should worry less about making Lindsey happy and more about making myself happy. Do you think she's right?"

"Yes," Susannah said firmly. She might have answered that way because making himself happy would mean making her happy, too. But she also felt he, like her, needed to stop letting the demands of others determine his fate. He needed to figure out what he wanted and to go after it.

Of course, Lindsey was just a child—one who'd suffered a terrible loss. Yet why should Toby and Susannah's pursuing a relationship make her unhappy?

"If you're happy, she'll ultimately be happy," Susannah predicted. "And anyway, you're not going to change. You're always going to worry about her."

He chuckled. "That's true." Lindsey's team and the opposing team were arranging themselves in formation on the field. "Come on—the game's about to start." He took her hand and pulled her toward the field. A few people stared at her in recognition, but she didn't care. She was with Toby, and they were there to cheer their hearts out for Lindsey, whether or not she wanted them to. They were there for each other, but also for her.

LINDSEY'S MOOD didn't change throughout the rest of the day. Even though her team won their game, she seemed apathetic about the victory. After showering and donning regular shorts and a T-shirt, she insisted she didn't want to see any movies, or even go to the mall. She remained indoors while Toby and Susannah surveyed Susannah's backyard and debated whether she should resuscitate the bedraggled flower garden the Robinsons had planted in the southwest corner of the lot, or seed it for grass and let it go.

Toby invited Lindsey to choose a restaurant for dinner, but she shrugged and said she didn't care. They went to an eclectic family place where the menu included pasta dishes, stir-fry dishes and quesadillas, along with burgers and steaks. At least a dozen patrons recognized Susannah and asked for her autograph. It wasn't a good time to be pestered, but she didn't want to raise a protest. Not when Toby was trying so hard to make this outing pleasant and Lindsey was trying so hard to make it unpleasant.

She watched Susannah each time a stranger approached with a pen and a napkin. Susannah was courteous to them all, asking their names, assuring them she didn't mind their intrusion on her meal. She used her acting skills to conceal her annoyance. But maybe, she thought, Lindsey might understand why Susannah was less than enthusiastic about her celebrity past, a life that made it difficult to enjoy a quiet dinner out with a special man and his daughter.

"This must seem so boring to you," Lindsey ob-

served after the tenth or eleventh person interrupted
their meal to request her signature.

She shrugged. "They mean well. They think they're
flattering me by asking for my autograph."

"No, I meant eating dinner at this place." Lindsey
gestured vaguely at Susannah's Caesar salad and then
at her own plate of spaghetti. "It's so, like, ordinary."

"I like ordinary things," Susannah told her. "And
the company I'm in is anything but ordinary."

Toby sent her a brief smile. Lindsey only rolled her
eyes and sniffed. "Everything in Arlington is ordinary," she argued. "Ordinary and boring. Soccer.
Work. School. Spaghetti and tomato sauce." She gestured at her plate again. "Anyone with half a brain
would get pretty bored with it, pretty fast."

"I'm not bored with it," said Toby. "Does that
mean I've only got half a brain?"

Lindsey shot him a look. "What do you think?"

"I think you're on a cynical streak."

"And I think you've gotta be really out of it if you
think this *isn't* boring. At least, it's boring for anyone
who has the chance be somewhere else."

"I could be somewhere else, but I'm happy here,"
Susannah interjected.

"You haven't been around long enough to realize
how boring it is." Lindsey nudged her plate away,
slouched low in her seat and folded her hands across
her chest.

They left soon after. Lindsey didn't want any dessert, nor did she want to stop at Paganini's for ice
cream on their way home. When they got to Toby's
house, Lindsey helped herself to the last few home-
made cookies, lying in plastic wrap on a plate on the
counter, and vanished upstairs into her bedroom. The

faint sound of music, a thin-voiced female singing a
bland pop melody, filtered out under her closed door.

"My world and welcome to it," Toby muttered,
gazing up the stairway.

Susannah wished she could come up with a clever
quip, something to reassure him. But the fact was, she
didn't even want to think about Lindsey right now. For
the first time since they'd made love, they were alone
together, Lindsey a flight of stairs away from them,
Toby's hand resting on the newel. Susannah covered
it with her own, savoring the feel of his thick, strong
fingers beneath hers.

She wished it had been a perfect day. But perfection
existed only in fiction. If this were *Mercy Hospital,*
someone could have written the script so that in the
end Lindsey would emerge from her bedroom, prance
down the stairs and spring into her father's arms, saying, "I'm sorry I was so cranky today. I love you,
Daddy. If you want to be with Susannah, that's fine
with me."

But it wasn't *Mercy Hospital.*

He rotated his hand so he could twine his fingers
through hers. "After a day like today, you probably
miss the glamour of Hollywood."

She grinned. "I think that was what Lindsey was
trying to tell me over dinner—that I should have stuck
with Hollywood."

"Is she right?"

"Let me put it this way. She thought today was
boring. I wasn't bored for an instant."

He turned to face her, then released her hand and
brought his arms around her. He planted a light kiss
on her brow. "I've been wanting to hold you all day.
Ever since Wednesday night, actually." He kissed her

again. "When I asked you to spend the day with us, I had in mind that you'd spend the night, too."

She nodded, her head rubbing against his chin.

"But with Lindsey acting the way she is—"

A dark ache twisted inside her. She loved that he was such a dedicated father, but... She wanted to spend the night with him. She wanted to make love with him again. Just because Lindsey was throwing a prolonged hissy fit didn't mean Toby and Susannah had to ignore their own desires, did it?

"I don't know what she'll do if she finds you here in the morning," he said.

Susannah recalled the first time she'd been in this house, when Lindsey had invited her to have dinner with the Coles. She'd been so taken by Toby's attentiveness to his daughter then, the tight, solid warmth of their tiny family. She'd envied them their coziness, wishing she'd had such a close relationship with her parents.

Now that closeness stood between her and Toby. "I'll leave," she said.

"Not yet," he whispered, sliding his hands to her head and tilting her face up so he could kiss her again.

His kiss was deep, sending heat down her throat and through her body. She took his tongue, took his passion and let the sensations wash over her, warming her blood, melting her flesh. Life would have been simpler if she'd fallen in love with a man who wasn't a father, but before she'd met Toby she hadn't known that, and now that she'd met him it was too late.

To kill time before going up to bed, they sat in the den, watching a bad movie on TV, holding hands and snickering over the inane plot. But both of them knew what they were waiting for. They knew what would happen once the movie was over and Lindsey was safely asleep.

At ten they tiptoed up the stairs. Music was no longer seeping from her room, and there was no strip of light under the door. Toby signaled Susannah to wait for him in the hall while he eased Lindsey's door open, moved silently across the room and smoothed the blanket over her. Susannah peeked through the door into the darkened bedroom. She could see only Lindsey's silhouette in the dark, peaceful and still.

Toby moved silently back to the doorway. He gave Susannah a shy smile, as if almost abashed that she'd seen his paternal doting. She smiled back, a proud smile, one she hoped would convince him she thought his tenderness was lovely.

He closed the door, then ushered her down the hall to his bedroom. Once they were inside, she let Lindsey slide from her thoughts. In this comfortable room, with its sturdy oak furniture, its king-size bed and leather easy chair and Persian rugs, he was no longer a devoted father. He was a man. Her lover.

In the privacy of his room, they wouldn't worry about a temperamental little girl. Only Toby and Susannah existed, two adults who yearned for each other. As Toby removed her clothing and his own, as he led her to his bed, as he kissed and caressed and aroused her, awakening her body to its own secret pleasures, awakening her mind to its capacity for love, nothing else mattered.

He took his time. In fact, he took more time than Susannah would have liked. He seemed to think it was necessary to trace the creases and curves of her earlobe, to kiss a path from her shoulder to her palm, to roll her onto her stomach and nibble the length of her spine. Finally she turned around, her body hurting from wanting him so much. But he wouldn't rush, wouldn't give her what she ached for. First he would massage her insteps and tease her toes. He would kiss the skin behind her knees. He would urge her legs apart and press his mouth to her there, making her dizzy with longing, making her fear she'd come too soon the way she had the last time.

Her desperate moans must have gotten through to him, because he raised his head and gazed at her, his breath ragged, his eyes burning with passion. "Susannah," he whispered, rising onto her. She took him in her hands and he was already so hard. When she stroked him he shuddered, and she smiled inwardly. She wanted him to be as desperate as she was. She wanted him to feel for her what she felt for him. She wanted him to love her as much as she loved him.

When at last their bodies joined, she could almost believe it. She could almost believe that even though she was nowhere near as deserving as he was—she'd never raised a daughter, healed a sick child, contributed to the world in the important ways Toby had—he could still love her. She could almost believe, as his body claimed hers, as her name tumbled from his lips again and again, as his fierce thrusts pushed her over the edge of sensation—she could believe she belonged in his world.

"Stay," he murmured as their bodies slowly cooled. He lay beside her, his arm slung around her so she could rest her head on his shoulder. "Don't go."

"What about Lindsey?"

"She'll cope." He let out a long breath. "I've spent the past five years putting Lindsey's needs first. And now..." He tilted his head and planted a kiss on the crown of her head. "It's time for my needs. I need you in my bed."

His tone was light, but it held a serious undertone. She accepted the compliment in his words, but misgivings nagged at her. "What about tomorrow morning?" she asked. "What happens when Lindsey wakes up and finds me here?"

"We tell her you stayed the night."

"Toby." It wasn't so simple. Surely he knew that.

"All right. She'll be in a worse funk than she already is." He sighed. "I don't get it. She really likes you."

"Maybe she doesn't like me as your sweetheart. She only likes me as a TV star."

"Then we'll have to bring her around. If I can't, you can. She admires you. You're the one who can convince her that this is a good thing."

It *was* a good thing...but those misgivings inside Susannah's brain began clamoring to be heard. Toby wanted her to help him with Lindsey—not just to discuss menstruation with her but to help him repair his rocky relationship with her. He wanted Susannah in his world—and in his bed—and he wanted her to make things better between him and his daughter.

But she'd already spent too much of her life making things better for everyone else. She'd left California to get away from that. She couldn't slide back into the role of the fixer now, supporting everyone else, doing what everyone else needed doing, giving everyone else's needs priority and putting her own needs aside.

She needed Toby. But she needed her freedom at least as much. She needed not to be the one everyone depended on to make things right.

"No," she said. "I think it would be best if I left."

WONDERFUL, Toby thought by late Sunday evening. Everyone was miserable: Lindsey, Susannah and he himself.

He'd called Susannah earlier in the day, but she'd been curt on the phone. He couldn't begin to guess why—unless, like him, she was in a touchy mood because they hadn't spent the night together.

Was that really too much to ask? he wondered. Could a thirty-seven-year-old man, a responsible, honorable fellow who paid all his bills on time and donated to charity, be allowed to spend the entire night with the woman he loved?

Evidently, it *was* too much to ask. Susannah had left him, and now she seemed irritated about it. "Last night was wonderful," she'd assured him over the phone. "But I have a lot of things to do today. Maybe we can get together during the week."

She was withdrawing from him, and it enraged him. He wanted to tear right through the hedge, across her lawn into her house, and demand that she explain to him just why she was pulling back from him. Last night *had* been wonderful. So what was Susannah running from?

"You're stuck on her," Lindsey accused him over a tense supper of grilled lamb chops. Judging by her expression, Toby concluded that she wasn't thrilled by the idea.

"I'm not 'stuck on her,'" he argued. "I like her. Is that a crime?"

"She's a star," Lindsey said witheringly. "You want her to be just like us, but she isn't. She's on another whole level."

"You keep saying that, but it isn't true. She's an Arlington homeowner. Self-employed. She buys groceries, takes care of her cat, worries about her garden and drives a car. She's living a normal life like everyone else.''

"She drives a weird car," Lindsey said. "It's an ugly color." She picked at her food and shook her head. "You just don't get it, Dr. Dad. The minute you start thinking of someone like Susannah Dawson as being like everyone else is the minute you ruin what she is.''

Toby wanted to retort that he was tired of her negativity, but her statement was too significant to brush aside. Was that what she thought? That Susannah was some kind of goddess, an idol worthy of worship, and that by viewing her as just an ordinary woman Toby was destroying Lindsey's concept of her?

"She's not like everyone else," he said quietly. "If she was, I wouldn't be stuck on her."

"You're turning her into just an ordinary lady. You're taking this incredible star and acting like she's just the same as you and me.''

"She is," he asserted, still quiet, his anger gone. He had to make Lindsey understand. "Susannah is a human being. She eats and sleeps and cares about others, just like any other human being. She's not an incredible star. She's a woman."

Something that sounded like a sob emerged from Lindsey. "She *was* incredible, until all this happened."

"All what?" Toby asked, but Lindsey had already pushed away from the table and stomped out of the room.

Slowly, he began to make sense of Lindsey's words. She seemed to be saying that by loving Susannah, Toby had knocked Susannah off her pedestal. Toby happened to believe that by loving him, Susannah had descended from that pedestal all by herself—and thank God. Who could love a woman on a pedestal?

But Lindsey was blaming him for Susannah's descent from the pedestal. Or blaming them both. Toby had stolen Lindsey's idol and made her human.

His own appetite gone, he stood and crossed to the wall phone. He dialed Susannah's number, aware that she might be as aloof with him as she'd been when he'd called earlier. But he needed to share his insight with her, to see if it made sense, if it was something they could work with to break through to Lindsey.

As soon as Susannah answered, he launched into his explanation. "I think I know what's bothering Lindsey."

"That's great," Susannah said, practically cutting him off. "I'm glad."

"It's about you," he warned.

"I figured as much." She sighed. "Toby, it may be about me, but it's between you and her. You're going to have to work it out on your own."

Dumbfounded, he didn't speak for a minute. He thought they shared something essential, something strong enough to bind them, to help them face their challenges together. Why did she not want to help him face the challenge Lindsey posed, especially since it was all about her?

"I thought you'd want to know," he said.

"I don't." Her voice wavered slightly. "I'm sorry, Toby—" her voice wavered again "—but I don't want to be the one you depend on to get you through this."

If he couldn't depend on her, what kind of relationship was that? "All right," he said. "I'll get through it myself. I'm good at dealing with things alone." He muttered a terse farewell and slammed down the phone.

The kitchen was silent, thick with the aroma of his and Lindsey's barely touched dinners. He was definitely alone, even more alone than he'd been when Jane had died. Then, at least, he'd had Lindsey to keep him going, to receive his love and return it. Now, she was off somewhere, indulging in a snit because he'd reduced her idol to human proportions. And that idol, that special woman, had informed him that she didn't want to help him through a difficult situation.

Maybe Susannah was right to back off, to force him to resolve things with Lindsey by himself. She was his daughter, and no one in the world loved her as much as he did.

Even so... He'd thought he could count on Susannah. But she was done letting others count on her. She'd been there, done that, and she wasn't going to go there or do it again. Not even for Toby.

CHAPTER FIFTEEN

HIS PAGER was beeping. He'd just finished his Monday-morning rounds at Arlington Memorial, and he glanced at the pager to see whether his office was calling him. But he didn't recognize the number.

Frowning, he strode down the corridor to the nurses' station. Allison Winslow greeted him with a grin and waved the clipboard she was holding. "Hi, Toby."

"Can I borrow the phone?" he asked, still scowling at the unfamiliar number on his pager.

"Sure." She reached over the desk and brought the phone closer to him.

He punched in the numbers, then hooked his pager back on his belt while the call connected. "Elm Street School," a woman answered.

Lindsey's school? Was she hurt? His heart kicked hard against his ribs. "This is Dr. Tobias Cole. I got a message that someone was trying to reach me."

"Dr. Cole. Lindsey Cole's father?"

"That's right."

"You didn't call us this morning," the school secretary told him. "The rule is, when your child is going to be absent from school, you're supposed to phone us."

"Absent?" His heart kicked again, harder. "What are you talking about?"

"We telephoned your home to confirm that Lindsey

was absent, but no one answered. So we contacted you at your office, Dr. Cole. All I need is confirmation that—''

''Lindsey isn't absent,'' he said. His throat felt tight with tension, and he had to exert himself to force his voice out. ''She got on the bus this morning. I saw her.''

After a pause, the woman said, ''She isn't in school.''

''Oh, God.'' He closed his eyes and tried to think. He'd definitely seen her get on the bus that morning. She'd eaten a huge bowl of Cheerios for breakfast, and her spirits had seemed upbeat. He'd actually felt optimistic that the cloud hanging over her all weekend was finally lifting. She'd polished off her cereal, dashed upstairs to brush her teeth and grab her backpack and bounded out the door. He'd watched from the window as she jogged to the bus stop on the corner, and then he'd stepped outside in time to see her board the bus. He was always discreet about observing her; she believed she was much too old to have her father watch her head off for school. But he liked to see her safely onto the bus.

He'd seen her safely onto the bus today. ''Where is she?'' he asked the school secretary, his voice threatening to shatter.

''I don't know. Ms. Hathaway reported her as absent. She never went to class.''

Oh, God. He was clutching the phone so tightly his fingers ached. He could hear the blood rushing through his brain in a raucous pulse. He had to concentrate on his breathing to keep it steady. ''This is bad,'' he told the secretary, because short of cursing, it was the most accurate description of the situation he could come up with. "This is very bad. My daughter is missing." He breathed in, breathed out. "I'll call you back." He slammed down the phone and breathed in again.

"Toby." Allison's voice reached him like a ray of light piercing through the encroaching darkness.

He turned to her. She appeared grim, measuring him with her gaze. "I heard what you said. Lindsey's missing?"

He nodded. He didn't think he could speak the words again. Speaking them once had nearly killed him.

"Do you think she might be at home?"

"The school called my house. No one answered."

"If she was playing hooky, she wouldn't answer the phone."

"Playing hooky." That sounded so safe, so innocuous. But Lindsey wouldn't do that. She'd never cut class before.

"Or maybe she went to the mall."

"How would she get there?"

"With her friends, maybe? There are lots of possibilities, Toby, and most of them aren't so awful."

"It's my daughter," he said. His feet shifted, as if they sensed the floor crumbling beneath him, the earth splitting open and threatening to swallow him. "My daughter's missing."

Allison touched his arm to console him, then reached for the phone. "Molly Saunders-Russo's husband is a police detective. I'll call him, okay?"

Toby nodded, too numb to thank her. A police detective. Christ. His daughter was missing, and Allison was calling a police detective.

"John Russo, please," she was saying into the phone. A pause, and then: "John? It's Allison. I'm calling for a colleague of mine, Toby Cole. He's a pediatrician affiliated with the hospital. His daughter is missing." She listened, then said, "She's about ten, eleven years old?" She sent Toby a questioning look and he mouthed *ten*. "Ten years old," Allison reported into the phone. "She got on the school bus this morning, but she never showed up in class. Toby is worried." She listened. "Uh-huh. Okay..." She eyed Toby again. "What school?"

"Elm Street Elementary."

"Elm Street Elementary," she told the detective. She listened, then handed the phone to Toby. "Why don't you talk to him yourself."

He took the phone hesitantly. At the moment, he hated it. He knew it was just a molded plastic object, but it had brought him wretched news. He would associate this particular phone with terror for the rest of his life. "Hello?" he said.

Detective John Russo spoke calmly, sounding focused but less urgent than Toby would have liked. He asked Toby for his phone number and address. "Why don't we meet at your house and start there," he suggested. "She might just be skipping school. Maybe we'll find something there. Meanwhile, I'll send my partner over to the school to talk to the kids on her bus. What bus does she take?"

"The number four, I think."

"Okay. We'll find her, Dr. Cole. Don't worry. Meet me at your house in ten minutes."

Toby nodded and handed the phone back to Allison to hang up. "Do me a favor and call my office. Tell them to cancel my appointments."

Allison gave his arm another affectionate squeeze. "I'll take care of everything."

"Okay." *Keep breathing,* he ordered himself. "I'm going home to meet with Detective Russo."

"He's the best," Allison assured him.

Toby didn't know if he was the best, but the tall, placid detective waiting for him at his house when he arrived there after breaking several speed limits appeared competent. He had a pad and pen in his hand, and he began asking questions while Toby was still unlocking the front door. "Who are your daughter's closest friends?"

"Two girls—Amanda and Meredith. I don't know their last names. They're in her grade but not in her class."

"Okay." Russo looked at him askance, and he realized he must sound like a neglectful parent because he didn't know his daughter's friends' full names. But they'd become her best friends fairly recently. "She used to be best friends with a girl named Cathy Robinson. But her family moved to Atlanta, and Lindsey's just started making new friends."

Russo nodded and took notes. "Do you have a recent photograph of her?"

Her school picture. He had one enlargement on his desk at the office, and another on his desk in the study. He strode across the paneled room and lifted the photograph to hand to Russo. Straightening up, he glimpsed Susannah's house through the bay window. He froze for a moment, then turned to the detective.

"Who lives next door?" Russo asked. He must have noticed Toby's reaction to the sight of the house.

"A woman. A woman I've been involved with." Russo's eyebrows twitched, and he added, "I'm a widower. She's single. She moved in a few weeks ago, and she became friendly with Lindsey. And me."

"Do you think she might have an idea where your daughter is?"

"No." But who knew? She might not want to help Toby, but damn it, if she had any idea where Lindsey might have gone… "I'll call her." He lifted the phone and started to dial.

Russo plucked the receiver from Toby's hand. "What's her name?" he asked. "I'll talk to her."

"Susannah Dawson." He hovered impotently by the window as Russo lifted the receiver to his ear. "Susannah Dawson? This is Detective Russo from the Arlington Police Department. I'm next door at your neighbor Dr. Cole's house. His daughter is missing…"

Toby couldn't listen anymore. He couldn't remain in the room while Russo talked to the woman Toby loved, the woman who'd abandoned him when she decided things were too tricky with Lindsey, the woman who didn't want to stand by his side when he needed her.

He stalked down the hall to the kitchen and searched the room. A couple of Cheerios lay on the table; they must have slopped over from her bowl and he hadn't had time to wipe the table down. Her chair was pushed out. Her soccer cleats were on the floor near the door to the mud room.

Lindsey! Where the hell are you?

He wasn't a praying man, but he prayed now. He prayed that wherever Lindsey was, she was all right. He couldn't survive any other possibility.

He heard footsteps behind him. "I'd like to have a look at her bedroom," Russo said.

Toby wanted to ask him what Susannah had said. Maybe she'd told him something terrible. Maybe she'd explained to the detective that Toby and Lindsey were feuding, that he'd pursued a relationship with Susannah even though he'd known Lindsey disapproved. He'd put his own needs ahead of his daughter's and made love with Susannah in his own house, just down the hall from where Lindsey was sleeping. And he'd wanted Susannah to be with him when he woke up, even though he'd known it would upset his daughter. He'd cared more about himself and his own needs than about his child.

She'd run away. It came to him like a stab in the solar plexus, sharp and deadly. "She's run away," he said aloud.

"You think so?"

"She was angry with me, and..." He cursed.

"Let's check out her room."

Lindsey's bedroom looked the way it usually did. Her bed was made haphazardly, books and papers were stacked high on her desk and her soccer uniform was crumpled in a heap on the floor, instead of in the laundry hamper where it belonged. Russo crossed the room to her desk, surveyed the clutter and then glanced at her computer. "Does she go on the Internet a lot?"

"No." Toby's heart clutched at the thought of the creeps vulnerable children met through the Internet. Thank God Lindsey had never been interested in chat rooms.

"What does she use this for, then?"

"Games and e-mail," he said.

Russo turned the computer on. "What's her e-mail software? Does it have a password?"

"Yes, and I don't know it." He sighed. "She e-mails her friend Cathy Robinson, though. The friend who moved to Atlanta."

Russo turned the computer off. "I'll need her phone number," he said.

They spent a few more minutes searching Lindsey's room. Toby's gaze lingered on the clutter heaped upon her desk for a minute. The pile was higher than usual. "I think some of these notebooks are what she usually takes to school with her," he said, shuffling through the textbooks and papers. "Here's her assignment book. She always takes that to school."

"Then she probably didn't intend to go to school today," Russo concluded.

"She had her backpack with her."

"Packed with something else, maybe."

That led Toby and Russo to go through her drawers. Toby honestly couldn't remember how much underwear she usually had in her top drawer, whether she might have stashed some of it in her backpack. He ducked into her bathroom. Her toothbrush was gone.

He cursed again, not in anger but in dread. He'd guessed right: his daughter had run away.

Susannah was standing in his driveway when he and Russo left the house. She was dressed in faded jeans and a T-shirt with palm trees silk-screened on it, probably a relic from her California past. Toby should have been immune to her. He was distracted to the point of madness over Lindsey, and he'd learned on Sunday that Susannah didn't want to be his comrade-in-arms when it came to fighting life's battles.

But the sight of her caused a different reaction in his heart—not the crazed thumping from the adrenaline flooding his veins but a deep knot of emotion, tight and constricting. He used to think he needed her for companionship and sex. But he needed her much more right now for support—the one thing she didn't want to give him.

She charged across the lawn to him. "Toby, what can I do?" she asked. Her eyes were wide and glistening, her face pale.

"This is Detective Russo," he said stiffly. He didn't want to be so glad to see her. He couldn't lean on her. She wouldn't let him.

"Anything," she said to the detective. "Anything I can do. Just tell me."

"Nothing right now," he responded. "We'll be in touch if we think of something."

She fell back a step, her gaze riveted to Toby. "I'm so sorry," she murmured. He didn't know if she was referring to Lindsey's disappearance or her retreat from him yesterday. He tried to convince himself he didn't care.

But when he got into the detective's unmarked police car, he felt his soul clench with a fierceness born of fear and grief and something more—the understanding that he wasn't strong enough to get through this ordeal alone, and Susannah wasn't going to help him.

SUSANNAH WAS inches from her telephone when it rang that afternoon. She'd been inches from it all day, prowling the house with her cordless unit, waiting, hoping, praying it would bring good news. She should have been with Toby. It pained her to be apart from him. But she'd seen the unforgiving look in his eyes in front of his house that morning, when she'd asked what she could do to help. *Nothing,* his expression had shouted at her. *You can do nothing at all. I don't want you here.*

She was furious with herself for not having offered

her help when his problem was so much smaller. Perhaps if she'd spent Sunday with him and Lindsey, easing the girl out of her dismal mood, Lindsey might not have disappeared. If Susannah had reached out to her, let the Coles depend on her, done whatever she could to make things better for them...

She'd wanted to spare herself from the fate she'd suffered in Los Angeles. Why hadn't she acknowledged that Toby wasn't Stephen or her father or any of the other people who'd taken advantage of her there? He was completely different.

She should have given herself to him fully. But she'd reflexively chosen to protect herself, and look what had happened.

The abrupt chime of the phone jolted her. She jammed her thumb against the connect button and lifted the unit to her ear. "Yes?"

"Susannah." It was Toby, not the detective. She hoped that meant the news was good—that he'd located Lindsey, that he wanted Susannah's help, that he didn't despise her.

"Yes."

"Susannah, we've contacted Lindsey's friend Cathy Robinson."

"Yes?" Did that mean Lindsey was with the girl who used to live in this house? Had she somehow traveled all the way to Atlanta?

"Cathy told us Lindsey sent her an e-mail last night telling her she was going to go to Los Angeles. She wants to be a star." His voice faltered.

Her pulse skidded. "Los Angeles?"

"Cathy forwarded the e-mail to Detective Russo. In it she said she thought you'd blown it by turning your back on stardom. You were just going to be a plain old lady—dating me, no less—and you were throwing away everything that made you special. Lindsey said she was going to Hollywood to become a star so you'd see how it was supposed to be.''

Susannah dismissed the intended insult. There was nothing she'd rather be than a plain old lady—Toby's old lady. She moved right past it to more immediate issues. ''Why didn't Cathy call to warn you?''

''She didn't think Lindsey was actually going to run away. She thought Lindsey was just sounding her out about the idea.'' He sighed. ''Of course Cathy told Lindsey to go for it.'' He sighed again. ''Some idiot at the Arlington bus station sold her a ticket to Manhattan. The NYPD has been alerted. They think she might have changed buses at the Port Authority terminal.''

''She's trying to take a bus to Los Angeles?''

''She can't afford an airplane ticket.'' Again his voice faltered. ''Susannah…there's so much that could happen to her on a bus. She thinks she knows everything, but she doesn't. I can't—I can't believe how much danger she's in, I—''

''Where are you, Toby?''

''I'm at the police station with Detective Russo.''

''I'll be right there.'' She disconnected the phone before he could tell her not to come.

Grabbing her purse, her cell phone and her keys, she hurried out of the house. She had a general idea where the police department headquarters was located, and after circling a couple of downtown blocks she located the building and parked. Inside, she stopped at the front desk to ask the sergeant where she would find Detective Russo.

''Up the stairs and take a left,'' he directed her.

"Say, you look like that actress, you know? From the hospital show—"

Ignoring him, she sprinted up the stairs two at a time. At the landing she turned left and entered a small squad room crowded with six desks. She immediately spotted the detective she'd seen with Toby that morning. He was seated at one of the desks. Toby wasn't with him.

"Excuse me," the receptionist called to her, trying to keep her from rushing through the entry and heading straight for Russo's desk.

"Where's Toby?" she asked the detective, tuning out the receptionist. "Where's Dr. Cole?"

Russo glanced up from the paperwork on his blotter. He studied her as if trying to place her.

"I'm his next-door neighbor. Susannah Dawson."

Russo nodded. He must have recalled what she'd told him on the phone: that she and Toby had a complicated relationship, that Lindsey wasn't happy about it, that Susannah was trying to keep her distance from Toby because of Lindsey. "He's in the coffee room, right through that door." Russo pointed to an open door at the far end of the room. "I'd join you, but I've got calls to make."

"Make your calls," Susannah told him. "Thanks." She wove through the maze of desks to the coffee room.

Toby stood in the tiny lounge, staring out a soot-streaked window, his back to the door. His jacket was draped over the back of a chair, his sleeves were rolled up and his shirt was wrinkled. From his posture alone, Susannah could tell he was dejected.

"Toby?"

He spun around. He appeared on the verge of smiling, but then he checked himself, apparently remembering he wasn't supposed to be glad to see her.

"I know people in Los Angeles," she said. "I'll call anyone you want. My old producer would know the best detectives in the city. I can afford any private eye in town, Toby. Let me do this, all right?"

He stared at her as if she were speaking a foreign language.

"A good private investigator will find her. We can get started right now. Should I clear it with Russo first?"

"You want to call your old producer?"

"I'll call anyone you want, Toby. I know people in Hollywood."

"You can't stand those people," he reminded her.

She pressed on. "I'll fly out there if you think it might help. I'll look for Lindsey myself. I can just imagine some of the places a kid might wander, trying to find a way to break into the business. That might be a better idea," she realized, her brain speeding ahead of her words. "I'll fly out to Los Angeles myself. I'll turn the whole damned city upside down till I find her."

"Susannah." He crossed the room, cupped his hands around her elbows and held her in place, as if he expected her to flap her arms and fly directly to Los Angeles from the coffee room. "She's not in California."

She tried not to react to his nearness, the strength of his hands on her arms, the intense beauty of his dark, sad eyes. "She's not? You told me that was where she was heading."

"By bus. She got on a bus in Arlington at eight-thirty. She's been traveling no more than seven hours.

There's no way she'd get anywhere near California in such a short time.''

"I'll go anyway,'' Susannah insisted. "I'll be there to greet her when she gets off the bus.''

"They'll find her before then.''

She let out a breath. If they found her, he was right—she would be nowhere near Los Angeles in seven hours. She'd be lucky if she was as far away as Pittsburgh.

If they found her.

She peered up into Toby's face. "This is my fault,'' she murmured. "This whole thing—''

"No.''

"I wasn't what she wanted me to be. She thought I should be a glamorous celebrity, and I disappointed her—''

"No. It's not your fault.''

"Whose fault is it, then?''

His hands relaxed the slightest bit on her arms. "It's Lindsey's fault,'' he said. "She was enraged with us both, and she did something stupid.'' He released Susannah's arms and prowled around the tiny room, evidently too nervous to stand still. "I learned something in that Daddy School class. I learned that no father is perfect, but if we give our children love and guidance, that's not bad. I'm a good father, Susannah. Maybe I could have gotten through to Lindsey, but I sure as hell tried and I didn't succeed. And maybe it's not my fault.''

Tears blurred Susannah's vision. "You're a very good father, Toby.'' She followed him into a corner of the room and blocked him so he couldn't keep pacing. "I'm here telling you I'd do anything for you and Lindsey.''

"What about your independence? What about not wanting to do things for other people?"

"This isn't about other people. It's about you and Lindsey. All day today I've been wishing I were with you, thinking of you and her and wanting to do something—*anything* to make this better."

"Because you think it's your fault?"

"Because I love you," she said.

Something relented inside him, his shoulders going less rigid, his head tilting slightly. "Is this a heat-of-the-moment confession?"

"It's the truth."

"Loving me means accepting that I've got a wild, exasperating, tempestuous daughter—"

"Whom I adore."

He let out a long breath, then tucked his hand under her chin and dropped a kiss onto her lips. "Lindsey warned me not to fall in love with you. Just one more thing she was wrong about."

Approaching footsteps caused them to move apart. Turning toward the door, Susannah saw Detective Russo hurrying toward them, smiling. "Philadelphia," he said. "She's in police custody. They pulled her off a bus. She's safe, healthy and very weepy."

Susannah grew weepy, too. She glanced at Toby and saw tears glistening in his eyes, as well. "Can I talk to her?"

"Sure. You'll have to drive down there—"

"Of course. But let me talk to her first. I just want to hear her voice."

Russo led Susannah and Toby out of the coffee room to his desk. He dialed a number, spoke to a few intermediaries in Philadelphia, then handed the phone to Toby.

"Hello? This is Tobias Cole. Can I speak to my daughter, please?"

Susannah stood next to him, her arm looped around his waist and his slung over her shoulders. She wasn't sure which one of them was holding the other up. All she knew was that she didn't want to let go.

"Hi, Hot Stuff. It's Dr. Dad," he said into the phone. "You're in big trouble, you know that?" He listened. "Yes, I'm mad. I'm furious. But I love you. With all my heart. And I'm going to come down to Philadelphia and get you. I'll be there in about four hours. Maybe less, if I drive fast." He listened. "We'll talk about whether you're grounded when we get home. Honey, stop crying. I love you. Lindsey? I'm bringing Susannah with me." He listened. "She loves you, too. She and I are going to come and get you. We're going to bring you home."

He listened for a moment longer, then said goodbye, handed the receiver back to Detective Russo and turned to face Susannah. She closed her arms around his waist and he gathered her close.

"I would do anything for you," she confessed in a whisper. "I don't care if this isn't what I planned for myself. I'll do anything for you, Toby."

"Hold me," he asked. "That's what I want you to do."

She held him, and he held her. This was the way it was supposed to be, she realized—two people giving as much as they took. Two people holding each other, stronger because they were together, strong enough to tackle any challenge. Strong enough to convince a girl in Philadelphia that there was no problem in life so great that love couldn't make it better.

HARLEQUIN®
SUPERROMANCE®

They look alike. They sound alike.
They act alike—at least some of the time.

Two Sisters by **Kay David**
(Superromance #888)
A sister looks frantically for her missing twin.
And only a stranger can help her.
Available January 2000

The Wrong Brother by **Bonnie K. Winn**
(Superromance #898)
A man poses as his twin to fool the woman he thinks
is a murderer—a woman who also happens to be
his brother's wife.
Available February 2000

Baby, Baby by **Roz Denny Fox**
(Superromance #902)
Two men fight for the custody of twin babies.
And their guardian must choose who will be their father.
Available March 2000

Available wherever Harlequin books are sold.

HARLEQUIN®
Makes any time special ™

Visit us at www.romance.net

HSRTWINS

Come escape with Harlequin's new

Series Sampler

Four great full-length Harlequin novels bound together in one fabulous volume and at an unbelievable price.

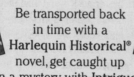

Be transported back in time with a **Harlequin Historical®** novel, get caught up in a mystery with **Intrigue®**, be tempted by a hot, sizzling romance with **Harlequin Temptation®**, or just enjoy a down-home all-American read with **American Romance®**.

You won't be able to put this collection down!

On sale February 2000 at your favorite retail outlet.